THE HOUSE-WIFE BLUES

THE HOUSE-WIFE WIFE BLUES

WARREN ADLER

CROWN PUBLISHERS, INC.

New York

Published by Crown Publishers, Inc.,
201 East 50th Street, New York, New York 10022.
Member of the Crown Publishing Group.

CROWN is a trademark of Crown Publishers, Inc.

Manufactured in the United States of America

Library of Congress Cataloging-in-Publication Data

Adler, Warren.
The housewife blues / Warren Adler.
I. Title.
PS3551.D64H68   1992
813'.54—dc20   92-8398
                                                              CIP

ISBN 0-517-59172-3

10   9   8   7   6   5   4   3   2   1

First Edition

For Sunny

Again and Always

THE HOUSE-WIFE WIFE BLUES

1

IF SHE hadn't placed her great-great-grandmother's spinet in that exact spot along the east wall and hadn't set aside time to polish it on this particular April day, Jenny might have avoided any confrontation with this bit of unsavory information.

First there was Godfrey Richardson letting himself into the main hallway, which was unusual enough, since he was rarely at home during the middle of a weekday morning. She heard him climb the single flight of stairs to the apartment he shared with his wife, Terry, just above hers on the second floor. The Richardsons rarely used the tiny mahogany-paneled elevator, and she heard his ascending footfalls on the steps, not because she was deliberately listening, but probably because his tread was lighter than usual, as if he were walking on the tips of his toes.

She realized, of course, that she was conscious of the difference because it was out of the ordinary pattern of sound and activity of the weekday life of their building. In the two months that she and her husband, Larry, had lived there, she had discovered that she was usually the only tenant in residence on most days. A couple of the tenants had maids in for an hour or two a week, but they came and went with barely a ripple.

There were five apartments in their converted East Side Manhattan brownstone, and all of the tenants were normally off pursuing their various vocations during the day. As a housewife, Jenny, too, was pursuing her vocation, which she took as seriously as the others in the building took theirs.

Godfrey Richardson's tiptoeing up the stairs, despite a rational dismissal of it as being none of her business, had alerted her to what followed. Looking out of the bay window through the lower branches of the budding sycamore tree that fronted the building, she had noted that a young woman had passed the building twice already, lingered in front of it briefly, looked up toward the Richardsons' apartment, then proceeded toward Second Avenue. She was now headed toward the building once again, this time coming from the Third Avenue side.

Jenny continued to apply polish to the spinet. She had it on her mental schedule to polish the heirloom once a week. This was exactly the way her mother had treated the spinet in their house in Indiana, and one of the conditions of the gift was that it be treated the same way in perpetuity. It had been purchased by her great-great-grandmother, handed down to each generation in turn, and had never left Indiana. So far it had fared quite well in its new Manhattan life, had not warped and had kept its tune, although she rarely played it.

Her concentration was deflected by this young woman parading in front of the window. The woman was no more than twenty and wore tight jeans, black cowboy boots, and a black leather jacket, which emphasized the fullness of her breasts. Hussy type, her mother might have said, but then her mother, like the spinet, had never been anywhere but Indiana. As a newly anointed Manhattanite, Jenny felt herself superior to such judgments.

With obviously contrived casualness, the woman stopped in front of the building, looked at her watch, then proceeded up the stone steps to the front entrance. When the woman could no longer be seen from the window, Jenny listened for the faint sound of the outside buzzer. Curiosity, she supposed, had made her hearing more acute than usual. She heard the return buzzer sound, then the door opening, and, after a short interval, the tiny elevator moving in the shaft, stopping on the floor above her.

It was, of course, the kind of information that she would have preferred avoiding, especially since she liked Terry Richardson, Godfrey's wife. Not that they had been overly friendly, considering Jenny had had them, over Larry's objections, for an informal dinner featuring her prized meat loaf recipe and they had not yet reciprocated. According to Larry they might never, which he told her would be a good thing. Neighbors, according to Larry, were a nuisance, sometimes a danger, and a good thing to avoid, but he had let her have her way just this once to prove the point.

New Yorkers were like that, Larry had explained, always too busy to reciprocate, although sooner or later they'd invite you out for an obligatory dinner at a restaurant. Such explanations did not jibe at all with her midwestern upbringing. New people were always welcomed by their neighbors, not the other way around.

Swallowing her pride and against her husband's wishes, she had decided nevertheless not to be standoffish with the neighbors. She wasn't going to change her Hoosier ways just because New Yorkers were crude and ignorant of the social graces. People were people everywhere, her parents had taught her. Prick them and they bleed. Their basic human instincts were the same as hers, the good with the bad. Above all, follow your own value system. Never stoop to theirs.

Larry thought this attitude naive, instructing her daily in the survival tactics of New Yorkers. Live defensively. Double-lock doors. Avoid carryout deliveries. The delivery man could be a thief, a rapist, or a murderer. Stay off the streets after dark, and in the daytime be wary. Trust no one. When in doubt, cross the street. Since she had never been to New York before their marriage, she had no other frame of reference than his various caveats.

Once, about two weeks after she and Larry had moved into the building, Terry Richardson had come downstairs and asked if she could borrow a screwdriver because Godfrey, who was "all thumbs," had misplaced theirs somewhere. Jenny had obliged and invited Terry in for coffee. It was Sunday morning and Larry was

3

off playing tennis with friends from the advertising agency where he worked.

Terry was an open-faced brunette with hazel eyes and a broad, toothy smile. To Jenny's surprise she had volunteered a great deal of information about herself. Not to pry was another in Jenny's catalog of values inculcated by her Indiana upbringing.

Terry was a vice-president of Citibank, which sounded very awesome and important to Jenny, to whom bankers and banks, at least in the Midwest, still ranked, along with doctors and hospitals, as trusted professionals and institutions.

"That's quite impressive," Jenny exclaimed.

"That's what my mother thinks," Terry said, sipping her coffee. "But the pay is not quite commensurate with the title, and I'm one of many. I will admit, though, that it does have a wow factor in certain circles."

"It does to me," Jenny agreed. Back in Indiana a woman vice-president of a bank would have had real prestige.

"Prestige shmestige, my mother says. She'd rather see me pregnant." Terry sighed and shook her head. But her hazel eyes revealed a stab of sudden pain. "We tried this fertility clinic three times and are about to go for number four. We're batting a thousand in strikeouts."

Jenny didn't quite know what to say. Encouraging Terry to continue her revelations seemed patronizing. It also crossed her mind that her own and Larry's fertility had not yet been tested, and she decided, probably on superstitious grounds, to make no comment that might encourage Terry to continue the subject.

"Puts a lot of pressure on Godfrey," Terry persisted, speaking into the brief vacuum of silence. "I'm the weak sister in the combination. Something about the sperm dying before it hits pay dirt. Like the fallopian tubes were a kind of gas chamber. Only the doctors don't quite know why. Anyway, we're going to try yet again." She contemplated the thought in silence for a moment, then turned her attention to Jenny.

"Don't wait too long," Terry said. "I'm thirty-seven. We didn't try until I was thirty-five."

In the pause that followed, Jenny held back any comment, except to offer her own age, which was twenty-five, and to point out that she and Larry were only married a little over two months and were not planning a family for a while. After all, friendship and intimacy took time to develop. That was another item in her value system. Perhaps that was the reason the conversation drifted away and Terry swallowed her last mouthful of coffee, thanked Jenny for the screwdriver, and went back to her apartment.

There was something open and fresh about Terry, and as soon as she had left the apartment, Jenny regretted not opening up more than she had. Telling somebody such personal information was, in fact, a confidence, which should really be returned. Jenny made a mental note to reveal something equally as intimate about herself, but she wasn't exactly sure what that might be.

Certainly she could never tell Terry what she was "witnessing" at this very moment. She tried to push the obvious from her mind and put a better light on the circumstances. Perhaps she was jumping to conclusions. Then why was the woman so cautious, passing the building a number of times before going in? And there was something about the woman that suggested, well, sex. Clandestine sex.

All right, she admonished herself, she was just a hayseed from Indiana, a Hoosier hick, but under that blond blue-eyed curly-topped adorable—some might say Lolita—look, she was not totally naive. She felt a strong rapport with Terry, who was at that moment, Jenny was dead certain, being betrayed by her husband.

The idea took some of the natural joy out of her day. Why couldn't he do his dirty work away from their home? A home was a sacred place, a nest. Birds never fouled their own nests.

Although she had never crossed the threshold of the Richardson apartment, she imagined that the deed was being done on the marriage bed, in the bedroom, exactly above where Larry's and her bedroom was located. As if to validate that point, she walked to the bedroom and looked upward at that point where she was certain the Richardsons' bed was placed. It had to be queen-size. A king or a double would simply not fit properly.

She admonished herself for allowing the silence to exist, knowing that she was deliberately listening for the sounds of lovemaking, feeling ashamed. Worse, she felt that telltale tingle of her own sexiness. The power of suggestion, she rebuked herself, taking a surreptitious glance at her face in the mirror and seeing the slight flush on her cheeks.

She went into the bathroom, ran the cold water tap, and patted her cheeks, then returned to the spinet and resumed her polishing. But she could not rid herself of the idea of those two up there and the sympathy and outrage she felt on Terry's behalf.

It hadn't occurred to her when they first rented the apartment that she would be the only tenant whose daily chores revolved around the apartment itself. Of course, she did have lots of errands outside the apartment. It wasn't easy putting a home together, and there was the regular shopping to do, although most of the food shopping was done on weekends with Larry, who particularly liked those fancy gourmet stores.

They considered themselves quite lucky to find the apartment. They both detested those big impersonal high rises, which made people feel more like transient cave dwellers than human beings. The location, too, was perfect, being on Thirty-eighth Street between Second and Third, which meant that Larry could actually jog the two miles to work at the advertising agency on upper Madison Avenue, where he was a vice-president in charge of the research department.

Mrs. Bradshaw, the rental agent who found them the apartment, told them she knew instantly when it became available that it had their name on it.

"I know this building intimately," she told them, her half-glasses perched on the end of her nose, as she stood in the middle of the living room reading the listing card and reciting the history of the building. The two brownstones joined together, both built in 1911, had first been converted to apartments before World War II, then refurbished in the early sixties.

Jenny marveled at the spaciousness of the apartment, which was on the first floor of the building. She inspected the high ceilings trimmed with wonderfully elaborate molding, the working fireplace, the exposed brick kitchen with shiny stainless-steel appliances and a gas cookstove and oven, the wall of bookcases, the little mahogany-paneled den, the dining room with a small crystal chandelier, and, best of all, the white-tiled bathroom with the marvelous bathtub that sat on sculpted claw feet. She adored the bathtub and could picture herself lying there enveloped by tingling soap bubbles. There was nothing like a good warm soak to settle the mind and calm the spirit. Mrs. Bradshaw was right about one thing: the apartment certainly had her name on it.

"A steal at three thousand dollars a month," Mrs. Bradshaw said, smiling, the laugh lines on the sides of her eyes crinkling. She had a grandmotherly air that Jenny liked and seemed sincerely interested in their welfare.

"You're right about that," Larry said without cracking a smile. He had told Jenny earlier that he had had one of his researchers check out comparable rental values in the area. "It's really way out of line. In fact, outrageous." He looked toward Jenny, who had stiffened inside of herself. Larry had warned her not to appear enthusiastic: "Please restrain yourself, Jenny. We mustn't give them the advantage."

All this was against her grain. She hated negotiating, exercising those little ploys and manipulations. The idea of it implied a sense of being sharp, of trafficking in rejection and hurtfulness. Larry, on the other hand, had no compunctions in that department. "In New York, it's screw them before they screw you," he had lectured her, part of his endless laundry list of advice about how to survive in the Big Apple. Above all, he cautioned, trust no one. No one!

"That seems like a mighty cynical assessment," she had countered, offering her own time-honored homily: "People are essentially good and the same everywhere."

"Everywhere but New York, Jenny. Trust me."

Why would he say that? she had wondered, especially after saying, "Trust no one." She put the idea quickly out of her mind. He didn't, of course, mean himself.

She hoped he wouldn't be too hard-nosed about the apartment. It was beautiful. Just what she had imagined living in Manhattan would be like. Surely he felt the same way. Then why was he bargaining so hard? It surprised her, too, that the grandmotherly

Mrs. Bradshaw didn't bat an eye at Larry's statement about the price being "outrageous."

"Out of range of your financial ability or out of line pricewise?" Mrs. Bradshaw asked. She had taken off her half-glasses and was distributing her gaze between Larry and Jenny.

"There is a clear line between fair and gouging, Mrs. Bradshaw. If I couldn't afford it, I wouldn't be wasting my time. And yours," Larry said smugly, shaking his head. Jenny wished she hadn't heard his remarks.

"What do you think, Mrs. Burns?" Mrs. Bradshaw said, turning to Jenny.

"Me?"

Jenny was startled at the question and looked quickly at Larry, who blinked his eyes in a kind of signal for her to stay out of it.

"Get real, Mrs. Bradshaw," Larry said, shrugging, turning his body as if it were a gesture of total rejection. Jenny felt her pulse throb with anxiety. Larry took a folded paper from his inside jacket pocket and unfolded it, then waved it in front of Mrs. Bradshaw. "I've got the comparable rental values in the area."

"You can't compare apples to pears, Mr. Burns," Mrs. Bradshaw countered. The cute little crinkly laugh lines had smoothed out, and her lips were tight as she waited for a response. When none was forthcoming, she said: "This place has charm, personality. Anyone can see it's one of a kind." She looked at Jenny, her eyes boring in. "Surely you can see that, Mrs. Burns."

Jenny shifted her eyes quickly to Larry, who was now assuming a pose of bored indifference.

"I'd say two thousand a month tops," Larry said casually, without apparent interest. Jenny felt a sinking feeling in her stomach. He couldn't. She loved this place and was already visualizing how she would decorate it. And that wonderful bathtub!

Mrs. Bradshaw started to arrange the papers in her hand and opened the clasp of the large pocketbook that hung from her shoulder as if she, too, were drawing the negotiation to a close.

"I don't know if I can show you anything better. Sorry about that," Mrs. Bradshaw said, snapping the clasp of her pocketbook with much fanfare. They had seen enough apartments to confirm that observation. Jenny knew that the woman was right, and she was finding it difficult to hide her disappointment.

"We're sorry, too," Larry said with indifference.

Jenny wondered if he really believed that. She supposed he was right about the price being high. That was his department. He had told her never to concern herself about money, only about properly managing her own allowance, which he would decide upon when they got their apartment. At the moment, Larry was providing her with pocket money "as needed."

Not that she was totally ignorant about managing money. In the past ten years, she had actually saved nearly twenty thousand dollars from her earnings in various jobs. Larry had complimented her on that and had insisted that that money be kept in her own name even after they had married. His gesture was somewhat confusing since her view of marriage meant that everything was to be shared between them forever and ever. She supposed that this was meant by him to be a gesture of generosity, although in her own mind the money was considered shared assets.

In Manhattan, Jenny had found, money had an entirely different meaning. Back in Indiana even two thousand a month was a king's ransom. This was nearly double her entire monthly take-home pay when she'd worked as an assistant to Dr. Parker. And even after paying her rent, food, and other necessities, she had enough left over for entertainment and savings.

The three of them now headed for the apartment door. Jenny was crestfallen, but still hopeful. Although she was uncomfortable about Larry's tactics, she had full confidence that he knew what he was doing.

After they reached the street, Mrs. Bradshaw turned to them.

"If you really want this place," she told them, addressing herself mostly to Jenny, "I could make a call."

"Suit yourself," Larry said, looking at Jenny sternly. "At the right price it might be considered."

Mrs. Bradshaw's gaze lingered on Jenny's face. Jenny hoped she was registering indifference properly.

"Yes," Jenny said. "At the right price." She noted Larry's quick glance of approval.

They walked to the corner, where there was a telephone booth. Mrs. Bradshaw picked up the phone and dialed.

"God, Larry. I can't stand it. I really love this apartment," Jenny whispered.

"Easy. You're her target of opportunity," he said. "Show her nothing. No interest. You had me worried for minute."

"My stomach is doing flip-flops."

"Stay cool. Remember this is the Big Apple, the hustler's paradise. Our top price is twenty-five. She'll come back at maybe twenty-seven."

"I can't stand it."

"Trust me," he said, preparing his face for Mrs. Bradshaw's return. It was a blustery day, but that did not deter people from being on the streets. In fact, nothing deterred New Yorkers in anything, Jenny thought. People looked so determined and intense, although she had observed that they scowled a great deal and did not smile often.

"Best we can do is twenty-seven, Mr. Burns," Mrs. Bradshaw said. Jenny noted that the woman's grandmotherly aspect was completely gone. "Frankly, I think that's very generous."

"Not in this market," Larry said. "The vacancy rate is staggering."

"I could call again," Mrs. Bradshaw said.

"Okay then. Here's my bottom line. Twenty-five with the first month free and a three-year lease with an option for another three at a five-percent yearly rise."

Jenny's level of anxiety soared. She couldn't bear to watch Mrs. Bradshaw's face.

"Really, Mr. Burns..."

"Make the call, then," Larry said.

"It won't do any good," Mrs. Bradshaw said, shrugging.

"Try," Larry said.

Mrs. Bradshaw hesitated for a moment, then, shaking her head, went back to the phone.

"I could never do this," Jenny confided when Mrs. Bradshaw was out of earshot.

"Worry not, Jenny. She's a whore. All real estate people are whores. And the biggest whores are in New York."

"She seems so nice."

" 'Nice.' That's a dangerous word in this town, Jenny. Nice is okay in Indiana. Not here. Get 'nice' out of your vocabulary while you're in this town."

Mrs. Bradshaw finished her call and came back to them.

"Twenty-five it is. Two-year lease with option. Six-percent-a-year rise for two-year renewal." She smiled, her crinkly lines back in place, and held out her hand. "Deal?"

Jenny's heart was in her mouth.

"I wanted three years," Larry said.

"Leave us some dignity, Mr. Burns." Mrs. Bradshaw winked. "Our pants are down."

He turned suddenly to Jenny.

"What do you think, baby?"

"Me?" Jenny searched his face. His eyes signaled that it was okay. She hesitated, then turned toward Mrs. Bradshaw. "I say deal," she said with mock assertiveness.

"The little woman has spoken," Larry said, putting out his hand. Mrs. Bradshaw took it and pumped.

"Now let's all get a cup of coffee and do the paperwork," Mrs. Bradshaw said.

"Masterly," she told Larry later as they lay in bed in their hotel room. They had made love the rest of the day, and she had been gratefully aggressive.

"You've got to know how to play the game," he said as she cuddled in the crook of his arm. She stroked his hard, muscular body, so well proportioned and sculpted by his regimen of pumping iron three times a week along with his daily jogging schedule.

"I married a very smart cookie," she whispered.

"Here in New York, you've got to base everything on the premise that the next guy is out to screw you. You want to make it here, you've got to learn survival skills. That goes for every human transaction. Every move you make has to be defensive. Watch your ass. They're out to do you. And, above all, never show your ruthlessness, unless you're ready to act on it. That's why I'm up there in the agency, not just some dumb numbers cruncher. And I've just begun to fight."

"Gives me the shivers," Jenny said, cuddling closer, her fingers following the contours of his naked body from forehead to penis.

"In this town never, ever take anything at face value," Larry continued. "People are never what they seem."

"That will take some getting used to," Jenny said.

"Just do it fast," Larry said, turning toward her.

"Some things work better slower," Jenny said, giggling, as she continued to caress his body. She was so happy. Nothing but nothing was too good for her Larry.

She had met him nearly a year ago when he came into Dr. Parker's office with a nasty gash on his arm that required some stitches. Apparently he had tripped on a rock while investigating possible sites in the area for a theme park that was being researched by the advertising agency.

She had assisted Dr. Parker in the procedure. In fact, she had actually done the stitching, since it was one of those mornings when Dr. Parker's arthritis was acting up. For a year after high school, she had taken courses at the Bedford Hospital preparatory to becoming a paramedic, where she had learned a number of emergency procedures. But then the job with old Dr. Parker had come along, and she'd decided to forgo the complete course, reasoning that it would be a good opportunity to be "on her own," get her own place, and not be a financial burden on her parents.

"Handy little helper," Larry had commented. She wore a white uniform and white stockings, and Dr. Parker called her "nurse." He told her often that she was "better than any graduate nurse," which flattered her enormously. In addition to his arthritis, Dr. Parker's eyes were failing and he relied on her to assist him to an extent that might have seemed borderline to the Medical Society of Indiana.

"Couldn't do without her," Dr. Parker had responded.

Jenny remembered that she had blushed beet red, not simply because of the compliment, which was well deserved, but because it was delivered in front of this handsome young man who had stirred in her a disturbing response to his presence. She sensed, too, that there might be a mutuality about it.

After he had dressed, he had lingered in the reception area and engaged Jenny in conversation between her answering the doctor's telephone calls.

"Didn't hurt a bit," he had told her.

"We aim to please, Mr. Burns."

"Do you do this often?" he had asked. "Stitching up the wounded?"

"Only on occasion," she had replied, compelled to be truthful as a point of sincerity. "I'm not really a nurse. More like a paramedical jack-of-all-trades."

She could tell he was interested, and by then she was dead certain that she was attracted to him. He was so handsome and confident and immaculately dressed in beige pants and blazer with a crisp striped shirt with tab collar and a wonderful perfectly matched tie. He seemed so worldly and sophisticated, so in charge of himself, and above all, so different from most of the men she had dated in Bedford.

"Maybe you can tell me about Bedford over lunch?" he had asked.

After a brief hesitation for propriety's sake, she'd consented. But she would always remember the thought that had passed through her mind at just that moment: There must be a God, because he just dropped this beautiful man from heaven right on my doorstep.

Attraction was a mysterious and magical thing and, almost always, unpredictable. She knew her own type, which was that category of woman whom people referred to as the "small packages" the "best things come in." Not that she was that small—five feet two—but well proportioned for her height, too small to win a beauty contest, but with the kind of figure that could and did turn a male eye. So far, heavy exercise was not a necessity, and no matter what she ate she never gained a pound. Her blue eyes dictated her colors, and she dressed to complement them.

In school she was considered perky, the type that made a natural cheerleader. Her mother had pressed her to pursue that phase of her school career, even sending her to baton-twirling lessons. As a baton-twirling cheerleader, she was automatically a kind of local celebrity. Fame of that type was very sought after in a small town like Bedford, mostly because that kind of visibility gave one entrée to date the best boys, meaning the local athletic heroes.

Despite being popular and visible in high school, she was also a conformer and definitely not a rebel, which meant, in that context, that she maintained a monogamous relationship with one boyfriend with whom she had sex, beginning around her sixteenth birthday, which seemed the obligatory age when one lost one's virginity in Bedford. The experience, as most of the girls agreed, was generally awful but was supposed to get better with time. She had looked forward to that with toleration and hope.

She had never had any plans other than to get married, have children, and stay in Bedford to raise her family as her mother and grandmother and great-grandmother had done before her.

Her mother had instilled in her the idea that when all was said and done, being a housewife and mother was the noblest profession a woman could aspire to. Nor did she envy any of her schoolmates who went on to college, determined to make it in the world at large. She knew, of course, that such an attitude was old-fashioned and totally contrary to the ideas fostered by the women's movement, but she saw herself as more of a traditionalist and felt no guilt about her well-defined ambition to run a happy home, have a loving husband, and raise two, maybe three children. She considered that a noble aspiration.

But being a traditionalist did not mean that she was not modern in her ideas. One did not have to be militant and outspoken to understand her own version of liberation, which to her meant being respected by men and consulted as an equal on those subjects where she could contribute. In her mind, however, there was a distinct separation between home and business. Home was, generally speaking, a woman's domain, and business, also generally speaking, was a man's.

Her own mother, for example, ruled the roost with tact and subtlety, never relegating her father to a secondary position in terms of respect and the illusion of command. He was always the man of the house, an authority figure to be deferred to and consulted for his wisdom and knowledge of the world. Early on, Jenny recognized that her parents' home was a repository of love and contentment. If she could replicate such a home in her life, Jenny decided, that would be the ultimate fulfillment.

Unfortunately, there were drawbacks to her fulfilling these dreams of love and contentment. The mating rituals in a small town did not provide much variety in terms of husband material. Not if you were choosy like Jenny, whose personality and good looks demanded that she choose a mate who was a cut above most of the boys who stayed on in Bedford.

The local boys who were going to make something of themselves had already moved out of town. This left the older men who had chosen to come back and set up shop in the professions and started to raise their own families.

It was slim pickings indeed, but this never depressed her. She adored her parents and her brother, who had married a local girl before he was twenty and already had three children, and he was just twenty-seven. She envied him, but in a healthy way, not to the point of despair, and she loved her nieces and nephew and never gave up on the idea that her man would come along one day.

Her family, naturally, wanted her to "settle down" and considered her too picky in her choice of men. Her defense was that she prized her independence, which she did, although in her heart of hearts she would have loved to settle down with the right man and raise a family.

Jenny, who had her own small apartment not far from Dr. Parker's office, loved to come over to her mother's house and help with the chores. Most of the girls in town were well schooled in what was still referred to in Bedford as the "domestic arts." They were taught cooking, the care and cleaning of household furniture, sewing, knitting, petit point, simple repairs, gardening, and little specialties such as putting up preserves and canning. Weekly family gatherings were a ritual, as was going to church on Sunday in your best clothes, having the neighbors in for barbecues, and generally participating in community activities.

This did not mean that Bedford was isolated from the realities of the surrounding world, the global village. It did, after all, have cable television and access to a wide variety of other media that provided a great deal of knowledge of what was happening beyond their cloistered small-town world. It even had its share of what were once considered exclusive aspects of big cities, drugs, crime, racial animosities, homosexuality, and, even in Bedford, AIDS. Bedford also had its Republicans and Democrats, its pettiness and gossip, its Gothic secrets, its hidden aberrations, its share of pain and poverty. For people with oversize dreams and ambitions, Bedford was a prison. But not for Jenny.

Her father worked for a carpet manufacturer, a good solid job with a pension and health benefits that paid enough for the family to own their own small home with a nice yard and two old cars and to have raised a son and a daughter. The concept of the family fortress, their good name, being thought well of, doing the right thing, having compassion for the less fortunate, and being decent to your fellow man was the bedrock of her family's value system.

Jenny's value system did, however, have its private exceptions, particularly in the practice of sexual congress, which carried with it an element of hypocrisy. The sexual revolution was a fact of life and the peer pressure extraordinary. It was the one value that couldn't, at this juncture, be multigenerational. It was simply not in her parents' lexicon of experience. Her mother had been a virgin until she was married, and, Jenny was certain, she believed in her heart that the same was true of her daughter, all the evidence around her notwithstanding.

Her one overt break with the family value system was when she had an affair with a doctor who had offices in the same building as Dr. Parker, Darryl Phipps, a man in his mid-forties who was going through a trial separation at the time of their liaison. Yet officially he was still a married man, which carried with it a stigma that made Jenny uncomfortable and forced them into a secrecy that also made her ashamed.

In retrospect, Jenny rationalized, their affair was part learning experience, part sexual awakening. Darryl Phipps was an import to Bedford, having married one of the local girls he had met on a skiing vacation. He was East Coast Ivy League with a level of sophistication that was unknown in her experience up until then.

By osmosis and intimacy, she felt somehow socially and culturally elevated by the relationship.

More important, Darryl had confirmed what she had suspected, that her teenage jock boyfriend, long gone by then, was a sexual illiterate and probably a premature ejaculator, a condition that, by the testimony of her girlfriends, seemed to afflict the young men of Bedford in epic proportions. By contrast, her mature lover was enormously patient, considerate, and wonderfully instructive. In the end he opted to return to his wife and children. Actually Jenny felt relieved by his decision and was enormously grateful for the experience. Discretion had left her reputation intact, her self-esteem enhanced, and her sexual nature understood and vastly reinforced.

This prior relationship stood her in good stead with Larry Burns, who had been married once before for a brief period and was still bitter about that episode in his life.

According to Larry, his former wife had been a journalist, far more interested in her career than in him and their marriage. That was, in fact, the hidden agenda of their whirlwind courtship and the one thing that set Jenny apart from his former wife. It was, she told herself, fate intervening, as if Larry Burns did indeed drop from heaven, right into the target's bull's-eye. In a wife he wanted exactly what she aspired to be, homemaker, mother, nurturer, devoted helpmate, lover.

To her family Larry was an awesome figure, a smashing success in the advertising business, handsome, intelligent, articulate, charming. He was extremely fastidious about the care of his body, and his grooming was tasteful and immaculate. She liked that. It showed that he had respect for himself and his good looks. Indeed, at that point in time she enjoyed watching him pose and primp in front of the mirror, and she was oddly pleased when she spotted him surreptitiously checking his image in whatever reflection was handy. Even the after-shave he used was deliciously enticing.

He was also enormously organized, fastidious in keeping records of his expenditures and allocating his time. This greatly impressed her. It indicated that he was a man in charge of his own destiny, someone who would be in control of his and his family's life, able to intelligently plan the future, not be a victim of circumstances, a rolling stone.

Her parents were proud of her for attracting such a marvelous man at the ripe old age of twenty-five. Her dad called him "a go-getter," which was his highest form of compliment.

She worried, of course, that the differences between them in terms of "worldliness" would inhibit or even destroy their relationship. A small-town upbringing carried a stigma of diminishment, not that she didn't have her defenses. When they were together, she made light of the idea that she was "a Hoosier hick" and he was a "city slicker," but like all humor, there was an element of truth hiding just below the surface of her words.

Of course, Larry's response was all the more disarming, since he assured her that "a Hoosier hick" was exactly what he had in mind. She wondered how he defined the image and hoped he hadn't equated it with naiveté or ignorance. Inexperience and innocence were other matters entirely, although she showed him that she was certainly not innocent in sexual matters. That, too, had given her pause. She had worried that too quick a sexual capitulation and the resultant evidence of her experience might frighten him off. It didn't. After three nights of consecutive dating, she was in his motel bed, an actively aggressive participant.

"Nothing hick in this department," he had commented.

"Can't fool nature," she had responded saucily. "If the conditions are right, it takes you there."

"You're exactly what the doctor ordered," he'd told her.

"Likewise," she had agreed, complimenting him sincerely on his manliness. She had, of course, been concerned about a possible disappointment in this area. Early on he'd admitted that his first marriage was dysfunctional. It didn't take long for her to discover that it wasn't his fault.

"Perfect fit," he told her.

"Uh-huh," she agreed.

She hoped that he attributed her knowledge to the fact that she was a medical person.

"Now wasn't he worth waiting for?" she proudly told her parents and brother when it was apparent that a genuine relationship had begun to spring up between her and Larry. Naturally they agreed.

Even the parameters he had laid down on the night he had proposed, which was exactly three weeks after he had come into town, were a perfect parallel for her own aspirations.

"Make me a home, Jenny," he had told her the night of his proposal. "Let me love you and protect you." They had been lying naked on his motel bed. "You can't imagine what it means to a guy who comes home after fighting the world to find a beautiful, loving woman waiting—"

"To fall into his arms," she interrupted. "Willing, wet, and wonderful. Who has spent her day making coming home special and has prepared a lovely meal."

"With a delicious bottle of wine."

"That, too."

"Sheer heaven," he said. "Far from the slings and arrows of outrageous fortune."

"Yes," she replied, vaguely remembering the words as a famous quote. "Far from those."

"Which brings up a question," he teased. "Do we make love before or after dinner?"

"Why not both before and after?"

"Why not? Every night of our lives."

"Mornings, too."

"Exactly my fantasy," he said. "A wife who runs my house and a whore in my bed."

"A whore?" She feigned offense, but she knew what he meant.

"I will aim to please in all areas." She giggled.

"Pinch me," he said. "I must be dreaming."

"I won't pinch. But how about a love bite on that?" Her lips closed around his erect penis. God, she thought, how grateful I am that you've sent me such a beautiful man.

She loved seeing him naked, and he enjoyed exhibiting himself, especially, as now, when his penis was in glorious erection. He was so perfectly proportioned, he reminded her of a picture of the Michelangelo sculpture of David. She loved the feel of the rippling tightness of his body, his hard buttocks, his ivory smooth penis. She loved wrapping her legs around him, swallowing him into her. It set off sparks within her body. Nor was she loath to try any new way to bring him pleasure, and she could be as compliant in sexual matters as he was aggressive and eager and vice versa.

She also enjoyed exhibiting herself in whatever manner he requested, and she refused him nothing. Pleasing him, even at that early stage, had become her mission in life. She had every reason to believe this desire was mutual.

"Between people who love each other, there are no barriers," he told her. "Only trust and honesty." She agreed with all her heart.

It gave her goose bumps to discover such a mutuality of ideas about what a true relationship meant. It was as if they were sharing some wonderfully deep and very private secret.

She was certain that there was something between them of real lasting significance, of which the body's pleasure was only a symbol, something spiritual and holy. This was, for her, a lifetime commitment. She had no doubt that it was for him as well.

There were of course some drawbacks to the impending marriage. Since his office was in New York, she would have to leave Bedford, which would be traumatic, but it would certainly be exciting to live in Manhattan.

"It's a lot different from Bedford," Larry told her. "But I'll teach you how to hack it."

There would be an adjustment period, of course. She had never been to New York and was well aware of her own lack of what he called "street smarts." Big-city life was intrinsically frightening to small-town folks. People might characterize her as a hayseed or a hick. But, she was, she knew, a quick learner, and she was determined to pull her weight as the wife of the brilliant and beautiful Larry Burns.

She was certain also that he would not opt for children immediately. Considering his first experience with marriage, he would be cautious, waiting perhaps a year or two to be sure of their compatibility.

He made a great living, he informed her, although he was never specific about the number. Six figures was all he would volunteer, which was good enough for her and more than good enough for her father, who thought he had reached the pinnacle of success at thirty-five thousand dollars a year. In their value system, the man was the provider.

"And that's only the beginning," he told her. "I've got plans, big plans, and someday I'll be the boss."

She certainly had caught a good one, the family agreed. She also assured them that she would be a frequent visitor to Bedford, certainly on holidays. They knew that, of course. Her heart would always be in Bedford. That was her upbringing. Family was everything, regardless of distance.

Not that they weren't truly worried. The big city, especially New York, to a small-town Hoosier was seen as a corrupting influence. She assured them that they had given her a good foundation and that she was beyond corruption, and with Larry protecting her, what was there to worry about?

Larry's family was practically nonexistent. He was an only child who had been raised mostly in boarding schools. His father was an accountant in Seattle who had married twice after leaving his mother and had acquired two additional families, which kept him perpetually strapped for money. He and Larry hardly communicated. His mother had died years ago. Obviously, Jenny reasoned, Larry was a man who hungered for the joys of home and hearth, of real family, and a wife to love and care for him and provide him with children. She vowed to be that wife.

On the day she left Bedford, Jenny and her mother had a real heart-to-heart, complete with tears and lots of hugs.

"Just be good to your man and everything will be fine," her mother told her.

"You know I will, Mom."

"And never, never stray from your real values."

"Never, Mom."

"Sometimes things will get tough. There will be ups and downs, but in the end it will be the wife who holds things together."

They hugged each other for a long time and dried their tears.

Then Jenny's mother gave her the petit-point poem entitled "The Wife," by author unknown. It was suitably framed and had been replicated from her grandmother's, one of those sentimental possessions that are handed down from mothers to daughters. Her mother, she knew, had hung it on the inside of her closet door, where it still remained through the years, a kind of very private and very cherished idea. Jenny knew that her brother's wife had also received one when they were married.

She took the petit-point poem from her mother and read it aloud.

THE WIFE

The heart of a home is a loving wife
Who protects it always from trouble and strife
Her sacred role is to love and to care
Always to nurture and forever to share
As helpmate or more, she can never lose
Unless she surrenders to the housewife blues.

Again mother and daughter hugged and cried. Jenny had never been happier.

Jenny set to work putting the apartment together with tremendous enthusiasm. Larry had given her a budget, and she was determined to stay within it and impress him with her own resourcefulness and good taste. He had also given her samples of the colors he favored and she did not make any purchases without his complete approval. She welcomed his hands-on attitude and his firm views.

They haunted the little antique stores tucked away in various Manhattan neighborhoods and bought numerous items that seemed to fit perfectly in their apartment. She favored American Colonial and he favored Victorian English, but they managed to compromise and get the apartment furnished with a minimum of new pieces. They did, however, purchase a new four-poster queen-size bed.

"And it had better be sturdy," Larry had told the clerk with a wink.

She particularly enjoyed putting together the kitchen. She always had a flair for cooking, and Larry let her buy whatever equipment was needed, including expensive copper pots, which she hung from hooks on the brick wall. She also bought a complete set of knives, which she kept in a wooden block with handy slots on the kitchen island. On a shelf over the sink she had put a wonderful antique spice rack. In the kitchen closet she put a wine rack that held thirty-six bottles. Larry considered himself an expert on wines.

She had known from the beginning that Larry loved the idea of coming home to a well-cooked meal, and she had done her best to oblige. Once, however, while working late into the afternoon in the apartment, she'd neglected to prepare a meal and was obliged to call a carryout pizza place for their dinner.

It was, of course, against Larry's ideas about how to conduct oneself safely in the city, but she was certain he would allow her to make this one little exception. Besides, she liked pizza, which went very well with a salad and a glass of wine.

Unfortunately, he got home almost at the exact time that the delivery man pressed the outside buzzer.

"Who can that be?" he had asked.

"The pizza man," she replied, pressing the buzzer that would allow the man to enter.

"Are you out of your mind?" he rebuked.

"You know I like pizza and I haven't had time ... "

"Jenny, how many times must I warn you? The carryouts in this city are a license to steal or worse. The statistics on this are appalling and I will not allow you to endanger yourself."

"Now, that's being paranoid. Lots of people order carryouts in New York."

A moment later the door buzzer sounded and Larry rushed to the door. She watched him opening it carefully, keeping the chain on the hook. After inspecting the delivery man, a black teenager, he asked the price and quickly exchanged the box of pizza for the money, then swiftly rechained the lock and slid the dead bolt into its slot.

"He was just a kid," Jenny said.

"Right. A black kid. The highest single group of crime perpe-
trators in the country."

"Really, Larry..."

"I'm not kidding, Jenny. No more of this. Not ever again. I want
a promise."

"You're taking this much too seriously, Larry."

"A promise," he repeated.

"If it means that much." She sighed.

"It does."

"Well then, I promise."

It was, after all, just to keep the peace. If it was important to
Larry, then it was important to her. She let it pass, put it out of
her mind, and did not let it interfere with her putting the apartment
together.

He fitted out one corner of their bedroom with a weight bench
set up between two standing antique mirrors that gave him a two-
sided view of himself when he lifted weights. He usually did it
wearing only a jockstrap, and he enjoyed having her watch him
do his sets. For Jenny it was sheer joy watching his muscles ripple,
and invariably she reacted sexually.

From the beginning Larry had harped on her not to be too pushy
in trying to get to know the neighbors. New Yorkers, he insisted,
were uncomfortable with neighborliness, and he didn't want her
to have to face what might be interpreted as rejection. She appreciated his concern, but exercising a mild assertiveness, she
reminded him that she had worked for several years as an assistant
in a doctor's office and was not totally naive about people and
their motives. She pointed out, too, that people who lived under
the same roof were obligated to get to know one another, if only
as a kind of insurance for emergencies.

"I've got to learn how to deal with city people," she told him.

"Forewarned is forearmed," he told her. "Most New Yorkers
have a siege mentality."

"People are people."

"New Yorkers are conditioned by a hostile environment. They
react to everything defensively. Even their offense is defensive.
Most people in this town are takers, not givers. Besides, what do

you need them for? My advice is keep to yourself, mind your own business. It's safer."

"I'm perfectly capable of making that judgment on my own."

"Of course you are, darling," he said, retreating somewhat. "But, remember, I grew up in Manhattan and it's gotten worse over the years. I can smell the hustlers, the phonies, the users. Lean on me in that respect. I know. Believe me, I know. All I'm saying is watch out. Next thing you know you'll be involved in somebody else's complications. Trust me."

With that in mind, she nevertheless felt obliged to make a modest effort to strike up some social intercourse with the neighbors. After all, in her comings and goings, how was one to avoid them? A smile and a kind word were certainly in order under those circumstances. So far, the easiest people to get to know were the Richardsons, largely because Terry was naturally approachable. Godfrey was less so, but had been gracious and charming at dinner.

Larry, although he had consented to her inviting the Richardsons, had been a reluctant participant.

"You know how I feel about getting too intimate with the neighbors."

"Just dinner, Larry. You never know when you'll need a little neighborly help one day."

"As long as it's just dinner," he told her.

The dinner had seemed to go well. She had made her grandmother's favorite meat loaf recipe. She also did her homemade biscuits and baked what she considered her inspired apple pan dowdy. A real "down home" meal with succotash and whipped-up mashed potatoes. Only the fancy French red wine served in big stem glasses gave a touch of Manhattan sophistication.

The Richardsons were pleasant and affable and seemed to like the meal, except that Godfrey hadn't touched the succotash. But the conversation seemed to steer clear of any real intimacy. Mostly the talk centered around contemporary art. Godfrey owned an art gallery, and Larry probed him most of the evening about which artists were on their way up for investment purposes.

"Now did that hurt?" she asked after the Richardsons had gone and she had finished the dishes.

"Depends on your definition of pain," Larry said.

"I don't understand," Jenny replied, confused.

"Meat loaf?"

"What's wrong with meat loaf?"

"Oh, it's fine for cafeterias and home meals, but for guests? Really, Jenny. Meat loaf?"

"It's my grandmother's recipe," she said, her stomach churning.

"Succotash?"

"What's wrong with that?"

"I hate to put it this way." Larry sighed. "You worked so damned hard. But it's . . . well . . . second rate. Not in taste or even intention. Just . . . lower order . . . not upscale."

"I did serve that fancy French wine," Jenny said. She felt rebuked.

"It's not important," Larry said. "You did tell them it would be no big deal."

"Yes, I told them."

"Call it gentle advice, Jenny. Not worth a hassle between us. Put it in the category of a learning experience."

"I am confused, Larry."

"Just trust me. I've got a handle on perception. Follow my lead. It's my fault, really. I should have put my two cents in. Anyway, forget it. Fact is, the meat loaf was yummy and the apple pan dowdy scrumptious."

He put his arms around her and kissed her forehead.

"You're wonderful, Jenny. Wonderfully Midwest. Don't ever lose that."

She wanted to explore the question further, but she decided that she would leave it for another time. She knew she had a lot to learn.

"Notice how Godfrey was hustling his artwork? Proof positive. Everybody here is hustling something."

"I wasn't paying much attention to that side of it," Jenny said.

"Well, I hope you learned something about the banking business from Terry."

"Actually we talked mostly about babies. Hers. They've been going to a fertility clinic."

"So much for opportunity," Larry said with a sigh. She glanced at him suddenly, wondering if he was serious. He must have felt her scrutiny. "She is a banker," he said. "We gave them dinner. There's a quid pro quo here somewhere."

"They're neighbors," Jenny said, confused by his remark. "Just neighbors."

"Nobody is just anything, Jenny. Not in the Big Apple," Larry said, reaching for her hand and leading her gently into the bedroom.

Two hours and ten minutes by the clock passed before she heard the elevator move in the shaft once again. It annoyed her that she was timing the liaison as if she were a private detective.

Yet as soon as she heard the elevator, she dashed closer to the window, hiding in the shadows at a spot that offered a good vantage to watch the street. Sure enough, the woman appeared on the steps, and Jenny studied her carefully, as if her physical aspect might reveal some confirming truth. She seemed to have combed her hair with some care and put on new makeup and did not look as furtive or as anxious as before. In fact, she seemed almost relieved, as if she had been through some ordeal and was glad that it was over.

Not ten minutes later she heard Godfrey's regular tread coming down the stairs. No need for him to sneak now. It crossed her mind that his earlier caution had been for Jenny's benefit, since it was probably apparent to him as well as the other tenants that she was the only one who remained in the building on most weekdays.

She heard the front door open, then Godfrey came into view. He was only visible in profile, his thin face seemed paler than before, his body hunched into his overcoat. She made a conscious effort to read his attitude, hoping that she might sense some element of saving grace, like guilt or remorse for what he had done. Without realizing it, her concentration made her less cautious. She had stepped closer, moving toward the center of the bay window.

Then, suddenly, her attention shifted to the sycamore tree in front of the house. There was that tabby tomcat climbing the tree again. It belonged to the men who lived in the downstairs apartment and was always getting out somehow. Frequently she would see it climbing the tree, posting itself on the branch opposite her window and looking into her apartment, which it was doing now. Larry, who was allergic to cats, hated the sight of it.

"Just don't give the bastard milk," he had warned her. "Then you'll never get rid of him."

Godfrey's attention, too, might have been deflected by the cat, and he had turned. Perhaps he had sensed her observation of him as well. She felt a blush of embarrassment rise to her face. Their eyes met and stayed locked together for a brief moment. He did not smile in greeting but turned quickly like a man caught in the beam of a floodlight, then headed swiftly toward Third Avenue.

He knows I know, she cried inside, burning with the discomfort of holding his dark secret, as if somehow she had become a co-conspirator in his act of infidelity and betrayal.

2

DAMN, damn, Godfrey Richardson railed at himself. He was wallowing in self-disgust. His insides were churning. It had been a gross idea. He should have gone to a hotel, overcome his guilt, his paranoia of being seen, suffered through the little ritual of checking in, the process of paying in advance, in cash, endured the stares and imagined snickers of the room clerk.

There was not a question in his mind that Jenny Burns had observed this ill-fated caper. If only the Kellys, who had the apartment before the Burnses, hadn't split up and were still there. At least both of them worked during the day like normal people. How was it possible that in this day and age, in Manhattan, there was such a thing as a professional housewife? It had irritated him that the woman seemed to revel in her role, as if she were doing something actually superior to what everyone else did.

"What is more boring than being a housewife?" he had asked Terry when they had returned from dinner at the Burnses. "Meat loaf, for chrissake."

"And succotash, your favorite dish," Terry teased.

He put a finger in his mouth.

"Barf."

"She is a doll, Godfrey. And just a newlywed," Terry had responded.

"I'll grant her that," Godfrey had replied. He had found her Lolita-like looks and her high small voice attractive and oddly sexy.

"A pretty little thing, isn't she? She was a doctor's assistant in this small town in Indiana. I found her by no means stupid."

"A doctor's assistant. Small town in Indiana. Meat loaf. Deliver me."

"Quite a snob for the son of a high school teacher," Terry snapped.

"Look who's talking. Your mother believes there are two places in the world—New York and out of town, with people from the latter mostly rednecks and KKK'ers with southern accents."

"She may be right."

"And I can be a snob if I choose. I am, after all, in the art world," Godfrey said, laughing.

"Speaking of snobs, Larry took the cake. He struck me as real puckered up. What's his story?"

"He's this big gun at this mega–advertising agency. Research. One of those guys with opinions up the wazoo. Dripping in yup values."

"You were working him pretty good," Terry said.

"Tight-ass guy like that will squeeze out all the aesthetics. He's looking to unlock the mysteries of finding gold in art."

"And you're helping him along."

"That's my racket," Godfrey had responded. "New York is filled with Larry Burnses. Guys that think they know exactly where they're going, destiny riders. He'll rise up the ladder like a hot knife through butter. And she'll be the dutiful wife, walking ten paces behind."

"Well, aren't you the dutiful husband?"

In a way he was. He knew how to play the game with her colleagues and her bosses. But, of course, he had his own ax to grind. He could sell the pompous sons of bitches art. Anyway, there was a limit on how far they would let her go. What do they call that? Glass ceiling?

"What does she do with her time all day?" Godfrey asked, his mind still focused on the Burnses. "I know. She makes meat loaf." "And biscuits." Terry laughed. "Don't forget about the home-made biscuits."

"Or apple pan dowdy."

"I thought that was great," Terry said.

"Apple pan dowdy, for crying out loud."

"You're being intolerant," Terry remonstrated. "Her agenda is different from ours." She had grown momentarily pensive. "Maybe."

Godfrey knew what she meant, of course, and it infuriated him. Her inability to conceive was driving him crazy. They had been together nearly twelve years, five of them married. In fact, that was exactly why they had gotten married. To begin a family. Terry had gone off the pill, and they had begun the so-called process.

To everything there was a season. He had lived by that concept. A time to plant. A time to sow. Finally they were established financially. He had his own gallery. Terry had become a vice-president of Citibank. It was exactly the goals they had planned for themselves. They had socked away a tidy sum for a house in Connecticut. Raising a child in Manhattan was out of the question. They had made plans, dared to dream dreams. It was as if they'd finished one chapter and were trying to begin another.

Their relationship had defied the odds, and they were proud of it. They had actually met at a bar on Second Avenue in the dwindling days, before AIDS, of swinging singles. His interest that night was pussy, strictly pussy. No encumbrances. No relationships. It was Friday night, and his objective was to cut a heifer from the herd. She was a bank teller then, and he was a contemporary-art appraiser.

Meeting in a bar was strike one. Strike two was that they had marched right up to Terry's place and gone right to bed. The entire operation had taken less than an hour, leaving up in the air the question of who seduced whom. It was an issue still in limbo between them.

"Just don't bullshit me," she had told him while they were still in the bar. "And don't pay me compliments," she'd said when they were in the cab. "Above all, don't tell me you love me, either before, during, or after."

"Who's in charge here?" he had asked her as they got out of the cab.

"We're about to work that out," she'd told him.

Sunday night, after a weekend of sex, talk, and carryouts, he told her that he loved her, and she went through the roof.

"Get out," she cried.

"I mean it."

"You're just setting me up for next weekend."

"You got it."

"Well, I'm busy," she told him. "And I'll be busy the weekend after that. In fact, for the next one hundred weekends."

"That's only two years," he told her.

"What are you, a mathematics freak?"

"I told you. I love you. Look, Terry. I'm thirty. I know what I've been looking for. I found it, and I want it forever."

"Liar."

"I am not."

"You're actually thirty-three. I picked your pocket when you were asleep and peeked in your wallet. I read your driver's license. Also, if it's any consolation, you're who you say you are. You were born in Elizabeth, New Jersey. And you are an art appraiser."

"You have character flaws," he responded. "I like that. Nobody is perfect. Even me. You work where you say you work. Your real name is Theresa, and you happen to be twenty-four, not twenty-two. You also don't weigh a hundred and twenty pounds, as your driver's license points out. I'd say..." He squeezed her breasts and buttocks and patted her stomach. "One hundred and thirty."

"I'm five seven. I can carry it."

There is such a thing as knowing, he had decided at that moment. Bar or no bar. First-night lay or not. This woman had his name on her. They made love again, and all of a sudden it was dawn on Monday morning and he opened his eyes to find her studying him, her head resting on her elbow.

"While you were sleeping, I looked you over carefully, from

stem to stern. Are there any major diseases in your family? My grandmother has mild hypertension."

"How old is she?"

"Eighty-seven."

"How old was your grandfather?"

"What do you mean, was? He's ninety-one. My parents are also alive and kicking. What about yours?"

"Both died before they were sixty," he told her.

"It would be like playing Russian roulette," she mused, continuing to study him.

"Life's a gamble," he pressed. "Why not roll the dice?"

"With those odds?" She started to laugh. "I'd have to be a fool. And be afflicted with infantile romanticism."

"That's my affliction, too," he told her. "Incurable. I've had to learn to live with it. You can, too. In fact, I'll teach you. It's a very long course. Might take a lifetime."

"That long?"

"Longer, I hope."

"Can I test it? See if it suits me?"

"Of course. But be forewarned. I'll teach my heart out."

"Where do I register?" she said haltingly, her voice breaking. Tears welled suddenly in her eyes, rolling down her cheeks.

"Right here," he said, kissing her cheeks dry, then taking off from there.

That Monday they never did get to work.

Now this business of conception was consuming their lives. Beneath their banter and the effort to maintain the familiar routine of their relationship was this dominating, corrosive, aching sense of frustration. Neither of them wanted to admit or, more appropriately, surrender themselves to the idea of failure.

The doctors had not found any organic reason for Terry's inability to conceive. She produced healthy eggs. Godfrey produced perfectly capable swarming schools of spermatozoa. But something went awry, as they say, between the cup and the lip.

"I'm so, so sorry," Terry had cried after the doctors had diagnosed that she was the problem. For weeks after that she had wallowed in self-pity and depression, and it had taken a massive effort on his part to pry her out of it. He had feigned indifference at first, but she knew better. He had wanted children, perhaps even more than she did, had fantasized about fatherhood, and had been quite vocal on the subject. She had come to the idea reluctantly, reasoning that there was still time. But he had been insistent, and she had finally consented. Their failure to conceive was completely unexpected, a cruel blow.

"Bet you're sorry we ever got hitched," Terry told him one day, a day engraved on his memory. They were scheduled to go through yet another fertility process. It was the third time. They had changed clinics, opting for one only two blocks away, a lucky find. All he had to do was ejaculate and rush the results and Terry over to the clinic for the procedure.

By then the whole idea of sex, reduced now to pure biological mechanics, had lost most of its allure. It had become merely a medical process, a far, far cry from the wonderfully erotic pleasure it had once been, the rich exercise in fantasy and sex games that they had indulged in with such abandon. Not once in all the years that they had been together had he failed literally to rise to the occasion. And if he showed signs of flagging after three or four consecutive episodes, Terry, who had a finely tuned sense of the erotic and knew his parts intimately, could always manage to squeeze "one for the road" out of him.

In fact, the menu of their sex life was daring, intense, and, they thought, quite original and always exciting. Sometimes they would call during the day and talk each other through mutual masturbation. She would be sitting at her desk wearing no panty hose, an idea that was a surefire inducer. Sometimes they would have sex adventures in uncommon places like taxicabs, ladies' rooms, airplanes, telephone booths, movie houses. They had tried tie-ups and paint-ups, making their own videos, and other oddments of a sexual nature that came of an active fantasy life and guiltless and uninhibited mutual trust. Everyone needed a hobby, they told each other, never tiring of the giddy humor they induced in each other.

But on this crucial day, nothing, but nothing she tried could muster any excitement, and his penis simply remained in a state of flaccid indifference.

"Where are you when I need you?" he said, addressing the uncooperative part, hoping the wisecrack might dispel the tension. After two hours of trying without success, she reached for the phone and called the clinic. He actually put his hands over his ears in embarrassment.

"The doctor says it's not uncommon," Terry said after she had hung up. "He said to cool it for a while."

"That's the problem, not the solution," Godfrey said.

"He also said that maybe a little porno might get it going."

He shrugged, then consented to the possibility, and she got dressed and went to the video store to rent some porno movies. While she was gone he tried to channel his thoughts into images of lewdness. Nothing worked. She came back quickly with three tapes, none of which, despite their salacious images, could induce an erection.

It was maddening, embarrassing, debilitating, and by the end of the day mentally and physically exhausting. Naturally the appointment had to be canceled. Consultations followed at the clinic. All agreed that the situation was a common by-product of tension, and it was recommended that they stop thinking about conception for a few months. Producing an erection was, after all, a mental thing, and there was nothing organically wrong with him. Impotence, like death, was something that happened to other people.

They tried to pretend that it was not affecting them profoundly. The fact was, though, that they still loved each other and that these events were actually bringing them closer together, an irony, since such closeness should have induced a natural sexual response. It didn't. Not at first.

Then, like a miracle, a few weeks later Godfrey's impotence went away as mysteriously as it had arrived. Except that there was no more talk of fertility clinics. Soon they were up to their old sexual gymnastics. Indeed, absence, so to speak, made the hard-on grow fonder. The episode brought with it a greater renewal of their love. They had come through a crisis, and it had strengthened them. Not that they had ever been, in any way, even temporarily alienated. He had always been faithful, and it was no leap of faith to believe that she, too, had never strayed from the marriage bed.

But somehow this setback, which both viewed as temporary, proved how deeply they cared for each other.

They resumed their regular sex life with even more intensity than before. Finally they felt that they had conquered the problem and were ready to try again. The strategy they decided upon was for them to cease and desist until the fatal day. Store up the jism, they joked. She assured him, by observing his nocturnal erections, that he was wonderfully normal and that she had exerted great willpower in not throwing herself upon him as she did her research. Indeed, all the evidence pointed to both a lack of tension and a good attitude.

Until the fateful day. Nothing. The more Terry tried, the more intractable the article. Finally the operation was terminated once again. There was another option, of course. In an interview the doctor had explained that in such cases of psychological impotency, the sperm, when produced and delivered within a short time, could be frozen for future use, meaning injected into Terry at a time of her choosing. On the surface this seemed like a splendid idea, except that the very suggestion of such a process had sent any recovery of potency into limbo.

For months now nothing had happened, although she had been alert to his nocturnal erections in the hope that they, or only one, could be productive. It continued to be debilitating and humiliating. At times she actually would begin to masturbate while he slept, the idea being that she would be ready to begin the process during the night at a moment's notice. Unfortunately he always awoke, which resulted in a complete collapse of the instrument. It was all so depressingly clinical.

Their nerves were stretched thin, and often their eyes would meet and they would break into tears. How long before this finally rips us apart? he wondered. It was awful. He felt inadequate. He couldn't concentrate on his work. The gallery was going to hell.

He got the hooker's name from another dealer who had admitted to using call girls as a service to his out-of-town clients. Godfrey had been appalled by the idea.

"You don't sell art with pussy," he had remonstrated with the dealer.

"You can sell anything with pussy," the dealer had countered. He was a fat, balding man with thick lips and a gravelly-voiced gift of gab so originally crude that it was memorable. "Besides, strange pussy is always exhilarating." It was that crude phrase that stuck in Godfrey's mind, that phrase that motivated his idea. He had even inquired at the clinic as to how the freezing process worked, including the specifics of time and distance. In his scenario the event would be the ultimate surprise gift for Terry, the means justifying the end. He would tell her he had masturbated.

"Welcome to the world of corruption," the dealer told him when he called with his request.

"I'll try your method," he told the dealer. "I've got one tough client."

"I'll give you Wendy's number. Wendy is surefire. She majored in art history and is an artist herself. Guaranteed to put a client in a great frame of mind for art appreciation."

"Is this what we've come to?" he found himself saying, as if to maintain his moral superiority.

"Your tense is wrong, pal," the dealer said. "In this business what difference does it make as to how you fuck the client?"

Godfrey made the assignation for a time when he knew Terry would be at her regular weekly loan-committee meeting. He couldn't bear the idea of having his assistant at the gallery lie about his whereabouts. The very centerpiece of his relationship with Terry was honesty, absolute, uncompromising honesty. And faithfulness. Even on the phone with Wendy his guilt was so acute that he offered her double her price, which came to two hundred dollars, an additional payoff to ensure her silence about his identity.

"Are you kidding?" she said as if she were insulted. "Silence is the given of my business." She sounded more like a professor than a prostitute, which did not augur well for what he hoped to achieve. But she did consent to the double fee.

"You'll earn it," he told her.

"I always do."

He gave her specific instructions. Above all, he did not want her to be seen entering the building. He had calculated that most of the people in the building were off to work, except, of course, for

Jenny Burns, who, he assured himself, would probably be in the kitchen making meat loaf. He chuckled at the flash of humor, which calmed him somewhat. Not that he wasn't concerned about her spotting them. He would be very uncomfortable about anyone living in the building possessing knowledge of his infidelity. People gossiped. There was no denying that.

Jerry O'Hara and Bob Schwartz, the homosexual couple who shared the ground-floor apartment, could offer a threat of revelation only because O'Hara talked too much, jibber-jabbered in his singsong fey way, not caring what came out of his mouth. They and their damned cat, whom they had named, appropriately, Peter. He was a tabby, a kind of little tiger with the stripes to match and a fierce wanderlust instinct. He hadn't been neutered, which might be expected from Jerry and Bob. They were always searching for him, and the constant drumbeat of "Where's Peter?" could rattle the teeth of everyone in the building. More than once Godfrey had begged them to fix him, as did almost everyone.

"How would you like it done to you?" was Jerry O'Hara's invariable response when any of the neighbors had the temerity to complain. Jerry worked as a showroom salesman for a Seventh Avenue clothing manufacturer, and Bob Schwartz was a partner in a design firm. They were rarely home during the day. Godfrey had sold them two paintings by Hollander, which was their only point of neighborly reference. Godfrey would hate to have them know anything about what he was up to, although he felt reasonably secure that they would be out, especially at that hour.

The same was true of the Sterns, Sally and Barry. Barry was in real estate in Brooklyn, dealing apparently in slum-type property, and Sally was an accountant with one of the Big Five accounting firms, he couldn't remember which. He and Terry decided that they were workaholics on the basis of how much time their son, Teddy, spent alone. He was about sixteen and went to some fancy private school in Manhattan. There didn't seem much risk in the Sterns being home.

As for Myrna Davis, who lived across the hall from them, she was off in the wee hours every weekday and didn't return until very late. She was an associate editor for *Vanity Fair* who always seemed to be hassled and disorganized.

She had offered them bits and pieces of her history, mostly on the run. She had been married twice. Both had ended in divorce. And she had lived with a rather handsome middle-aged man for six months in the apartment, a Ronnie something, who rarely spoke, as if he were hiding from someone, which was probably true. He had simply disappeared.

At the moment Myrna had a mysterious weekend lover, of whom they had yet to catch a glimpse. He'd apparently arrive very late on Friday night and leave very early on Monday morning. Their routine was to send in from carryouts and never leave the apartment all weekend. He and Terry speculated that Myrna's lover was a celebrity cheating on his wife.

After one of those weekends Myrna always looked exhausted. All fucked out, they agreed. Myrna could be depended upon to be working, especially at that time of the month, deadline time.

Except for Jenny Burns, he felt reasonably secure. Jenny did not seem to be the prying type. Nevertheless, it would bother him that anyone who knew Terry might find out that he had betrayed her. That's the way people would see it, notwithstanding the mitigating circumstances.

He had let himself in the front door with his key and had walked up the stairs like a thief, counting each little squeak of the steps. The place seemed quiet. Occasionally, he knew, one or another of the tenants would have a maid in a couple of hours a day, but he didn't count them as any threat. They were mostly invisible people. Besides, they didn't know him or Terry.

His anxiety level did not decrease when Wendy finally arrived at his apartment door. He was already worrying about her leaving the building without being seen.

"Nothing untoward to report, *mon capitaine,*" Wendy said as she entered the apartment, offering a salute.

"Voice down," he whispered, inspecting her. She was young, well endowed, with black hair and olive skin. He took her for Italian. She looked more like a student than a prostitute with a carryall slung over her shoulder.

"What's the protocol?" he asked.

"Usually payment in advance," she said, smiling coyly and shrugging. "We all have to eat."

He put two hundred-dollar bills in her palm, and she put them into the carryall, unhooking it from her shoulder.

"Where is the bedroom?" she asked.

"No," he said. "Here. On the couch."

Not in their bed, he decided. The couch seemed less culpable, a hollow idea since the entire apartment might be said to be bearing witness. Terry's presence was everywhere.

"You seem nervous," she said, taking his hand. "And your hand is like ice."

"Everything is like ice," he said nervously.

"We'll see what we can do about that."

"I have condoms," he said, placing the box on the end table beside the couch. He also had the little cup the fertility clinic had given him, hidden behind a picture on the end table within easy reach. His idea was to remove the condom at the moment of ejaculation and use the cup for storage. The clinic preferred the cup.

"I come supplied as well," she said. He sat on the couch and stood before him. He felt tense, sitting up straight, his hands on his knees. "You have an art gallery?" she asked as she began to undress.

He watched, half listening, offering perfunctory answers. He sensed a growing anger in himself as she slowly revealed what by any measure would be a sensual body. She posed and gyrated in what was certainly a provocative performance.

Then she began to undress him. He closed his eyes. He felt ashamed. He hadn't expected such a reaction, and he knew from the moment that she touched him that this would result in one more failure. Yet he allowed her to persist, and she was quite resourceful and imaginative.

"I'm sorry," he whispered.

"Don't be. It happens."

"So does shit."

She was kind and knew exactly what to say under such circumstances. After a while he did feel more relaxed, but empty of any excitement or reaction. He did tell her that he was going through this bout of impotency, although he could not bring himself to mention the conception problem.

"It'll come back. As long as it's nothing organic." Then she proceeded to tell him of the various procedures that had been developed by the medical profession. "I've serviced men with implants and pumps."

"Do they ejaculate?"

"Yes, they do," she said, going into details on how these devices worked. She seemed expert on the subject.

"Very informative," he acknowledged.

"A man has it tough," she told him. "He just can't fake it."

In a strange way he felt relieved that nothing had happened. This couldn't count as unfaithful. After a while they got dressed and talked about contemporary artists.

"I'd like to see your work sometime," he told her.

"And I'd be grateful," she said.

By then nearly two hours had passed, and he told her that she had better get going. He also told her he appreciated her understanding and, of course, her knowledge. That in no way mitigated his utter sense of hopelessness and failure. This had been a terrible idea, a desperation measure, and it left him more depressed than ever.

She kissed him on the cheek as she left. "Don't worry," she whispered. "I'll be as quiet as a mouse." He listened, heard the elevator move in the shaft. Again he had forgotten to tell her to use the stairs. It was as if he consciously wanted to be found out, to be caught.

From the window he watched as she went out the door and headed quickly toward Second Avenue, losing her in the parade of pedestrians. Relieved, he washed, then quickly but carefully straightened the apartment, and, as if he even had to exorcise her aura, he sprayed the apartment with Lysol. Then he let himself out and walked down the stairs. There no longer seemed any need to be cautious.

He got down the front steps okay, then suddenly his attention was arrested by something in the tree. Turning, he looked up. That damned cat. But there in the window of her apartment, looking directly at him, was Jenny Burns. Yet neither of them made any effort to acknowledge the other. No nod. No smile. It was as if both of them were determined to render themselves invisible.

If only you knew my pain, he said to her in his heart. It is not at all what it seems.

Then he turned away and hurried down the street toward Third Avenue. He did not look back, but he could feel Jenny Burns's eye observing him as he fled.

3

JENNY met Myrna Davis, who lived in apartment 3 directly across the corridor from the Richardsons, when she went upstairs to deliver a package from Bloomingdale's that she had consented to take when the Bloomie's delivery man rang her buzzer one afternoon. That was another thing that being home most weekdays entailed. She was open to delivery men leaving packages or messages.

"Oh, my God, my shoes," Myrna exclaimed, taking the package from Jenny. She was a tall, very attractive brunette in her mid-thirties with an air of cocky assurance and a bearing to match.

"I'm Jenny Burns down in apartment one. The driver left it with me. I was home, you see...."

"You can't imagine how much I appreciate this, Mrs. Burns," Myrna said, offering a plastic smile with just enough warmth to show gratitude but not friendliness.

"Jenny. We've just moved in and—"

"Well, I do owe you one, Mrs....Janey."

"Jenny, and don't mention it."

"It certainly was nice meeting you, Jenny."

"Same here"—Jenny hesitated before continuing—"Myrna."

Giving one the right to use one's first name was, in Jenny's value system, a transaction that made first-name use acceptable to both persons.

Further conversation was deflected by the ring of the telephone from the interior of Myrna Davis's apartment.

"Damned phone," Myrna said, shaking her head and offering what was clearly a mock look of exasperation. From that expression, Jenny deduced that Myrna was relieved by the interruption.

"Well, it was nice..." Jenny began, letting the sentence drift away.

"Thanks again," Myrna said, the plastic smile disintegrating as her life apparently turned to more pressing events.

"Don't mention it," Jenny said, feeling suddenly awkward, hating the idea that she was repeating herself, nodding and smiling with more energy than she wished, then backing away. What had she expected? she wondered, trying to shake off an undeniable sensation of intimidation.

"In love with her own self-importance," Larry told her at dinner that night after she had reported her encounter with Myrna Davis. "I was married to a journalist, remember. I know the type well. All of them are ambitious, self-centered bitches."

His inflammatory comment made her regret that she had recounted the incident in a negative way, and it had slipped her mind that he had once been married to a journalist. Actually her comment about Myrna was only mildly negative. She had merely mused aloud that it would have been a nice gesture on Myrna's part to have invited her inside the apartment, not simply letting her stand in the hallway like some messenger boy.

She acknowledged to herself that perhaps she was also reacting to her own irritation, independently of Myrna Davis. Her prime rib had been overcooked, and the chocolate soufflé had collapsed. Larry, too, was in a bad mood, having fired one of his assistants for a sloppy interpretation of demographic information during a pitch to a major client. He had called her from the office to vent himself, as he often did, and to lift his spirits, she had planned this special dinner.

"Overdone," he had complained, forcing a tolerant smile. At that point she had told him about the incident with Myrna, realizing instantly that it reflected other irritations as well, both past and present.

"She could have had a lot of things on her mind," Jenny said, retreating. After all, the telephone had rung and that became a priority. Or did it? It always upset her to think ill of people before giving them a fair chance to absolve themselves. Myrna had not been impolite, merely self-absorbed.

"The issue is that you went out of your way to be nice. Am I right?" Larry pressed.

"It seemed like the neighborly thing to do," Jenny pointed out, knowing she was setting him off again on his favorite subject: staying clear of the neighbors and minding one's own business.

"It was neighborly," Larry assured her. "And look where it got you."

She had not told him about Godfrey Richardson's paramour. He might have called her a gossip, a term of opprobrium she did not wish attached to her. Her mother's characterization of gossips was people who suffered from boredom and got their kicks creating negative and mostly false ideas about people. Jenny agreed, and she did not want Larry to put her in that category. She was not bored. She liked running her little household, despite the prevailing attitude of women her age.

"She's a hotshot magazine editor for *Vanity Fair,* which puts her right up there with the worst of them," Larry went on. "Probably thinks she's on the cutting edge of trendy, and with people kissing her butt most of the day, she's lost any connection with reality."

"That seems a wee bit harsh, Larry," Jenny said, pouring the last of the wine into Larry's glass.

"I know the type well. Superior. Deliberately intimidating. Too sophisticated for words. She continues to be uppity, I just won't recommend any more advertising buys for *Vanity Fair.* I happen to have a bit of power in that department. The agency does do some business with that book."

"I could be misinterpreting her attitude," Jenny said, fearful that she had done enough to stir his hostility. "I think she was just rushed."

"Sure, rushed," Larry said. "She wouldn't be so rushed if she knew what I did for a living."

Why couldn't he stop? she wondered. Myrna hadn't been that rude.

"I really don't think she warrants that much anger, Larry."

"That's because you've never really been exposed to people like that. I have. She's one of those ball busters. Trust me. I know these career-obsessed women. No softness. No sweetness. Hard-edged. Experts at the put-down. Never give you the right time." Suddenly he mimicked in falsetto, "Oh, so you're Jenny Burns, the sweet little housewife in apartment one. How wonderfully quaint."

"She didn't say anything like that," Jenny countered. She was getting confused by Larry's overreaction and decided that she had best deflect the conversation. The soufflé having collapsed, she had put together a quick peach melba.

"I hope you like this as a substitute," she said, beginning to eat hers. She concentrated on the taste. "Not bad if I say so myself," she said, looking across the table at her husband. He hadn't touched his dessert.

"You're so damned naive, Jenny. You think all the people in this town are as honest and forthright as the folks back home. They aren't. Why can't you take my advice? Believe me, I know. Why open yourself up to insult?"

"It wasn't exactly—"

"Oh, yes, it was," Larry remonstrated. "You can't deny it, Jenny. No way."

She studied her husband. What was going on here? She felt terrible for pushing him into a foul mood. She remembered her mother's prescription for dealing with a husband in a funk. "Tiptoe through the tulips until he works it out of himself. He's probably reacting to something at work and is using the subject at hand to vent his anger."

"Eat your dessert, Larry. You're missing out on something good," she said pleasantly, hoping to close the issue. She spooned up the last of her peach melba. He still hadn't touched his.

"I think you should stop serving desserts," he said, patting his flat stomach and getting up from the table. "And stop being Mrs. Goody-Goody."

He couldn't seem to get it out of his mind, which was disturbing. She tried another tack.

"Are you saying, Larry, that you would not have accepted the package?" Jenny asked. It came down to that, she had decided.

"Probably not," he declared. He had gotten up from the table and had begun to unbutton his dress shirt in preparation for weight lifting in the bedroom. "In fact, I wouldn't. She should have had it sent to her office. She knew she wouldn't be home for a Bloomie's delivery, which happens only in the daytime. She also probably knew that you were the only person in the building who didn't work."

After he had gone into the bedroom she began to load the dishwasher, mulling over his comment. Not work, she wondered. Then what is this I'm doing?

Sometime later, after she had cleaned up the kitchen, she found him in the bedroom lifting weights. She sat on the bed and watched him, a process he greatly enjoyed. After a while he turned to her and she could see that his mood had changed.

"Like what you see, baby?" he said.

"Love those buns," she told him coyly.

"Then come on over and butter them up."

She did, watching the activity in the two standing mirrors.

It was, in fact, impossible to ignore the other tenants. Despite all Larry's caveats, she was not the kind of person who could pass someone in the hallway, turn her eyes away, and refuse to acknowledge their presence. Admittedly the episode with Myrna Davis, particularly Larry's reaction to her explanation of it, made her a bit gun-shy.

There was also no way not to observe them or to prevent herself from speculating about their lives. For example, there was Teddy Stern, who lived with his parents in the apartment on the third floor, the only floor that contained only one apartment.

Jenny had seen them in the hallway on weekends. Barry Stern, Teddy's father, was a chunky man in his early forties, balding, with the beginnings of a paunch and jowls and a serious, self-absorbed expression, as if his mind were perpetually occupied with weighty thoughts. When she passed him in the hallway while he waited for the elevator, she would always nod and smile pleasantly and offer the time-honored platitudes about the weather.

"On the chilly side for May," she would say as she headed for the front door.

"A bit," he would grunt indifferently, as if the statement had interrupted his far more important contemplations. His wife was only slightly more forthcoming and looked harassed and sickly with a sallow complexion and a glazed expression. There was a dark puffiness under her eyes as if she were on the verge of exhaustion.

Jenny had first seen Teddy Stern with his parents one Sunday as the three of them emerged from the elevator just as she was entering her apartment. She had smiled politely, and they'd all nodded and moved past her to the entrance of the building.

She'd observed him again one late afternoon through her front window. She guessed he was about fifteen or sixteen years old, a lanky, handsome boy, still at the awkward age. He had jet black hair and a sallow complexion like his mother's and wore blue pants and a gray sweater that had some kind of insignia sewed on to it, and she'd speculated that he probably went to some private school. Instead of coming in the front door, he had walked the few steps down to the entrance of the ground-floor apartment. There he'd fished in his pocket for a few moments, then let himself in with a key.

It seemed rather odd, since he lived on the third floor. She knew from the nameplates on the front door that the two gentlemen who lived there were named Jerry O'Hara and Robert Schwartz. She had met one of them, although she wasn't sure which one. He was a handsome blond man in his mid-thirties who had rung her apartment buzzer one late afternoon looking for his cat.

"I'm so sorry to bother you," he had said, smiling, showing even white teeth. "I seemed to have misplaced Peter."

"Peter?"

"My cat," he said.

She had seen a tabby sitting on the branch of the sycamore directly across from her apartment window, assuming it was merely an alley cat that had wandered about all night and was taking a morning respite. She hadn't thought about it much until that moment.

"A tabby?" she asked.

"You saw him?"

"Not today," she added quickly when she saw his sudden eagerness.

"Every time the maid comes this happens," the man said, shaking his head. "Hates cats. Something very ... very unfeeling about people who hate cats, don't you think?"

She knew Larry hated cats, but only because he was allergic to them. It was not the kind of information to pass along to a cat lover.

"I haven't thought about it much," Jenny said. "Growing up, I had dogs, standard poodles...." She remembered that she had begun to reminisce, but he had interrupted her.

"I must get on with the search," he said, hurrying away through the little lobby and out the door.

But when she saw Teddy enter their apartment with a key, she noted that there seemed to be a furtive air about him, as if he were doing something illegal or forbidden. Admittedly she became mildly curious, especially when it appeared to happen with some regularity.

Bearing in mind Larry's caveat about not getting involved, she forced herself to put it out of her mind, not mentioning it to Larry. Yet it was Larry who brought it back to her attention.

He had come in from his Sunday morning regular tennis game, which by then had become a kind of ritual. She always had a wonderful breakfast feast ready for him when he returned, mimosas, mushroom-and-cheese omelet, homemade muffins and jam.

Larry usually showered at the tennis club and came home in a jogging outfit. But on this particular Sunday he had showered at home and come to the table in his wine-colored terry-cloth Polo robe. As always, they chatted about his game. He loved to recount his tennis prowess, cataloging various killer shots that he had made to overwhelm his opponents. Larry liked to win. When he didn't, he returned deeply depressed and was often irritable for hours after.

On this particular Sunday he had lost and was in a foul mood. Married nearly three months by then, she knew these moods and had learned that the best way to ride them out was to ignore them and proceed with any conversation as if his mood were placid and content.

"It was meeting those two fags that threw me off my game," he said sourly, picking at his omelet.

"Oh," she exclaimed, not knowing what he was discussing.

"Talked my ear off. Somehow the others managed to avoid them by watching the ball game." Suddenly he pushed away the omelet with disgust. "It's cold, Jenny."

She rose, took the plate, and put it in the microwave.

"Talk about being neighborly. They had me trapped. All they could talk about was their damned cat. Peter this. Peter that. You know how these damned fags are. Everything trivial becomes so damned important."

"You mean the men who live downstairs?" Jenny asked, somewhat surprised. It hadn't occurred to her that there was more to it than their being roommates.

"Two fruits," Larry muttered. "I wouldn't even shower there. They finished their game the same time we did."

"I had no idea," Jenny exclaimed.

"I guess you wouldn't." Larry sighed, shaking his head as she put the warmed-up omelet in front of him and sat down beside him.

"We did have homosexuals in Bedford, Larry," Jenny responded. "I'm not that naive." But she apparently was and knew it. She hadn't even suspected.

"Right below us, Jenny," Larry said, pointing to the floor. "Performing unspeakable acts on each other. I admit to some lack of tolerance, especially when I imagine what they do in bed together. I hope AIDS isn't caused by proximity." He chuckled joylessly.

His remarks had triggered an odd, unwelcome sense of panic in Jenny as she summoned up the image of Teddy letting himself into their apartment with his own key.

"Maybe you're reading something into it that isn't there," she said hopefully. "They could be simply roommates. Such arrangements do exist."

"Trust me, Jenny. I can sniff them at fifty paces. We have quite a contingent in our business. Take my word for it. O'Hara and Schwartz are fags."

"One of them, I'm not sure which one, came up here a couple of weeks ago," she told him cautiously. "He was quite handsome and not obviously effeminate. All he wanted was to find his cat."

"Well, if the cat ever wanders up here, drown it. That's all they talk about." He finished the omelet, but without relish. "Microwaving destroys the taste," he said.

"I only warmed it up in there," she said with some irritation. She could not get Teddy out of her mind. Apparently it affected her, because when she poured Larry another cup of coffee, her hand shook and she spilled some on his robe.

"Shit, Jenny. It stains."

"Sorry."

She went through the ritual of pouring salt on the spot, then soda water.

"Never mind. Bring it to the cleaners tomorrow." He looked up at her. "What is it with you today, Jenny? You seem upset about something."

He studied her face, and she turned away quickly, then stood up to remove the omelet plates. She had always prided herself on being a tolerant person, accepting all human beings at face value, whatever their race, religion, ideology, sexual preference, or anything else that made them "different."

In Bedford she had encountered prejudice of every stripe, and although she didn't preach or become militant at every sign of bigotry, she considered herself the kind of person who could "live and let live." It therefore annoyed her to feel this sense of menace concerning Teddy Stern.

She hadn't given much thought to homosexuality. She had heard rumors about some of her classmates in high school, but they had not been part of her circle and, therefore, had been out of her frame of reference. Like most people, she wasn't quite certain how people became homosexual, assuming that they had either been born with the tendency or had been conditioned to it by other homosexuals. This latter idea somehow became tied in her mind to Teddy Stern.

Why did he go into the ground-floor apartment? Did his parents know? Teenagers were impressionable, easily influenced. Had the two men designs on the boy? To tolerate gay people was one thing. It wasn't her mission to approve or disapprove of the life they had chosen or that had chosen them. But she could not bring herself to accept such a way of living as "normal." Which didn't mean they were bad people. She tried to beat away such speculation.

It was too weighty a subject, too confusing. Above all, it wasn't any of her business. Yet she could not rid herself of the troubling memory of seeing this teenage boy enter the apartment of two gay men with a key of his own. However she tried to dismiss the idea, it did have the connotation of seduction, of innocence corrupted.

"Couldn't be your period," Larry said, observing her. Her expression must have revealed her disturbing feelings.

"I'm fine," she responded, forcing a smile. "Besides, I'm not due for another two weeks."

"I know."

There was, she decided, a limit to his thoroughness, but she didn't confront him with that. He got up from the table, wandered into the living room, and began to read *The New York Times,* leaving her to her own thoughts. There was no point in dwelling on Teddy Stern's dilemma, she finally told herself. Good sense must prevail. She remembered what her father once told her: Never worry about the things you can't do anything about.

To get Teddy out of her mind, she deliberately made certain that she was not near the window at the approximate time she knew that Teddy entered the ground-floor apartment. Then one afternoon, when she was in the midst of sewing together a bedspread for their four-poster bed, she heard the familiar buzz of the inter-com. Although she had become wary of answering it in the middle of the day, depending on her mood, she decided that perhaps she was becoming too reclusive and that Larry's constant barrage of foreboding was becoming too suffocating. She responded to the buzz.

"I'm Teddy Stern, apartment five upstairs. I lost my keys. Could you let me in, please?" His voice was young and appealing, and all sense of defensiveness disappeared.

"Of course."

She rang the buzzer and heard the door open. It seemed appro-priate for her to open her apartment door and greet the boy.

"I really appreciate this," Teddy said, nervously pressing the elevator button. She could hear the grinding mechanism as the elevator lumbered downward.

"Isn't that what neighbors are for?"

"Yes, Mrs. Burns," Teddy said politely.

Up close, he looked just this side of puberty, with a thin fuzz of black mustache on his upper lip that barely set off his complexion. His eyes were a limpid dark brown with long black lashes, which was his most striking feature. A shock of curly hair fell over his forehead. A prominent Adam's apple bobbed in his thin neck as he spoke. Slender and already taller than Jenny, he carried a much abused carryall over one shoulder.

"It's not much fun losing your keys," she said.

"It was dumb."

She realized suddenly that she was staring at him. Worse, she knew she was inspecting him for any signs of femininity or any telltale characteristics that might be interpreted as homosexual. The idea of it was appalling and embarrassing.

The elevator came and Teddy opened the metal gate and peered at her from inside the cab.

"My dad thinks I'm absentminded," he said. He closed the metal gate but still did not press the button.

"I guess you have the key to the apartment," Jenny said. It was a question in the form of a statement. He peered at her from behind the metal latticework of the gate.

"Actually, no. I was going to sit on the stairs and do my homework," Teddy said. He was, she realized, neither a boy nor a man, but that hybrid that occurred just before a boy began to shave. An image of her high school days intruded, and she remembered how swiftly the change took place. One moment the boys were more interested in their own company, and the next they were trying to play with the girls' breasts. The memory triggered a more ominous image.

"That's silly. You'll be far more comfortable in my apartment." She wanted to add that she would be happy to give him milk and cookies, realizing instantly that he would probably resent the offer.

He seemed to be mulling over her invitation. Finally he shrugged and reopened the elevator gate.

"You wouldn't disturb me. I'm just doing some sewing."

He followed her into the apartment, inspecting it as he entered.

"I was just making myself a cup of tea," Jenny lied. "Can I get you a cup?"

"Great," he said.

"Sit anywhere you're comfortable," Jenny said, flourishing her hand toward the living room. He sat stiffly on one of the upholstered chairs, pulled out a book from his carryall, and began to read.

She went into the kitchen and put the kettle up to boil, peeking into the living room occasionally. She noted that Teddy did more staring into space than reading.

When the water was at a boil, she poured hot water over tea bags, put the two cups on a tray along with brownies, and brought them into the living room. She put the tray on the cocktail table in front of the couch.

"Mind if I take a break with you?" Jenny asked, sitting on the couch opposite the chair on which Teddy sat. Not waiting for an answer, she patted the pillow next to where she was seated, and the boy rose and sat down beside her.

"I can't believe I lost them," Teddy said.

"I'm sure they'll turn up,"

"Typical, I suppose," Teddy said, a frown creasing his smooth brow. "My dad thinks I'm a screw-up anyhow."

She hadn't expected such swift intimacy, and knowing what she knew, it made her both uncomfortable and expectant. Strangers on a train, she thought. Perhaps he wants to reach out.

"Sometimes fathers need a bit of growing up," she said, biting into a brownie, feeling compelled to ally herself with the boy. His brown eyes seemed to indicate a deep, troubling vulnerability, as if he were carrying a heavy secret too weighty for his years.

"He's got his own problems these days." Teddy sighed.

"Does he?"

The boy shrugged, and she could hear warning bells go off in her mind. But before she could build up any defenses to deflect further intimacy, he was blurting out family events that were better left unsaid.

"Mom's not well, and the recession has really hurt Pop's real estate business."

"That's too bad," Jenny said.

"They really can't afford to send me to private school anymore," the boy said. "And here I am getting rotten marks." Teddy had been looking into his teacup. Suddenly he raised his eyes and his gaze met hers. "We may even get evicted from this place."

"Evicted?"

"Thrown out," Teddy said, sighing.

"How awful," Jenny said.

"Pretty hairy."

"If that happens, what will you do?" Jenny asked.

"I'm not sure. I don't even like to think about it. Mom pushes herself to go to work. Doctor says she got a bad heart and shouldn't be working. But we need the bread. Dad's trying to hook up with another real estate company, but business stinks everywhere. I feel guilty even going to private school. Dad says that no matter what, beg, borrow, or steal, they won't take me out of private school. Which I think is stupid. But what the hell do I have to say?"

It was an entirely unexpected litany, and she regretted having put herself into the awkward position of having to listen to it. At that moment she sensed the correctness of Larry's warning. Worse, she felt so terrible for the boy, for whom this burden was so unfair. This, along with the other.

"Things have a way of getting better," she said stupidly. When in doubt, try optimism, she assured herself. Besides, there was absolutely nothing more than lip service that she could offer the boy.

"You got a nice place here," Teddy said, looking around. "What do you do?"

"I guess you'd say I'm a housewife. I know it's kind of an old-fashioned thing to do. But frankly I prefer it."

"I mean what kind of work do you do?"

"I just told you," she said. "I keep house for my husband. I'm a homemaker."

"Mom says you stay home a lot. I thought maybe you were sick or something."

"Before I got married I was an assistant in a doctor's office." It annoyed her that she felt compelled to say "assistant" rather than "nurse." She felt herself growing impatient with the conversation, and as if to call it to a halt, she upended her cup and swallowed the last bit of tea. But Teddy's curiosity seemed boundless.

"Is your husband a lawyer?"

"No." She hesitated for a moment, watching the boy's face, hearing the echo of Larry's admonition. "He's a vice-president of an advertising agency." She deliberately held back on offering him any more specifics. But he was relentless.

"Bet he makes a lot of money," Teddy said.

"I have no complaints," she offered, standing up. He still hadn't finished his tea and hadn't touched the brownies.

"If they move," Teddy said with an intonation as if it were an announcement, "I may not go."

"Won't go?" She had been heading toward the kitchen with her cup in hand. Now she stopped dead in her tracks and studied the boy, who had averted his eyes, looking into his teacup. She was suddenly frightened, as if she had crossed some forbidden boundary.

"I'd stay right here with Bob and Jerry," Teddy said firmly.

"Bob and Jerry?"

The question was purely rhetorical. She knew whom he meant. Far too much revelation for one day, she rebuked herself, a part of her wanting to send the boy packing. But this other part was yearning with curiosity. She braced herself for what might be coming next, yet she made no effort to flee to the kitchen.

"Right below us," he said, looking toward the floor. "And Peter. That's their cat." He paused and smiled thinly, shaking his head. She did not offer a response, feeling increasingly uncomfortable, still standing above him, caught on the what-happens-next aspect of his revelation, expecting him to confess his—

"Actually I should be down there now, doing my homework, with Peter. I have a key to their place, but I've misplaced that as well. It was on the same key ring." He sighed and finished his tea, which must have been quite cold by now, although he didn't seem to mind. Then he put the teacup back on the tray. "I really am a screw-up," he said.

Without another word she put her own cup back on the tray and bent to grab both handles.

"Sure you wouldn't like a brownie?" she asked.

"No thanks." He got up and walked to the chair beside which was his book. Then he sat down and began to flip the pages. Before she could carry the tray into the kitchen, he looked up at her.

"I hope you don't tell my parents," he muttered, casting her a brief sideways glance.

"I wouldn't—"

"I mean about me going to Bob and Jerry's every day. Dad has seen me with them on weekends. You know, just chewing the fat. He'd really be pissed if he knew I was there after school every day. Actually it's Peter. I come in and feed him, see if he's okay. Better than just going upstairs to an empty place. I'd get a pet, but Mom is sick and all."

"I won't say a word." Jenny winked. "Word of honor." She raised her right hand.

"If they weren't gay . . . " He shrugged.

"Are they?" She hurried past him with the tray. In the kitchen she put the tray beside the sink and began to rinse the cups, furious at being on the receiving end of all these revelations.

"My father would beat the shit out of me."

He had come up behind her, and his voice, so close, startled her, and she dropped one of the teacups into the sink, breaking it.

"Damn," she cried, reaching into the sink and carefully picking up the shards. The accident didn't deter the boy.

"He thinks that I'll become one if I associate with them," Teddy said, growing thoughtful, as if he had left something unsaid. When he spoke again it seemed as if he had recalibrated his thoughts. "Probably thinks I'll get AIDS by just playing with the cat. Shows how much he knows. Calls them 'fruits,' 'queers.' Tell you the truth, they've been great to me. I really hate doing my homework up there." He glanced toward the ceiling.

She continued to concentrate on picking up the shards of the teacup and throwing them into the garbage can beside the sink. She deliberately didn't respond or turn to face him. Why is he telling me all this? she asked herself, angry with him now.

"I mean, the whole idea that you can get AIDS from a cat or by being around them is really stupid. He must think I'm really a dummy. He keeps harping on the subject. If he knew that I was doing my homework there, he'd split a gut. I usually tell them that on weekdays after class I'm out with the kids from school. That's very important to my father. He says that he wants me in private school not only for the education, but for the contacts I make among my school chums. Actually I don't have any school chums. I come up by seven, just before they get home. Sometimes I hang out until one of them gets home. Usually when Jerry comes home we sit around and shmooze for a while...."

Finally she could stand it no longer, and she turned to face him.

"I'm sure they're very nice people," she said. It wasn't what she had intended. She supposed she should be more forthright, tell him that she didn't want to hear any more, that it wasn't any of her business, knowing that it wouldn't be the truth.

"They're terrific," Teddy said. "But it's like I'm always feeling guilty being friendly with them. I mean..."

Again she sensed that he was recalibrating the conversation. She searched her mind for some way to stop him.

"You don't become gay by hanging around gay people." He paused, but she did not turn to face him. "Do you?"

It was a question she was hardly qualified to answer, although she suspected that the issue was hardly clean-cut. Instead of answering, she opted for a complete evasion. She looked up at the kitchen clock. But Teddy was persistent.

"Who knows? Maybe they have the right idea."

"You think so?"

"If they're inclined that way, who cares?"

"Different strokes for different folks," Jenny said stupidly, unable to disengage. She could tell that the boy was aching to open up further.

"I can see my father's point, though." He grew thoughtful, and his forehead creased into a frown. "I'm an only child."

"Are you?"

"I try to explain that you don't become gay by just being around them. I mean, you are or you aren't. Like it's sort of built in."

"I guess so," Jenny said, sensing that some response was required to keep him going. Despite all of Larry's warnings and her own discomfort, she could not hold herself back from wanting to know more.

"Fact is, they're my only friends. The boys at school aren't my type."

"And the girls?"

"Stuck up. All stuck up."

He shrugged again and sucked in a deep breath, studying her. Their eyes locked.

"Do you think I'm . . . you know."

"Gay?"

"Do you?"

"I don't think it's for me to judge," Jenny said, turning her eyes from his, not wanting to share his anguish.

"Jerry and Bob treat me like a friend." He hesitated, obviously wrestling with whether or not to delve deeper into the subject. Realizing this, she kept silent. It wasn't her place to prod or probe. "Although we did talk about it. You know, feelings and things. You know what I mean?"

"I'm not sure," Jenny said, which was the truth.

"People having feelings for people of the same sex. Stuff like that." He shook his head as if responding to some inner dialogue.

"I'm afraid it's not within my frame of reference," Jenny said.

"It's something that I think about a lot," he muttered.

"Maybe you shouldn't think about it so much," Jenny said, despite her resolve not to get involved.

"How can I not?" Teddy snapped, frowning, as if he were about to pick an argument with her. She sensed how deeply disturbed he was about the issue.

"Could be people are putting ideas in your head," Jenny said, realizing that she was taking sides despite her better judgment. His reply was surprisingly benign.

"You either are or you're not," he said.

"I'm afraid I'm not very knowledgeable on the subject."

It was increasingly apparent that the boy was confused about his sexual orientation. At that point she sensed that she had had quite enough. Avoiding his eyes, she looked up at the kitchen clock.

"My goodness. I hadn't realized the time passed so quickly. I have to start dinner." It was after five. Larry would be home by six-thirty. As Teddy had said, his parents usually came home by seven. She already knew that. Just as she knew that Terry Richardson, on most days, was home by six and her husband, Godfrey, was home by eight. Myrna Davis was more erratic, sometimes coming in near midnight, except on weekends when she stayed in all day.

All this knowledge was hardly subliminal. In a bit more than three months she knew every sound of coming and going in the house. There was simply no way to stop this flow of information from coming into her mind, becoming part of her life, despite Larry's admonitions.

"Do you want me to go?" Teddy asked. It would mean he would have to sit on the steps in front of his apartment. But not for long. Jerry, whose arrivals and departures were sometimes erratic, would be home in a little while, probably before six. She knew that as well. Bob would be home about a half hour later.

"I don't want you to think I'm throwing you out. But really, I've got to get to work." She smiled and reached out for a flowered apron, tying it around her waist. "We're having cassoulet."

"Sounds good," Teddy said. "Anyway, I'll just take a walk, get some air. Jerry should be home in a little while."

There was no avoiding a stab of guilt. Am I throwing him into Jerry's arms? The image nettled her.

"It's perfectly okay. You can do your work in the living room. It won't disturb me. Really it won't."

She wondered suddenly what Larry's reaction might be if he found Teddy there, and her irritation became even more acute.

"Tell you the truth, Mrs. Burns, I really don't feel like doing any homework now." He turned and headed back to the living room. At first she remained in the kitchen, trying to busy herself with dinner preparations. Then she remonstrated with herself, annoyed at her vulnerability. She came back into the living room, where he had just slung his carryall over his shoulder.

"I've got a great idea," she said. Actually it was an idea, quite obviously prodded by guilt, that had just popped into her mind. Teddy had turned to face her, frown lines of curiosity creasing his forehead. Not responding, he waiting for her revelation.

"Why don't you stop by...well, anytime after school. I mean after you feed...what's his name?"

"Peter."

"Could even bring him up if you like. Why be alone at all? Chances are I'll be home. I won't bother you. I promise."

"You won't mind?"

"Not if you leave before my husband comes home. He's allergic to cats."

Teddy's face lit up into a smile. "Might be a good idea," he said, nodding. "I really appreciate that." He started toward the apartment door, then turned to face her. "You've been great, Mrs. Burns." Then he dashed out the door.

What's wrong with that? she asked herself as she went back into the kitchen. It was a perfectly neighborly thing to do. Wasn't it?

4

ARRY STERN felt awful about it. Teddy's keys were like a big blob in his side pocket, weighing him down, bearing witness to his deception. It was, he knew, a desperate act. In fact, everything he did lately was a desperate act, and everything he thought about was even more desperate.

How was it possible that everything had gone sour in less than a year? Sitting in the anteroom of Glover's Real Estate in Hicksville, Long Island, he pretended to be reading a trade magazine, *Homebuilding*. The words of the articles did not enter his consciousness. Three strikes and you're out, he thought, trying to find a sliver of humor in his predicament.

Nothing helped. He was merely sleepwalking through his days, trying to keep up the pretense of normalcy by going through the ritual of what was really his former life. Six months ago he had a real estate business, buying and selling modest-price homes in Queens, the homes of working men and women.

Then suddenly it was all over. Nobody was buying because of the recession, and nobody was selling, hoping that good times were just around the corner. It didn't look to Barry like there would be good times ever again. There was no point in paying rent and salaries to employees. Staying afloat was impossible. His only alternative was to close down. He wondered if it had been his fault. Other small real estate companies had survived. Not many. The reality was that despite his illusions, he had always been a marginal player without financial depth, living far above his means.

Four years ago he had his peak year and had grossed three hundred thousand dollars. It was fat city then, and he'd thought it was going to last forever. That was the year they were able to move out of the apartment in Astoria and get that brownstone apartment in Manhattan and register Teddy in private school. Not bad for a guy who barely finished high school and whose father never made more than ten thousand a year working behind the counter of an appetizer store.

That was also the year he bought his parents that condo in West Palm Beach for $23,900, not exactly the height of luxury, but perfect for his folks, who thought they had arrived at Nirvana. At least he hadn't leveraged it, and they owned it free and clear and could manage on their Social Security. They could make it no matter what happened to him.

Even now, especially now, as he sat in the anteroom of Tom Glover's office, he could not chase the idea that his only way out of this mess was to cause something to happen to him, something deliberate. Removing such an idea from his thoughts was becoming more and more of a chore. What might be saving him from taking such an action, however unspecified, was the fact that he had borrowed heavily on his one-hundred-thousand-dollar whole-life insurance policy and Sally would net only about half. But even half was becoming more and more of an attraction as he sank deeper and deeper into the mud of depression.

The irony was that if ever there was a time to have cash, this was it. The deals were a dime a dozen. All kinds of sweet deals were being made now by people with cash. Hell, if he had cash now, he could make a quick fortune. Buildings were for sale at a steal.

He hadn't even told Sally and Teddy that the business had failed completely or that he had closed the office and fired his two employees. Kaput! So much for the American dream. At least they had Sally's salary, $27,000 gross, which was enough for the bare necessities, although considering her health problems there was no telling how long that might last.

That, too, had been a burst from the blue, Sally getting a heart attack two years ago. He had thought heart attacks were a male thing. Well, he knew better now. She was going downhill, too, with the doctors suggesting a heart transplant rather than a bypass, which was scary considering the odds. That, too, had become a catch-22. She had to keep working to be eligible for the company health plan, but the continued working wasn't doing her heart any good. At this point she didn't have the option of quitting.

In a way, he supposed, they were lucky that they had only one kid. When Teddy was born, they had vowed that they would give him all the advantages they hadn't had, the best education, the best environment, all the things children of poor parents wanted for their offspring.

This fucking recession had ruined everything. He felt the anger swell inside of him. Don't do that, he cautioned himself, not before this interview with Tom Glover, with whom he had had dealings when he was in business, which seemed ages ago. That much he knew about salesmanship. It was like show business. If you brought any downer baggage to the presentation, it was sure to queer the deal.

Queer the deal! There was no way to escape the inescapable. Teddy was about to become, or had become, a homosexual. Barry wasn't dead certain, of course. Maybe it was his imagination. But the kid showed no interest in girls. He had seen him in heavy conversation with those two who lived in the ground-floor apartment. At first he had thought nothing of it. Then when it was repeated he had actually warned him about getting too close to their kind, but obviously it hadn't made a dent. Perhaps he should have been more diplomatic in the way he approached it.

He had told Teddy to steer clear of those men on the grounds that they were fairies. He had used that word as a weapon, along with "fag," "fruit," "queer," "three-dollar bill," and other such terms of opprobrium, not that he had anything against how they lived and what they did. He just didn't want his son to become one of them.

He had also raised the specter of AIDS, which was frightening as hell. Of course he had exaggerated the possibilities of transmission, and Teddy had accused him of being hysterical, reeling off various statistical information that he had probably gotten from the boys downstairs. If Teddy ever got AIDS, he was dead certain that would clinch the deal that was floating ominously in his head. There would be absolutely no point in going on.

Yet he hadn't the guts to confront Teddy with the ultimate question, fearing that his answer would be affirmative. That would be an unacceptable blow to him and to Sally, from whom he hid the knowledge of his suspicion.

But all his venom-laden warnings and scare tactics apparently had made no difference to Teddy. That had been confirmed the day before yesterday. Barry had tried to keep up appearances that he was still running his business and had been coming home at his usual time. But on that day he was feeling so lousy he decided to go home early, maybe take a long nap.

Coming down the street, he had actually seen Teddy open the door of that downstairs apartment with a key and let himself in. What was going on here? It curdled his stomach just to recall it. For an hour he'd debated with himself about confronting Teddy in the apartment, but he was so damned depressed, he wasn't looking to find yet another nail for his coffin.

He went to the movies instead but could hardly concentrate on the story. The prospect of Teddy being one of them gave rise to a lot of heavy thinking on his part. It was not something he wanted to talk about with Sally. No sense aggravating her about it. Being homosexual was something that happened to other people, not his only child. Coping with it was far out of his frame of reference. Such a possibility was not even remotely included in those traditional dreams of fatherhood, where the son somehow picks up the relay stick from the old man and keeps sprouting branches on the family tree.

He wondered how other fathers—and mothers—dealt with it.

He was all for everybody having equal rights and hadn't considered himself a homophobe. "Live and let live" had always been his motto. He had nothing at all against them, and he was totally supportive of their right not to be harassed, to be left alone to live their lives in peace. All right, they were different. Some people were left-handed, some right. So what!

But his own kid being a fag didn't square with his hopes and dreams for Teddy. Toleration was bullshit on this issue. He loved his son, loved him fiercely, deeply, but somehow, despite all the politicizing of the issue, all the good public relations for gay people, all the rationalizing that this was only a matter of sexual choice, which was supposed to be no big deal, Teddy being a homosexual seemed worse than his being a criminal. It was pretty awful to think that, but he couldn't help himself. At the very least, he had to be honest with himself. He hadn't raised his son to suck dicks and take it up the ass. God, the images that floated through his mind. He hated them, hated the idea of it, hated his intolerance, but mostly he hated that such a thing could happen to his only son. And to him.

Of course, he assured himself, he would learn to be accepting. What else was there to do? He could not disown his own child. Never that. But it would never be the same. A foreigner would always be there where his son once stood. He'd have to bear the pain of his broken heart, keep it hidden from his son and paste a smile on his face. Could he really do that? He wasn't sure.

Not that he was dead certain that Teddy was one, and at first it seemed harmless for the boy to be friendly with them. Teddy liked animals, and had wanted a cat, but Sally was allergic to both cats and dogs, and that finished that. Now, along with all the other gloomy shit, this thing with Teddy stood on top of his agenda, along with going broke.

What the hell had happened to his street smarts over the years? He had grown soft, he supposed. Or maybe he was being punished for past actions, which had a logical ring to it. Once he'd had absolutely no conscience in the way he bought and sold. He could rationalize any shady deal. Well, they weren't really shady, just sharp. Buy low, as low as you could get and for as little cash as possible. Then sell high, as high as you could get. Wasn't that the American way?

He had been damned good at blockbusting, scaring the shit out of the Jews, Greeks, and Italians that the blacks were coming in. Start a panic. Buy low. Then sell to the blacks at inflated prices. Even that was long over. People got wise. Besides, the market was saturated. All right, it was shameful. So now they were paying him back, and he deserved what he got.

Somewhere down the line he had lost the stomach for it. Perhaps that was his downfall, this development of a conscience. One day he had awakened with scruples. Perhaps he had looked at Teddy and said to himself that this was no legacy to leave one's kid, the memory that his father was nothing more than a street hustler.

Now what he needed most was to recover some of those qualities they used to call moxie. Once he had had moxie.

There was good moxie and bad moxie. Bad moxie would have given him the balls to do outrageous things, like blackmail. There was an idea that had blasted into his head the day he saw and recognized Jack Springer, the junior senator from the great state of New York, sneaking up the stairs to the second-floor apartment of Myrna L. Davis.

The man was wearing sunglasses and a hat pulled low over his face, and he had a mustache, which Barry knew was a phony after he'd taken a look at a picture of the senator in the papers. Problem was the man had a prominent clefted chin that gave him away. He would have done better with a beard. Would make a damned good tip for the tabloids, he knew. Those supermarket rags loved stories about self-righteous politicians dipping their wick in strange places. He wondered how much the tip would be worth to them. In desperation, he thought, a man could rationalize anything, however sleazy. God, here he was sinking again, taking the low road.

He had passed Myrna Davis a number of times in the hall, offering the usual neighborly noncommittal smile. He wasn't much at mixing with the neighbors. Never did you much good. Besides, who wanted them to know your business? Especially now. He knew that Myrna was an editor at *Vanity Fair.* Mid-thirties. Cute. Good legs. Snotty look. But then he had caught sight of a familiar face skulking up the stairs to Myrna Davis's apartment. It had taken him weeks to figure it out.

The guy would hole up with her all weekend, arrive at odd hours, leave at odd hours. Shacking up. That was no secret. They never left the apartment all weekend, sending for carryout two, three times a day.

The real secret was who the man was. Barry recognized him from a big picture of him on the front page of the *New York Daily News*. It showed him along with his wife and children on the occasion of his announcement that he was going to run for a third term. He figured that this business with Myrna Davis had been going on for nearly six months when he saw that picture in the paper. Fucking hypocrite.

Actually, he never told Sally about it. He wasn't sure why, except maybe he did have this larcenous thought in his mind. Here was this family-man, big-shot senator, spending his weekends shacked up with their neighbor. No wonder they didn't go out. Wouldn't do much for the family-man image. Lately it had crossed his mind that that kind of information might be worth something, a great deal, maybe. To the senator. To the senator's opposition. To the media.

We're talking here of survival, he tried to tell himself. But that kind of an act would put him in that whole other place, the hole he had climbed out of. That wasn't good moxie. That was blackmail, beyond the pale, with the risk of being charged and put away. Then again, desperation was a great motivator. Certainly it pushed his imagination to great flights of fancy.

Even to robbery. Hell, he had Teddy's key to the apartment downstairs. He could simply walk in and take whatever was quickly convertible to cash. Maybe he'd even find some cash, lots of cash. But that idea quickly sank out of sight. That woman on the first floor, Burns. She had a bird's-eye view of the stairs leading to the apartment. Once he had seen her watching him as he came up the front steps. Of course, he could wait until she was gone on some errand, then make his move.

No, he decided. Desperation was making him crazy. Besides, it was never a good policy to shit where you ate, which brought his thoughts back to Teddy once again.

This thing with Teddy was devastating. He could remember the pink little bundle of flesh he had seen through the maternity-ward window and how proud he was to show everyone who passed that this was his kid. He also remembered how much he had fantasized about what his boy would become and how he, Barry Stern, would dedicate himself to building a great financial base so that his kid wouldn't want for anything.

Watching little Teddy in that maternity-ward window, he was absolutely convinced that this child would amount to something really important, something impressive and wonderful, a person famous throughout the world. He could remember very clearly thinking such thoughts, thoughts that crystallized into a father's dream. He was certain that all fathers felt like that. Yet nowhere in this equation had the idea of homosexuality even entered his mind. His son, a queer?

Not that he didn't love Teddy with all his heart and soul, but the idea that he would live a life as a kind of exile and, in some circles, even an object of ridicule and defamation was depressing. His son, having sex with other men, with no possibilities of children, a loving wife, a normal life, was, well, face it, pissing on his dream. It wasn't fair.

Perhaps he was just overreacting to the idea, based on only circumstantial evidence. All optimism had faded. He was on the mat, broke, over his head in debt, on the verge of eviction, his wife ailing and working beyond her strength, his son a possible homosexual. Clearly, even now, he was better off dead than alive, although he was not comfortable with the idea of being a cop-out.

All this horror pulsed through his mind as he waited for Glover to see him, hoping and praying that Glover would provide him with an opportunity of financial recovery. So far he hadn't been successful in hooking up with another real estate outfit that might be willing to pay an advance. They were all in deep shit. But Glover had stuck it out all those years making a market in Levitt's houses in Hicksville, and in the good years Barry had thrown a lot of business his way.

Once he got a little financial breathing space, he could direct his attention to Teddy and Sally with a clear mind. It could be that he was just reading things into Teddy's odd conduct. It was a brief flash of optimism, but intruding on it was the memory of what he had done about Teddy's keys.

Stealing Teddy's keys was a shabby act of which he was greatly ashamed. But he couldn't think of any other way to keep him away from the two queers, acting on the idea that the way people became homosexuals was by being turned on by other homosexuals. He could not bring himself to believe that people were born that way. How, then, did it come about? Older men seducing younger ones, making them like it so much that they could renounce women altogether. He wondered if it was too late.

"Barry Stern," Glover called from his office. "Come on in. Sorry to keep you waiting. Have a cigar."

It was an old-fashioned way to welcome someone into his office, and in an effort to keep the mood, Barry took one of the cigars from the humidor and allowed Glover to light it for him. Glover relit his own stub of cigar, then the two settled back on their chairs and studied each other.

Glover was a short man who wore his pants high, nearly up to his chest. When he was sitting, his feet barely reached the floor. His eyes were set back deep in his face, giving him a hawklike appearance despite his thick, moist lips.

"It stinks," Glover said. "They fucked us real estate guys good."

"Better believe," Barry said. "Not that we haven't been through this before. But this one is for the books. Nobody's buying. Nobody's selling. The S and L's are fucked. The banks are on the balls of their asses."

He looked around the room. Outside, he could see the rows and rows of Mr. Levitt's ingenious idea for the American family, now individualized, as if the owners were determined to mock Mr. Levitt's method of mass-producing the American dream of home ownership.

"Maybe it was a blind fluke," Glover said. "But this place turns over. Not as much as I'd like these days, but I think I can get through it."

"Paid to specialize, Tom," Barry said. "Here you got a following."

"Forty years in the making, Barry," Glover said.

"I'm a helluva salesman, Tom," Barry said, hoping he did not sound as if he were gilding the lily.

"That you are, Barry," Glover said.

"I sent people your way."

There it was, Barry thought, the reminder. Pulling on the guilt chain.

"And you never screwed me."

Barry was encouraged by Glover's response. "That's very important to me, Tom," he said, seeing the opening. "My reputation is everything." He took a deep puff of the cigar, too deep. He was growing nauseated. He was not a cigar smoker. Sweat began to creep down his back. It put a damper on his salesmanship.

"I know what you mean."

"I'd like you to put me on," Barry said, watching Glover's face. The man's eyes had drifted away, and he was inhaling and blowing smoke out of the side of his mouth.

"Long trip in from Manhattan every day," Glover said.

"Oh, I'd move. Get an apartment somewhere out here. I need this, Tom." It felt as if desperation were flowing out of every pore of him along with the perspiration.

"Worth considering, Barry," Glover said.

"You don't know how grateful I'd be," Barry said, suddenly finding the courage to put the cigar down on the glass ashtray. The nausea was still there, but the sudden optimism had a calming effect on his guts.

"It's slim pickings, though," Glover said in a cautionary way, as if he had noticed the effect his consent had had on Barry.

"Tom, I promise you I'll sell the shit out of this place."

"I know you will, Barry. That's why I'm taking you on."

"A couple a thousand a month will tide me over until the commissions roll in. Maybe sixty, ninety days at the most." Barry felt oddly relieved. There it was. Out in the open, and his throat hadn't tightened.

Glover shifted his weight on his chair and puffed deeply, this time blowing the smoke directly in front of him, enveloping Barry until it dissipated.

"Wish I could, Barry," Glover said. "Unfortunately the phrase *cash flow* doesn't exist in this business anymore. But, hell, there won't be any grass growing under your feet, Barry. I'd say ninety days max you could be pulling down two, three thou a month."

Barry felt his stomach churn. "I'm tapped out, Tom," he mumbled, his eyes watching his restless hands as they massaged his thighs. "If two thou is too much, say one thou and more if the sales roll in."

"Nothing rolls in anymore, Barry. There's only two salesmen able to make a living on this turf now. This bullshit about the recession being over is just that. I got a feeling that the real estate boom is gone with the wind for you and me, Barry. I'm sorry. But no advances."

"Sure, Tom, I understand." Barry stood up. His head was spinning, and the feeling of nausea had surged back. He managed to put out his hand. Glover took it, pumped.

"I wish I could, Barry. You know that," Glover said.

"Sure, Tom," Barry said, forcing himself to be pleasant in the time-honored way of salesmen who hadn't sold their wares on the first pitch. It was the rule of the game never to burn your bridges. He managed to make his smile last until he got to the anteroom.

He held on to his nausea until he reached the station platform, then he threw up in one of the litter cans. In the midst of his retching he had the sensation that the process was ridding his being of the last vestige of hope.

5

TEDDY'S afternoon visitations with Jenny became somewhat of a routine. On most weekdays he would arrive at Jenny's apartment with Peter in his arms. She would provide Teddy with a snack and Peter with a saucer of milk. Then Teddy would proceed to do his homework and Peter would curl up in a ball at his feet and she would proceed with her household chores.

Just before six o'clock, as if it were a silent agreement between them, Teddy would leave with Peter and go downstairs to Bob and Jerry's apartment. Jenny knew that having Teddy in each afternoon would be contrary to Larry's wishes. It was, after all, an involvement with a neighbor.

But to Jenny it was more than that. She viewed it in far more complex terms. Teddy was a troubled boy, an adolescent living in a shadow world, unsure of himself and vulnerable. What was wrong with people helping each other, sharing, confiding? She wished she had someone to confide in, someone wise and objective. Of course, she had her mother, but it was becoming increasingly obvious that her mother's experience was aeons away from life in Manhattan.

Bedford, Indiana, might as well have been in another solar system. There was no way that she could present Teddy's dilemma to her mother for advice and counsel, and both her mother and Larry would have objected to the relationship, each in her or his own way.

From Jenny's own vantage, she was simply being kind, a good neighbor. In some ways it brought out her maternal instinct. She wished she could offer Teddy solid advice, but she was not exactly an expert on the problems of teenage boys.

Her teen life, compared with Teddy's, had also had its moments of uncertainty and angst, but she had not experienced any massive gender identity crisis. In Bedford teenagers lived within understood boundaries on the issue of sex, and accepted silent conspiracy between parents and children.

Parents of girls, naturally, prized the idea of virginity, while the girls themselves prized a monogamous relationship with a member of the opposite sex, with virginity considered an old-fashioned concept. Most of her friends had had their first sexual intercourse experience before they were sixteen. Even getting pregnant did not carry with it the stigma of an earlier generation, although it was considered inhibiting to one's ambitions and future, and those girls who allowed it to happen to them were looked upon more with pity than with scorn.

There was, therefore, nothing in her own experience that she could draw on to deal with Teddy's dilemma. Larry, she was certain, would have been shocked to know that Teddy and his problems had become a part of Jenny's daily experience. Such involvements, she assured herself, were simply part of being in the life of a community. The apartment building encompassed this community, a kind of mini-Bedford. Something in Larry's city upbringing, she decided, had made him overly frightened and distrustful about other people, almost to the point of paranoia.

She understood, of course, that city life was not without its crime and violence, and that security precautions had to be observed. She read the papers and watched the news on television. Her apartment door had a dead bolt and a chain lock, and people had to be identified before she buzzed anyone inside the building. But, surely, such reports and precautions didn't mean that everybody was suspect and had to be automatically feared and distrusted.

The danger of physical violence was no excuse to keep yourself hidden from your neighbors. She hoped that someday she would persuade Larry to be more open about people, especially those in their immediate community. Human beings weren't meant to be isolated and fearful of their neighbors. That attitude made for unhappiness. Sooner or later, she was certain, she would get him to understand. Now, while they were still adjusting to each other, was not the time. She knew that this meant withholding any mention of her relationship with Teddy. Nor would she put it in the category of keeping secrets from Larry. Well, not deliberately. But not mentioning was very different from telling lies. That would have been contrary to her concept of marriage.

Besides, where was the harm in it, especially since she was certain that Teddy wouldn't tell his parents about his afternoon visits and risk their finding out that he hadn't any school chums. That also meant that there was less chance of Larry finding out.

Of course, it soon became apparent that the relationship with Teddy was not without its responsibilities. But wasn't that, too, the price of friendship? It was natural for people to need other people. Teddy apparently had no one who could understand, and what was wrong about his using her as a sounding board?

The pressure on Teddy from his father was causing him a great deal of unhappiness, and the distance between them was widening each day. Events in his household were making things worse. His father's business had fallen apart, his mother's health was failing. Arguments between father and son were increasing.

She noted, too, that Teddy seemed to come to her apartment less to do homework than to talk, and the subject matter was taking on a more and more intimate tone.

Despite the fact that he was half a foot taller than she and his seriousness made him seem older than his sixteen years, she had never broached the bounds of propriety by allowing him to call her anything but "Mrs. Burns."

"Funny," he told her one day. "You look so much younger than you are. Sometimes it feels strange calling you Mrs. Burns."

"The fact is, young man, that I'm nearly a decade older than you."

"You're twenty-five, then. God, that's old." He lowered his eyes. "I didn't mean like old old."

"Just remember that. Older is wiser."

"But you don't seem that much older. Maybe it's because we're ... like friends."

"Yes," Jenny told him. "I guess we qualify on that score."

"I think your husband is a very lucky man, Mrs. Burns."

As time went on, Teddy grew more and more curious about Larry.

"Does he make you happy?"

"Of course he does."

"How?"

"By being a good husband, a good provider. In fact, he's good in every way." She felt a blush heat her cheeks.

"And you like being married?"

"Yes, I do. Of course I do."

She was deliberately sparse in any answers that required more intimacy on her part.

One day he asked her: "Do you have fantasies, Mrs. Burns?" When she didn't reply immediately, he expanded on the question. "You know. About men."

"I wouldn't be normal if I didn't," she answered, deliberately noncommittal.

"Bob and Jerry were talking to me about that," Teddy said. "They asked what kinds of fantasies I had."

"And what did you tell them?"

Teddy shrugged. "I wasn't sure what to tell them."

"Why don't you tell them that it's none of their business. That your fantasies are your private property and that they don't have a right to ask."

"They keep asking."

"Of course they do."

Teddy seemed confused by her comment. But she had begun to imagine that Bob and Jerry were trying to get this boy to cross the line into their world. Still, she tried to maintain a level of neutrality. It was, after all, Teddy's life, and even Teddy had been told or had decided that you either were or you weren't that way from birth, which might or might not be true. Yet it bothered her to think that Bob and Jerry might be contributing to Teddy's confusion about his sexual identity. Worse, they might be manipulating him for their own nefarious purposes.

The idea began to gnaw at her, not only because of her fears for Teddy, but also because she hated thinking ill of people and, above all, treasured the concept of fairness in her judgment of other human beings. But this did not stop her from worrying about Teddy's naiveté and vulnerability being taken advantage of, of his being seduced into a life-style for which he might not be ready.

She turned such a possibility over and over again in her mind. She hadn't bargained for that kind of emotional involvement. It was burdensome and distracted her. Again she began to think that perhaps Larry was right in warning her not to get entangled in other people's lives.

"What is it?" Larry asked her one evening at dinner. "You seem worried about something."

"You're imagining things," she replied.

Call it a little white lie. The fact was that she was preoccupied about Teddy and his concerns, although she tried to block it from her mind when she was with Larry. It was so difficult to compartmentalize one's life, she decided. Yet she did recognize it for what it was, a disruptive force that should never have been allowed to enter her home. Unfortunately it was too late for such remorse. Naturally she blamed it on herself, not the idea of being a good neighbor, but the inability to control such an involvement. She began to think of disengagement.

She would, of course, have liked to discuss Teddy and his problems with Larry, but that was out of the question. He was not well disposed to Bob and Jerry and seemed blatantly homophobic, which ruled out any objective discussion of the subject. Besides, he would certainly admonish her, emphasizing rightly that Teddy's sexuality was none of her business. Nor had she meant it to be.

She determined to tell Teddy at the first opportunity that she had no wish to discuss the subject of his sexuality anymore and that if it came up again, she would bar him from spending his afternoons in her apartment. Hard-hearted, perhaps, but certainly practical.

One afternoon, after three weeks of coming to her apartment, Teddy arrived earlier than usual and without Peter. Jenny had just taken a bath and was wearing a terry-cloth robe when she came to the door.

"Something wrong?" Jenny asked.

He seemed nervous and harassed, and his eyes had a wild unhappy cast. "I ... I didn't go to school today," he said. "I just ... sort of walked around."

"And Peter?"

"He's still downstairs. I didn't want him around."

"Would you like a snack?" Jenny asked.

"Nothing," Teddy said. He came into the living room and threw himself on the couch. Tears welled in his eyes.

"What is it?" she asked, sitting beside him on the edge of the couch.

"I had this dream, Mrs. Burns."

"Now really, Teddy," she rebuked him. "Everybody dreams. You can't take them seriously."

"This dream was scary," he said, brushing away the tears that had spilled over his cheeks.

"We all have scary dreams."

"I dreamt ... I dreamt ..." He couldn't go on.

It was obvious that the dream had made a profound impression on him. A warning flag went off in her mind. Perhaps this is something I should not hear, she told herself, standing up, crossing the room. She looked out of the window as if she were seeking the means of escape.

"I dreamt I was doing things ..."

"Teddy, really, it was only a dream and probably not worth repeating."

She cautioned herself that if she let herself listen, she would be drawn in further. Except that it was too late.

"I was doing things with a man," Teddy said. "And I had a wet dream."

"God, Teddy," Jenny snapped. "Why are you telling me this? It's so...so personal. You must learn not to be so...so revealing. Frankly, I'm embarrassed."

"I'm sorry," Teddy said, turning his face toward the wall, his shoulders racked with sobs. He was forlorn and pitiful, and she felt awful for him.

"It was only a dream," she said lamely, sitting down beside him again. Turning toward her, he embraced her and continued to cry. "There, there," she kept repeating, patting his back.

"Does this mean..." he began, then dissolved once more into tears.

"I really don't know what it means, Teddy."

I mustn't be part of it, she told herself. This boy needs counseling from experts. This is none of my business. But he continued to cling to her, and she continued to pat his back.

"I'm so confused," Teddy whispered. "I don't know what to do."

"Just...just live your life," Jenny said, equally as confused as Teddy. She continued to hold him. The sobs abated, and he partially disengaged. But as he did, she realized that the belt of her robe had become undone and the robe's flaps had opened, revealing her nakedness from neck to thigh. Teddy, too, became aware of it and began to pull away, averting his eyes.

"No," Jenny said. "You can look."

She wondered why she was doing this, yet she felt oddly content, as if she were doing someone a good deed. What harm could there be in this? Let him see for himself if he was capable of being aroused by a woman. It felt purely clinical on her part, sort of experimental.

The boy turned his head and studied her. His expression was one of dead seriousness.

"Would you like to touch my breasts?"

The boy nodded. Although she could feel her nipples harden under his tentative touching, she continued to feel no sexual arousal. In fact, she was inspecting the boy as he did so, as if he were an object to be studied.

"Have you ever seen a woman naked?" she asked.

"Only in pictures," he said, his lips trembling.

"Do you like what you see?" she asked gently.

"Oh, yes. Very much so."

She took his hand and guided it downward.

"Now you've touched the place," she whispered, allowing his hand to wander over her. Watching his face, she saw it redden, then she reached out to discover his erection. His first reaction was to move away from her touch, then he relented and allowed her to stroke him. She opened his zipper and stroked the bare flesh of his hard penis.

"Have I given you something else to dream about?" she asked.

"Oh, yes."

"Are you still confused?"

He shook his head. "Can I . . . "

He moved toward her, but she arranged herself so that any penetration on his part would be impossible. Instead she stretched herself lengthwise on the couch and held him against her naked flesh. His body trembled, his breath came in gasps. He had ejaculated against her thigh. She allowed him to embrace her for a long moment, then she got up and tied the robe together. He sat up and fixed his trousers. Then their eyes met.

"I would rather we didn't discuss it, Teddy," Jenny said. "Not ever." She wanted to dismiss it from her mind. "Call it a one-time experience, perhaps a lesson."

"I understand," he replied. "And I promise never to tell anybody."

"I know you won't, Teddy. Also, I would prefer that you didn't come here in the afternoons."

A shadow passed across his face. Then he smiled. It was the broadest smile she had ever seen him make. She smiled back at him.

"Doesn't mean we shouldn't be friends," she said.

"I'll always be your friend, Mrs. Burns. No matter what."

He started toward the door, then came back and kissed her on the cheek.

"I'll never forget this," he said.

When he was gone, she felt a giggly sensation bubble up inside of her. Assessing what she had done, she felt no remorse, no contrition, and no guilt, none. She was not even sure it would have any effect at all on Teddy's life, although she hoped it would.

"Can't say I haven't been a good neighbor," she said aloud, the giggle bursting out of her mouth.

6

YRNA L. DAVIS had often wondered if the name her father had given her had profoundly influenced her behavior. The "L" stood for Loy, and Myrna Loy was his favorite actress. Her mother had objected to it, but then all of her mother's objections were feeble against her father's overbearing and demanding ways.

She took after her father. Everybody told her so, and she had become convinced that his strong genes had overpowered her mother's wimpy ones and that she was created in his image. Physically she was, with the same firm cleft chin, blue-gray piercing eyes, jet black curly hair. People said she had also inherited his charisma and his manipulative ways. Like him, she could turn on the charm when she had to but could be arrogant and demanding when that conduct was called for.

As for her name, once people realized that she was named after Myrna Loy, especially people from her father's generation, they always remarked that that's probably where she got her gift for clever banter, meaning that she took after the Myrna Loy of the *Thin Man* series, as if the real Myrna Loy made up her own sophisticated one-liners. Few people in her age group knew who Myrna Loy was, although the *Thin Man* series had come out on cassettes and younger people were rediscovering her mastery of light comedy banter. For years Myrna considered her name one of her father's cruder jokes.

He was a trial lawyer of awesome reputation in Los Angeles, where she had grown up under his thumb and tutelage. The divorce between her parents when she was sixteen had hardly fazed her, since she had expected it for years. Living with her father was impossible unless you were prepared to be a doormat for the rest of your life. This had not been her mother's original wish when she'd married, but that's what she had become, finally winding up a horrid life as an alcoholic who had choked to death on her own vomit.

This, of course, would not have been Myrna's fate even if she had chosen to stay in Los Angeles, living in her father's shadow. She was too much like him to fall into that trap. He had fully expected her to follow in his footsteps, joining the firm after dutifully finishing Harvard Law School, as he had done.

She did graduate from Harvard undergraduate as an English major and had opted to stay in the East and pursue a career in journalism, a profession her father detested but one that suited her just fine. His detestation, in fact, actually enhanced the idea. Although she and her father were constantly at war, neither of them had ever chosen the path of complete alienation from each other.

They talked by phone and in person when each happened to be in the other's territory. Their conversations were never less than contentious and argumentative, and he was always prepared to offer a critique of every aspect of her life, usually ending in his negative judgment.

It was almost an article of faith that they took positions that were exact opposites of each other's on every subject imaginable. Even if they didn't at first, they would quickly polarize. At times their arguments disguised themselves as political, since they were both passionately interested in "larger issues." The more conservative he became, the more liberal her position.

It had taken her ten years of therapy to exorcise the invasion of her father's demons, but even the painful acquisition of personal insight did not end the need to continue the war between them,

although it did make it less painful and sometimes actually enter-
taining, as if their relationship had become a game.

This acquired insight had gone a long way toward explaining
the reasons for the failure of her two marriages, each to a man
who could not withstand the rigors of her demanding nature. Each
had buckled within a year, even though each had begun with
flaming passion. Her shrink, actually a series of shrinks, had differing
explanations for her crippled relationships with men, but all hinted
at some dark need of wanting to fuck her father to death. She found
the diagnosis interesting and probably correct, assuming that this
was exactly what he wanted to do to her.

Fortunately, time had withered the obsession, and the qualities
of manipulation, charm, and nut-cutting ambition that made her
father successful were doing the same for her. As an associate
editor of *Vanity Fair* she was acquiring both power and cachet,
and through her job she was meeting some of the most celebrated
people in the country, putting her in exactly those circles in which
she wanted to operate.

She enjoyed her job and she was good at it, both as an editor
who could come up with exactly the right angle for a sugarcoated
hatchet job on an important celebrity and as a personality who
perfectly represented the trendy, sophisticated, know-it-all bitchiness that was at the heart of the magazine's persona. Also, it fitted
precisely with her agenda, which was to surpass her father in
everything, especially importance. With her job had come the
opportunity to use every facet of her talents and personality, the
good with the bad.

Now on the cusp of forty, she had, however, not given up the
idea of finding a mate who could satisfy the requirements of her
dreams, ambitions, and physical needs. She was not one of those
people who ever gave up on anything, another of her father's
inbred traits. But, unlike her father, she did not want progeny,
certain that any child of hers would suffer the same fate at her
hands that she had suffered at her father's.

Let's face it, she told herself, underneath all her hubris was a
dyed-in-the-wool fourteen-karat bitch. Her moodiness alone would

have tried the patience of a tranquilized saint, and it took massive self-control to keep that beast caged.

Since her last marriage she had entered into a number of affairs, only to find the same sense of disillusionment and defeat. She couldn't blame the guys. But for the last six months she had been carrying on a torrid affair with Jack Springer, the junior senator from the state of New York, a Democrat. At last, she decided, she had met her dream man. So far.

Since it was impossible for her not to compare any man she bedded to her father, she had concluded that Jack was as close to the real thing as one got, without the toxin-ridden personal agenda. He was opportunistic, charming, and charismatic, all essential tools of his occupation, along with hypocrisy and duplicity. His public positions were tailor-made for his constituency, which was an interesting mix of the liberal and the conservative. At heart he was the latter. Worse, a closet bigot.

"Better than being a closet fag," he'd said, chuckling, when she had first used the term. But his public hypocrisy by no means neutered their relationship. In fact, the arguments they engaged in added spice to their affair.

"Politics," he assured her, "is not about conviction. It is about power, and the most essential ingredient of that power is having it, which means getting elected, then reelected."

There were moments, though, when his pronouncements could be genuinely irritating. Like her father, he was a bred-to-the-cloth elitist, a product of old New York wealth, which was, aside from providing the money, a considerable advantage for a Democrat. The great unwashed, Jack had assured her, liked rich candidates on the assumption that the rich wouldn't have to cheat and steal. It was, he pointed out, a false assumption, since the rich were more likely than lesser-endowed mortals to have greed pro-grammed into their genes.

She fully understood his paranoia about being discovered doing what would be perceived by voters as dirty business in his personal life. Voters' perceptions, they both knew, had little to do with the inner man, but he was married and had three grown children as well as an image, painstakingly manufactured for public consumption, as a strict family man with deep moral and religious convictions and a staunch upholder of traditional values. It was an image that allowed upstate conservatives to partially swallow some of his liberal positions, designed to win the needed portion of the city vote.

It was a source of enormous ego satisfaction to Myrna that Jack chose to spend every weekend possible with her, despite the risks and dangers, which to him were considerable. His wife accepted his weekend trips to New York from Washington as the usual business of politics, and his staff protected his privacy without question and without explanation. Naturally they speculated about his whereabouts. But they didn't know. Fortunately his wife was deeply involved in a career as a real estate broker, and weekends were especially busy for her.

It wasn't easy for him to carry on this affair. Everything had to be completely hidden. No financial records could attest to his whereabouts. No telephone calls could be made. He had to be anonymous and invisible.

He entered Myrna's apartment building, literally, in disguise. He had even refused to accept a key of his own to her place, afraid that if found in his possession, it might be traced to Myrna's apartment. It was an unlikely assumption, of course, but it did indicate to her the parameters of his paranoia.

With election coming up in less than a year, he had to maintain his public political persona to the letter, knowing that there were forces among his opponents that would love to get their hands on information that could destroy his career, especially anything that had to do with chasing women.

The media loved to crawl into a politician's pants. Not that he had been a notorious womanizer like Ted Kennedy, which was seen to be a traditional expectation for a Kennedy, or an arrogant womanizer like Gary Hart, who had deliberately triggered the media blood lust that brought him down.

Jack's previous sexual peccadilloes, the senator had explained to Myrna, were reduced to quickies under the safest circumstances, and they were extremely infrequent. His relationship with Myrna was, he assured her repetitively, vastly different. As a media person, Myrna completely understood the realities of their affair, noting that the danger of potential discovery actually added to the excitement.

To both of them, it had been an instant conflagration. Myrna had gone down to Washington to supervise a photographic color layout of Senator Springer. Ironically, most of the pictures were taken in his Chevy Chase home, and she and his wife, Nell, a postcard-perfect political wife, had gotten along famously.

That had been the beginning. Myrna and Jack both knew that they were at the mercy of a mysterious magnetizing force with inevitable consequences.

"No one escapes from fate," he had explained even as he posed for pictures. She knew exactly what he meant.

The very next weekend he had met her at her office in Manhattan to go over the pictures. The sexual tension between them was patently obvious to both of them, and as soon as the business between them was over, they were off to her apartment to spend the next two days in bed, keeping the pizza and Chinese carryouts down the street busy for sustenance.

At fifty-three Jack was remarkably virile, literally a sexual athlete of awesome powers. The more they saw of each other, the more their addiction to each other increased and the more serious they became about spending their future life together. This was, they could tell, even on that first weekend, no quick roll in the hay.

"As I see it," he told her after a month of weekends, "we've got two choices. I could confront Nell now, ask for a divorce, but it would be a real long shot for reelection. Upstate, I'd have a tough time, and up there are the numbers I need to mesh with the downstate liberals. If I stay in this racket, the best bet would be to wait until after the election. Between elections, divorce is quite acceptable for a senator."

"That's only one choice," Myrna replied. As usual, they lay in bed, waiting for desire to intrude on the conversation. It was remarkable, Myrna thought, how much "quality" time they did spend together being shacked up like this for forty-eight hours at a stretch.

"Actually three choices, then. I could divorce Nell and stand for reelection with you at my side, take my chances. Or I could just divorce Nell and say fuck it and go into law practice, make even more money, and have you to myself without worrying about what the great unwashed thinks."

"I like the part about the fuck it," Myrna said, reaching out to caress him. "But let's face it, Jack. Senator is what you want. In fact, I want it, too, even though I'm totally opposed to some of your agenda." She felt his penis begin to stiffen. "Well, not to all of it." She laughed, then bent down and kissed it. "It's what you want, too, and you know it. Nor would I want to be the cause of your losing the election and maybe your chances for higher office." Up till then he had been deliberately evasive about any reference to higher office, which both knew meant the presidency. But her exposure to politicians had taught her that the "big P" was always on their minds, especially if they had all the right physical and political credentials, like Jack Springer.

"It's a pipe dream," he had said with a sigh, although he could not quite hide the yearning.

"Hey, pal," she had countered. "This is little Myrna. The only pipe around here is that." She had pointed to the obvious. "Besides, you don't smoke."

"All right. It's more than a pipe dream."

"A lot more. A possibility."

"And old Ron was divorced."

"Nuff said."

"So you'd like to be First Lady, would you?" he had joked.

"Get laid by the president? In the White House? Who wouldn't?"

"You're using me to fulfill your sexual fantasies."

"Exactly. So I say we wait, then you do your split, and we get married and live happily ever after. White House or not. Really, Jack, that makes more sense."

"Light as lain," Jack said, still in a playful mood. "I'm getting a yen for some more flied lice. But first let's do something about this election."

"I love this election more than anything," Myrna said, kissing it again. And again.

But once it was firmly decided to take no chances and wait until after the election for him to ask Nell for a divorce, his paranoia increased. A misstep, they both knew, could be a political disaster, and therefore the mechanics of their weekends grew more com-plicated as the fear of discovery upped the ante considerably. It boiled down to his need to continue to be a senator, thereby keeping his options open for higher office, and her new compulsion to be a senator's wife or more. How will that grab you, Pop? she fantasized secretly.

"Maybe we should cool it until after the election," Myrna had suggested from time to time, knowing it was only a test. They were always testing each other. An affliction of lovers, she had told him. Never quite trusting the joy, the miracle, of it. It provided its share of pain as well. The pain of parting, the uncertainty of such love between them being sustained. "Suppose we're not in love like this after the election? Suppose you fall out of love with me?"

"Or you with me?"

"Never," she would attest. "Never. Never. Never."

"Why so sure? You fell out of love with others. Your two hus-bands."

"I never loved them."

"Then why did you marry them?"

"I was trying to fuck my father."

"And did you?"

"No. They were imposters."

"And me?"

"I want to fuck you, not my father. My father is yesterday. It's all over. I've taken over the blame." It had, she knew, the ring of truth. Only she could hear the hollow note.

"One day you'll stop loving me. Find out I'm an imposter, just like the others," Jack said, another test, just to bait her. It was all part of it, the testing, the fear, the delicious insecurity, the exquisite danger.

"And you? Didn't you once love Nell?"

"There's love and love."

"And this?"

"It takes some maturity to understand the difference between the original and a knock-off."

"And which are we?"

"The original."

"Then why do you keep knocking me off?" They both giggled at that. In fact, they spent lots of time giggling. At times she wondered if she had actually become the Myrna Loy of the *Thin Man* series. And he was the William Powell character. The irony amused her, despite its Pyrrhic victory for her father.

At times during their weekends they would hear sounds in the hallway or on the stairs or the movement of the elevator.

"You suppose any of them knows?" he would ask.

"How could they know?"

"They could have seen me, seen through my stupid disguise."

"In this building? Everybody seems to be hiding something around here. It's a miracle if you even get a hello. Which is exactly the way I want it. All I need is to face a lot of bullshit from the neighbors. Hell, we couldn't be doing this if I had gotten friendly with them. Some yenta would be ringing the buzzer at the most inappropriate moment, wanting to borrow some herb tea, for chrissake."

"But you still couldn't be certain, dead certain."

She contemplated his challenge for a long moment. "Certain. But not dead certain," she agreed. "What about you? Can you be certain that you got here clean and unspotted? I mean, how can you be so sure you weren't followed?"

"I know how to shake a tail."

"Yessirree. I vote yea to that one."

"Good. That's exactly my immediate intention."

"Okay. Here's my tail."

She loved this easy banter between them, the sex, the closeness, the letting go, and she was sure the same went for him.

One weekend, he asked her: "Is there anything you want?"

At first the question confused her, and she had hesitated to answer it, but he had prodded her.

"Something material, something you have on the top of a wish list, something personal." On other occasions he had expressed some guilt in the fact that they spent the weekends holed up, hiding out like fugitives. This request, she assumed, obviously came about because of those feelings.

"You don't have to, Jack," she told him. "My cup already runneth over."

"You don't understand. I want to. No, I need to. And not just a token."

She had thought about it for a number of weeks, deciding finally to tell him the truth, sure that it would be beyond his means. She had seen what she wanted at Henri Bendel one day. It had arrested her attention, and she had actually tried it on. Wanting a material thing had never turned her on. Except this.

"A certain full-length sable coat," she told him, giving some specifics about her experience at Bendel's. "Pure frippery, I know. Against all liberal principles about animal rights and such. But you really wanted to know. I don't like jewelry. You said personal. So that's it, that full-length sable coat. The one that said 'Come and get me at Bendel's.' I'd love to go out with you in that sable coat. In fact, we don't even have to go out, I'll wear it with nothing on underneath. How's that for fantasy."

She watched his face, expecting some expression of either ridicule or frustration.

"Perfect," he said. "I'm of an age when I can still remember that once a woman's most fervent material desire was to have a fur coat."

"See how traditional I am."

"That's my girl. You want that full-length sable, you got it."

"Come on, Jack. We're talking more than a hundred thousand dollars. I know you're loaded, but it's not easy to hide a purchase like that from the people who administer your private funds. Some one of your various retainers is bound to raise a red flag. You asked. I told you. It was meant to scare you, not to encourage you. Besides, you give me your love and your loving, and that's quite enough."

He was silent for a long time after that. She let him alone, hoping he was in the process of rejecting the idea as foolhardy and dangerous. Finally, when he did not speak, she embellished her earlier note of caution.

"First of all, in your position, you'd have to buy it in cash. No records, remember. Then you'd have to be sure that the name of the chippy, me, was totally hidden. Can't you see the headlines: 'Sable Coat to Secret Mistress in Senator's Love Nest.' The *National Enquirer* would have a field day."

"That's exactly the point. We'll outsmart the bastards. Fool them."

"Now that is crazy."

"Crazy? Better yet, dangerous. I love the idea of outsmarting the bastards. Let's just figure out how to make it happen. Can the coat you want be described on the telephone?"

"Of course. Actually, it may already be gone."

"Did you ask the price?"

"One hundred twenty-five thousand five hundred, plus luxury tax. So there. So much for fantasy."

"Do you know the salesperson? Were you recognized?"

"You can't be serious," she muttered. "But the answer is no."

"Okay. So we keep you anonymous. Now getting it to you..."
He mused for a while over the detail. Idle speculation, she decided.
"We have it delivered to someone untraceable to me or you. A casual acquaintance, perhaps. The thing about this business is that you've got to protect your flanks."

"Why bother?"

"Because it's there."

"What's that supposed to mean?" she said.

"It means," Jack said, "that I'm going to do it. I need to do this. I need to show you how far I'm willing to go."

"It's adolescent," she protested. "Like playing chicken."

"Sort of," he admitted. "One way or another I'm going to do it. With or without your complicity."

"You don't have to prove anything to me, Jack. I love you. Nothing can make me love you more."

"And I love you. And I want to do this."

"But, Jack, if the media, or some legitimate investigative body, or, for that matter, some illegitimate body, a private detective hired by an opponent, wants to dig up dirt, this will be a bonanza."

"I'm all a-twitter," Jack said.

"You have that much untraceable cash?"

"In my stash."

"What does that mean?"

"It means that most politicians have campaign cash hidden, un-accounted for. Even me."

"Is that legal?"

"Not legal. Just done. Standard practice. So you see, not to worry. Believe me, I can get the nicely laundered cash for the purchase. Like Nixon in the Watergate tapes saying he could get the cash. Anonymously. Then we get a private delivery service to deliver it to someone of your choice."

No matter what she said, however convoluted her scenarios of doom, she knew that he had already figured things out and there could be no dissuading him. In an odd way she was glad that she had told him about it, although she still worried about the terrible risk to him.

"You realize you're jeopardizing your career," she told him.

"That's exactly the point. I want to risk it. I want to illustrate how much you truly mean to me."

"Sounds like you want to get caught."

"Psychobabble," he replied. "No. I want to get away with it, and I want you to have this gift. I've bought enough gifts for people that meant nothing. I want you to have a gift from me that means something."

"It's romantic stupidity."

"I know. Isn't it wonderful?"

It did not take her long to be a party to it. The issue finally got down to who would be the perfect go-between. She wrestled over that one. It was not a matter of trust, more of naive ignorance, someone who would simply accept the assignment, relegating it to no more than a simple favor.

That cute little woman downstairs! She remembered how she had dutifully delivered Myrna's shoes, how fresh, sweet, and naive she seemed. And apparently, from what Myrna had observed, she spent most of her time at home, the perfect little homemaker. What was her name? Burns. Janey or Jenny?

Thinking about her caused Myrna to expand her thoughts about the people who occupied the building. Myrna had lived here for five years. It was perfect for her needs, spacious, high ceilings and thick plaster walls, well kept, and most important, away from the gossiping curiosity of concierges, doormen, and janitors who hung about high rises with their palms out and their eyes open.

She considered finding such an apartment in a small building a stroke of luck. It would have been impossible for Jack to visit her like this if she lived in one of those luxury high rises. Someone was sure to spot him. Not that she was totally secure that he had not been recognized coming in or out of her building. But the odds seemed a lot less, and six months had passed without any suspicious incident.

She had maintained a bare minimum of sociability with the neighbors, offering a pleasant hello or a trite comment about the weather. Invariably she kept her distance. The Richardsons, who lived in the apartment across from hers, seemed pleasant enough, and she heard their comings and goings without interest. Mr. Richardson had introduced himself to her, volunteering that he was an art dealer, which had immediately put her on alert. Art dealers were always hustling paintings.

Upstairs, just above her place, were the Sterns. She looked like gloom and doom, and he seemed always self-absorbed and unfriendly. Their son, too, was equally strange. When they waited on the first-floor landing for the elevator, she would be sure to offer the most perfunctory acknowledgment she could think of, then dash up the stairs. Actually it was difficult to ascertain who was being more standoffish, she or them. Either way it suited her just fine.

Then there was the gay couple on the ground level that were always losing their cat. Three times in the last year one of them had rung her buzzer looking for that damned cat. Once or twice she had spotted the Stern boy sitting on the steps stroking the cat, a tabby that looked like a miniature tiger. Beyond that, she had little or nothing to do with the couple.

Which left the obvious, that sweet little thing on the first floor. Myrna remembered that she had this midwestern twang and a fresh, open, trusting look. It was obvious that she would have liked to come into Myrna's apartment and pass the time of day. That, Myrna suspected, would be fatal, since the woman seemed to have lots of time on her hands.

Perhaps she stayed home because she was pregnant or unemployed or had been cowed into accepting the role of housewife by what could be her overbearing twit of a husband. Indeed, she knew the type well from paternal experience.

Her suspicions had been confirmed when she had observed the husband a couple of times as they passed in the hallway. He appeared to be a sleek, conceited, hard-body type. She felt certain that he was one of that vast army of nose-in-the-air, tight-ass, take-no-prisoners superyuppies, always dressed in the latest designer suits or jogging clothes. She had encountered hordes of them between husbands. They were always so cocksure of making it big and expected the world to bow down and admire them.

She got her jollies ball-busting them, making them feel like shit, especially in the sack, where they really thought they were showing their stuff. She chuckled to herself, remembering how she had faked indifference to their lovemaking, after coming to beat the band. That really pissed them off. This Burns fellow, she decided, was a classic specimen.

Actually, even though she was determined not to befriend the neighbors, he seemed to go beyond the pale, not even looking her way when they passed in the hall, offering not even the slightest impersonal grunt of recognition and leaving in his wake the stink of his trendy after-shave.

"Sounds like a great idea," Jack told her when she broached the subject of this Janey or Jenny receiving the coat. By then the situation was a fait accompli, both of them treating it as a challenge to be faced, with this last detail of delivery to be accomplished.

"If you don't hear from me to the contrary," she told Jack, "the coast is clear."

"Great. Next weekend we'll have a party."

"Don't we always. I'll wear it when we make love."

"I can't wait."

"So I see."

Then it was decided. A perfect shill. Myrna was certain the

woman would cream in her jeans at this opportunity to be a good neighbor.

Even that first brief visit had indicated the whole story; the woman seemed so open, so natural, so midwestern, so corny, that the potential request actually gave her a pang of conscience, as if she were using her for some nefarious purpose. In a way, she was. Hell, it was only a delivery, for crying out loud.

Myrna Davis rang Jenny's buzzer at exactly nine-thirty in the morning on a Wednesday in June, precisely when the tall antique clock Jenny and Larry had bought at a Soho store chimed the half hour. Jenny was drinking her second cup of coffee and making a list of ingredients she would be buying later for chicken Kiev, which was to be the centerpiece for Friday's dinner Larry had arranged for Vincent and Connie Mazzo. Larry had on occasion mentioned Vincent, referring to him as the only one in the agency who knew his ass from first base.

Although she was quite confident about being able to put together a wonderful meal, Jenny was not as confident about meeting the wives of Larry's colleagues, although she didn't express these reservations to Larry. Up until then he had not made any demands for her participation in any social obligations that had to do with his work.

Not that she didn't have expectations of this happening one day. Larry had on occasion expressed the necessity of husband-and-wife teamwork effort in the corporate world, and she assured herself repeatedly that she was fully prepared to shoulder the burden. But now that it was imminent she wasn't so confident. Worse, Larry had told her that the dinner was not merely socially important, but crucial.

"Crucial?" She was surprised that he had elevated the occasion to such importance. That part was unnerving.

"It's a bonding mechanism," Larry told her. "Vincent and I have made big plans together, and we both think it's important to put the wives together. At first we were thinking of going out, but I told him that my little woman is one great cook. After all, why not step out with your best foot forward?"

"I'll do my best, Larry," she had replied, hoping that the nervousness about meeting one of his colleagues' wives wouldn't hurt the dinner.

"Wives need to feel part of it, Jenny," Larry said.

"But I do feel part of it, Larry. Whatever happens to you happens to me, doesn't it?"

"In that respect, yes," he agreed. "I'm not particularly worried about you, Jenny. You know your place in the scheme of things. But Vincent and Connie have a different kind of relationship. She's a lawyer and a lot more involved than you are in business. Anyway, Vince thinks it's important that the wives meet and that the four of us get together."

"I hope I'll make a good impression."

She admitted to herself some concern about dealing with Vincent's wife. It was hard to envision what kind of a woman she was.

"It wasn't my idea, Jenny. I prefer the gals to stay out of the way. Just be the way you are."

The discussion had taken place in the kitchen. He had embraced her from behind as she stood in front of the sink, and the entire conversation had taken place in that position. "Some wives can be real bitchy. You know. Influencing their husbands when they don't know beans about anything. Vince and I are setting up this partnership, and I don't want anything to louse up the deal."

"I certainly won't."

"You? No way. But Connie could. Vince says she's got a good sixth sense about people. That always worries me."

"Why so?"

"It implies that her judgment about people is infallible, which it can't be. And even if it's pretty good, some people are very clever about hiding who they really are. What they really think." He pressed her closer to him and whispered, "Not you baby. What you see is what you get."

Did that mean he thought she was transparent? She wasn't sure, but it did not seem the time to raise that particular point. Instead she asked another question that was rattling around in her mind.

"Are you saying that if Connie Mazzo doesn't like me, you and Vincent wouldn't go ahead with whatever you're planning?"

"I'm not saying that," Larry replied. "But the fact is that some wives have more to say than others. Who knows. She might wonder why Vince wants to get in bed with us in the first place. People make judgments based on emotion, first impressions. Not me. I want to know the facts first. That's why I'm in research. I want to know hard facts."

"So in a way it's some kind of a test...for me."

"Let's say for both of us."

"But mostly for me."

"What happens to you happens to me."

For the first time in their marriage a flicker of doubt crossed her mind. "But you've met her," she said, taking a chance that it was true.

"Yes, I have," he admitted, averting his eyes.

"So it really is a test for me," she persisted. "I'm the one on the hot seat."

He seemed to sigh with resignation. "For us, Jenny. Why are you being so defensive? Neither of them has been to our home, met us as a couple."

Yes, she decided, there was some truth to that. But then she hadn't been to their home.

"But suppose I can't stand her? Or him? Would you still go into business with them?"

"There it is," he snapped. "That's why it's really better for the women to stay out of it."

She decided it was a good moment to change the tenor of the discussion. "And you're satisfied with Vincent?" she asked, wondering if she had overstepped. It was quickly apparent that she had.

"Would I be inviting him if I wasn't?" he asked, showing a flash of irritation. "I'm telling you, Jenny. He's the best. He controls two of the agency's biggest clients, and we could be in business in ninety days. He'd be Mr. Outside and I'd be Mr. Inside."

"Sounds terrific, Larry." I think, she told herself.

She sensed an undercurrent that wasn't to her liking. Were they planning to steal the two accounts away from their present employer? She didn't pursue the idea. That wasn't her place.

"I hope she doesn't think I'm just a Hoosier hick, unworldly and naive."

"And if she does? Maybe that's a plus. One thing she'll know, and that's that you're never going to interfere with the business. If you came over as some pushy bitch, she might think you were a threat."

"Suppose I think she's a pushy bitch?"

"She probably is. But I'm not prepared to queer the deal because of that. Wrong timing. I need Vince now. But I'll promise you one thing. Soon as we get rolling, she'll have to keep her nose out."

"I'll do my best," Jenny sighed.

"You are the best," he whispered. "That's the point."

"No. This is the point." She giggled, caressing his erection. He began to raise her dress, and she felt his fingers reaching for the elastic of her panties. "Here? Right now?"

"Well, you've already loaded the dishwasher," he said, and she could feel his nakedness behind her and her own rising desire as she braced her hands against the rim of the sink and arched her body.

Certainly Larry could guide her in what was required of her in a business sense, and she was determined to fulfill his expectations. Business was his. The house was hers. At least in theory. But he was a bit overprotective in his attitude about New York and New Yorkers, and she was finding herself less and less in step with his opinions on this subject. Yet she did not feel secure enough to challenge his attitudes on a regular basis. She also found herself beginning to question his judgment on some issues about what did and did not go on in the real world. In fact, sometimes she felt vaguely confused by his assertions.

Just yesterday she had discussed the subject of neighbors with her mother on the telephone.

"You mean you don't know your neighbors?" her mother had exclaimed after Jenny had told her that it was not generally accepted in New York to be neighborly.

"Well, I've met them. We had one couple for dinner. But I don't know them in the way you know your neighbors," she had admitted. "Sensible people find it better not to get involved." The episode with Teddy passed through her mind. For a brief moment she was tempted to tell her mother what she had done, then thought better of it, although in her heart she felt her mother would understand.

"Surely you've made new friends," her mother said with an obvious twinge of alarm.

Her mother's notion of "friends" had an entirely different definition from what she had encountered so far in New York. Jenny decided it was far too complicated to explain the gap that had opened between her mother's world and her own.

"Mostly Larry and I have spent the time getting to know one another," Jenny said. It was, she thought, a reasonably honest answer, as near to the truth as she could get without it becoming an outright lie.

"That probably makes a lot of sense," her mother replied. "But sooner or later you'll want for friends. And you never know when you might need a neighbor."

At that point Jenny's mother began a long recitation on the subject of neighbors, citing the Robinsons, who had been an integral part of their lives, and how their fortunes had intermingled and how they had come through in emergencies. Penny Robinson had been her best friend in high school but had married a naval officer and had drifted away. And Celia Robinson, Penny's mother, was to this day her mother's best friend. After a while it sounded to Jenny like a voice from an alien world, a kind of rambling lecture on the subject of people needing people. There was only one way to stop the lecture.

"This is New York, Mom. Not Bedford, Indiana."

At that point her mother branched off onto another of her favorite subjects, people being the same everywhere. Jenny listened with less than complete attention until her mother exclaimed with a prescience that seemed a bit scary:

"You mustn't become like them, Jenny."

It was, of course, the heart of her mother's worry, and it came out in the most seemingly benign but telling ways. Jenny supposed that all mothers of children brought up in small towns were afflicted with the same fundamental fear of the impersonal corrupting alien world that confronted their offspring in the big city. And despite her dismissal of her mother's remark as typical, she had not challenged it, although she was completely convinced that she could never, ever, become like "them." How could she? Nevertheless, the idea that her mother would be concerned about such a thing happening was worrisome and disconcerting and brought on a mild depression.

Finally Jenny began the withdrawal from the conversation with the usual regards to the rest of the family and the promise to visit Bedford for the Fourth of July if Larry could manage the time. This last cautionary note was designed to soften the blow, since it was more likely that Larry would decline the trip and she would, of course, not go without him.

The lingering effects of her depression were still bothering her when she opened the door to Myrna Davis on that June morning. Myrna, whom she had barely seen since delivering the shoes from Bloomingdale's and getting snubbed for her effort, was beautifully groomed in a yellow cotton suit and matching shoes. Around her neck she wore a silver pendant, which she fingered nervously as she stood in the doorway, offering a broad, pink-lipsticked smile that set off her very white, even teeth. She was quite striking, in marked contrast to Jenny in her loose sweats.

Larry was usually long gone on his jogging trip to the office when Jenny awakened. At first she had attempted to rise with him to make him breakfast. But that had ceased when she'd discovered that all he had for breakfast on weekdays was a cup of coffee and a piece of whole-wheat toast. She would have been content to make even that, except that he was not very communicative in the morning, preferring the company of *The New York Times.*

She also discovered that he was quite content with this arrangement, and after a while she fell into the pattern of sleeping a bit later without the slightest guilt. It was just one other dose of reality that separated New Yorkers from Hoosiers.

Her mother had risen to make breakfast for her family every day of her life, and she still made it for her father. And breakfast was abundant, with juice, hot cereal, eggs, sausage, bacon or ham, toast, rolls, jam, and fresh-brewed coffee. Just thinking about it these days summoned up memories that often brought tears to Jenny's eyes.

"I hope I haven't disturbed you," Myrna said, looking beyond Jenny to the interior of the apartment.

"Not at all," Jenny said, again feeling the same awkwardness that she had felt in her first confrontation with Myrna Davis. For some reason this woman, with her air of superiority and confidence, made Jenny feel diminished, a clumsy hick.

"I have a favor to ask," Myrna said.

Despite her own sense of intimidation, Jenny sensed Myrna's nervousness, as if she were more ill at ease than Jenny. It gave Jenny the courage to invite her in.

"Of course," Jenny said, standing aside as Myrna entered the apartment. Jenny observed her as she inspected the place. She seemed to fill it with her presence, her tallness, her coloring, her wonderful perfume.

"Nice," Myrna said with an air of someone who hadn't quite expected what she saw.

"Thank you," Jenny said as if she had been anointed. The approval further sparked her courage. "I was just having some coffee. Would you like some?"

"That would be wonderful," Myrna said, drawing out the "won" in wonderful as if she were being offered vintage champagne. The acceptance surprised Jenny, since it was obvious that Myrna was dressed and ready to pursue her day, which from the look of her seemed to promise marvelous and exciting events. Why waste time with little me? Jenny thought, instantly hating her own reaction.

She went into the kitchen to get the coffee, intending to prepare a nice tray and bring it into the living room. But Myrna followed her into the kitchen.

"What a wonderful place," Myrna said, again emphasizing the "won" in wonderful. "You must love to cook."

"I do," Jenny said, pulling two mugs from a shelf and placing them on the kitchen island. She poured the coffee into the mugs. Myrna took hers, and her nostrils twitched as she inhaled the aroma. "Nothing like freshly ground coffee."

"It's a great blend. We get it at Zabar's."

"Don't you just love that place?" Myrna said, almost girlish in her enthusiasm, as if the ultrasophistication of her dress and attitude were only a contrived pose for business purposes.

"It's, it's wonderful," Jenny said, trying to extend the "won" but stopping midway, feeling suddenly uncomfortable and clumsy with the affectation.

"How I envy you," Myrna said, shaking her head as if in admiration.

"Me?"

"You know what I mean."

"No, I don't."

"Being a wife." Myrna paused, studying Jenny. "I've never been," she said with obvious regret. "Oh, I've been married. Twice, actually. But I wasn't a wife either time. There's a difference." She trained her eyes on Jenny. "Now you. There's a contentment about you. I noticed it the first time I saw you."

Jenny sipped her coffee and shrugged. She hadn't thought of herself as merely content, which had a passive connotation about it. But Myrna would not give her any time for reflection.

"Sometimes we women out in the so-called big bad world can't see the forest for the trees," Myrna continued. She put her hand on her chest. "Hell, in my business we push the idea that the competing, upwardly mobile, ball-busting woman offers the best of all possible lives for our gender. We design our pitch so that housewives are portrayed as the drones of the female sex, slave to man's whims, put-upon, unrewarded, lesser beings. And we do it deliberately." She paused, looked at Jenny, then winked. "Make 'em insecure and they'll swallow anything."

"In a way you sound like Larry," Jenny said. "He's a vice-president in charge of research for Payne and Magruder." She put a deliberate emphasis on the name of the advertising agency.

Registering the name, Myrna nodded in acknowledgment, widening her eyes as if impressed. "Then, surely, he knows whereof I speak."

"Actually we've never discussed it."

She inspected Jenny's face. "I guess you wouldn't. Why bring such slop into your lives? For him this place has to be an oasis, free of the grit, a refuge from the madding crowd." She took a deep sip of her coffee.

"Little things like a good cup of coffee can make your heart sing," Myrna said.

"I'm glad you like it," Jenny said, hoping that Myrna was sincere. There was no way she could tell. Sophisticated women like Myrna were so articulate and worldly that it was hard to read them. Not like us ordinary mortals, she told herself as if to satirize her own sense of inferiority in the presence of such a queenly creature. Again she found herself resenting her own attitude. Why does this woman make me feel this way? she asked herself.

"Here I am babbling away and I've not even broached the object of my visit." Jenny noticed that Myrna took a quick, furtive look at the face of the kitchen clock. "I need your help on a matter of great delicacy." Jenny didn't reply, wondering what possible favor Myrna needed that required such an elaborate buildup. "All I need from you is your willingness to accept a package for me."

"Is that all?"

Suddenly Jenny remembered Larry's displeasure at her acceptance of the shoes from Bloomie's. In fairness, Jenny thought, she had portrayed Myrna as ungrateful and unfriendly.

"No, that isn't quite all, Jenny," Myrna said, her glance roaming everywhere but directly into Jenny's eyes.

Jenny was genuinely puzzled. On the surface it seemed like a simple request. Then why was Myrna being hesitant and obviously uncomfortable?

"The package will come in your name," Myrna said, lowering her voice to what was a distinctly conspiratorial tone.

"My name?"

"I mean it will be addressed to you, but it will really be for me." Jenny started to respond, but Myrna cut her off abruptly. "It's nothing illegal, just something...well...for me." Myrna winked. "Oh, all right...it's a gift from an admirer who wants to keep a secret that it's from him. Am I making myself clear here? It seems that I'm doing this rather badly."

"No. I think I understand." Jenny wasn't completely certain that she did, but the favor itself seemed simple. "It comes to me in my name and I bring it upstairs to you."

"It's just a wee bit more convoluted than that," Myrna said. "Oh, nothing really complicated. I'm being silly about it. It will probably arrive here sometime tomorrow or Friday. The thing is...well... it should be brought upstairs on Saturday. Say noon, if that's no trouble. Just ring the buzzer and leave the package against the door."

"It doesn't seem to be very complicated," Jenny said, wondering why Myrna was making such a fuss but determining that to pry further would cross the line between respecting privacy and no-siness. Aside from the favor being asked of her, it was really none of her business. Not that she could totally dismiss normal human curiosity. Myrna had said that this was a gift of some sort from a secret lover. Obviously, Jenny reasoned, that lover was the person with whom she spent her weekends. It didn't take a genius to figure that the man was very married and ultracautious.

Which brought her to another point about this situation. Did Myrna think that Jenny was too much of a hick to understand such matters? She remembered her own brief affair with a mar-ried, albeit separated, man, but the same conditions of extreme discretion, even secrecy, had existed. There she was overreacting again. The fact was that there was an air of exciting complicity about Myrna's proposal. A dollop of rebellion as well, since she was certain that Larry, if he were to find out, would object to the arrangement.

"I'll be eternally grateful, Jenny," Myrna pressed, perhaps reading in Jenny a sudden note of caution.

"No need for that, Myrna," Jenny said. "It's just a small favor between neighbors."

The statement seemed to relieve Myrna, and when she looked at Jenny her eyes were not roving anymore. "Above all, Jenny, I knew you were the kind of person I could truly trust. People sense things. I knew it instantly." Again she lowered her voice. "The truth is, Jenny, you're the only person in this building I believe I can trust. Maybe anywhere, including at the office." Speaking that last phrase, her voice had drifted away, as if she hadn't meant to say it.

"Just good midwestern stock," Jenny said, half joking but nevertheless proud of Myrna's attesting to her trust. She knew she was, above all, trustworthy. Such a trait was inbred, the very heart of her family's value system. At last something truly neighborly was occurring. Inspecting Myrna's face, Jenny decided that beneath all the so-called sophistication was a sincere, vulnerable person reaching out for trust and friendship.

"Believe me, Jenny, there is nothing untoward about it. Nothing out of line. Nothing you'll regret later. Not drugs or stolen goods or anything like that." Myrna seemed to be rambling onward, unable to stop, as if she were on the verge of making a clean breast of it, a confession. "If you have any questions. Any at all ..."

"Why should I have any questions?" Jenny said. "It seems like a totally straightforward request. I accept the package and bring it up to you Saturday at around noon. Not exactly like a spy mystery." Jenny laughed suddenly. "Or is it?"

"I hadn't thought about it in that way," Myrna mused. "Maybe you have something there. All this mysterious subterfuge must have you baffled."

Again Jenny sensed that Myrna wished to explain things further, perhaps bare her soul.

"I'll do my job, neighbor," Jenny said, offering a version of a military salute and, she hoped, a happy smile.

"Of course you will," Myrna said. Again her glance started to roam and she pressed her upper teeth against her lower lip, as if she were contemplating a subject not yet addressed. "I hope you don't think I'm going too far." It appeared to be a prologue to something more that she wanted to say, and Jenny held her silence, waiting. Whatever it was, it seemed to be a subject requiring great, perhaps agonizing, reflection on Myrna's part.

"I'm not sure I should ask you this. I mean you've been great so far...."

"I've always found it better to say what's on your mind," Jenny said, repeating something her parents might have said, which experience had taught her was not always realistic.

"Well then, here goes," Myrna said, shaking her head, as if what she was about to say were against her better judgment. "Do you think we can keep it, you know, in the sisterhood?"

Jenny must have frowned or otherwise revealed some gesture of uncertainty. If that was so, it was an involuntary act. It did, however, require some mulling over. She was being asked to break a kind of bond between her and Larry.

At first blush such a proposal suggested betrayal, and her first reaction was indignation. Then it occurred to her that such an attitude was motivated by Myrna's asking, not the truth of the situation.

Actually she had kept a number of things hidden from Larry, deliberately. Take the case of Teddy. Where was it written that every incident, every detail, every private thought, had to be communicated to one's spouse? Suddenly she was indignant at her own indignation. Certainly he, too, kept things hidden, which was appropriate to all human beings. Absolute honesty could be a form of nakedness and, therefore, discomfort.

"This is between us. You and me," Jenny said. "Only us."

"I'd better quit while I'm ahead," Myrna said. Again she started for the door, and again she turned to face Jenny. "Someday I'll explain all this."

"Really, it's not necessary."

Myrna's eyes glistened with tears as she concentrated her gaze on Jenny. "Tennessee Williams had it right. At one time or another we all have to depend on the kindness of strangers." Then she turned and went out the door, closing it softly behind her.

7

VINCENT MAZZO wore a wrinkled beige jacket, matching pants, and a black silk shirt, all amply cut in what Jenny supposed was the cutting edge of style in men's clothes. She had seen such outfits on television, and they'd always looked to her as if they needed a good pressing before they were carted over to the Salvation Army clothing drive. On his feet, Vincent wore black lizard loafers and no socks.

With his dark curly hair and what looked like a few days' growth of beard, he was hardly the kind of man she envisioned to run an advertising agency. At first she had wondered why he hadn't shaved, suspecting that he had some temporary skin condition. It was only halfway through their first drink that she discovered after some scrutiny that the beard was obviously trimmed on a regular basis. This was apparently the look the man wanted. To Jenny he simply appeared rumpled and dirty.

His deep-set eyes had a feral look, and his hawk nose, low forehead, and thick lips completed the picture of a very intense man. He did not smile often, and when he did the corners of his lips barely lifted.

His wife, Connie, a tall brunette, was wearing tight black jeans that looked as if they had been painted on her sleek body and a colorful and obviously expensive silk blouse. Around her neck she wore a gold chain that threaded through a teardrop ruby pendant. Although her long hair covered her ears, Jenny was sure she wore matching ruby earrings and that sometime during the evening they would be treated to a glimpse of them by some errant and deliberate movement of her fingers through her hair.

On her feet she wore black tooled leather cowboy boots, the bottoms of her jeans tucked into the stems of the boots. Her large brown eyes peered over knobby cheekbones. On meeting her, Jenny was instantly intimidated. The woman gave off an air of awesome self-confidence that hung over her thicker than the scent of her expensive perfume.

Jenny wore a long Laura Ashley dress that was supposed to be a surprise, and she deliberately hadn't previewed it for Larry on the grounds that this dinner was to illustrate how capable she could be on her own. It was something of a shock to discover that her dress was totally out of sync with her guests' outfits. Larry's quick glance of disapproval confirmed to her that somehow she had committed an unpardonable gaffe.

Larry had very appropriately worn his blue double-breasted blazer with the brass buttons over a button-down white shirt and blue striped tie. His pants were pearl gray knife-creased flannels. Larry had an instinct for always presenting himself in exactly the correct way, the conservative counterpoint to his more trendy partner.

The two couples, Jenny noted, seemed a pairing of opposites, at least on the surface. She cautioned herself to reserve judgment as she passed around a plate of hors d'oeuvres while Larry took their drink orders. Vincent asked for a Campari and soda, and Connie opted for vodka and water with a squeezed lime. Larry poured two white wines, one for him and one for Jenny.

She had set the table with a centerpiece of flowers and her best dishes and silverware, researching the pattern in which it should be set with three specimens of stemware, one for water, one for the wine, which was white and had been carefully chosen by Larry, and one fluted glass for champagne. A fork and spoon for dessert were set at right angles to the other silverware just above the plates.

"Not bad," Larry had commented when he had seen the finished setting. She was proud of his approval, since it was she who had decided what food to serve.

"Just stay out of my kitchen," she had warned when he came home from the office. "I've been working at it all day." Which, indeed, she had been, using Julia Child's recipes for the fettuccine Alfredo and the chicken Kiev. She did allow that he was to signal her when it was appropriate for her to begin dinner.

"What an absolutely charming pad," Connie had commented when she'd inspected the apartment. Vincent nodded his head in agreement. Almost immediately Larry spirited him off to his den, while Jenny and Connie chatted in the living room. Jenny assumed Larry had done this deliberately, although she wished that he had waited until she had finished her first glass of wine. Jenny felt her pulse pounding in her neck. The woman seemed so sophisticated and superior.

"I understand you're from Indiana," Connie said, raking her fingers through her hair. There they were, Jenny noted, the matching ruby earrings.

"Ever been?"

"Never. But one of my law partners is from Illinois. Talks with a twang like you. I love those out-of-town accents. Vinnie and I are sort of dyed-in-the-wool New Yorkers. I doubt we'll ever leave Manhattan even when the kids are ready for school. No need. Everything you ever want is right here in this city."

Connie had crossed the room and had been looking out of the window into the street. Suddenly she turned to face Jenny. "Bet it's been somewhat of a culture shock. You'll get used to it." Jenny felt the woman's eyes inspecting her as if she were a piece of meat in the butcher shop.

"I'm trying," Jenny said, sipping her wine.

"Of course it's got grime and crime. You've just got to know how to walk through the mine fields."

"Larry is teaching me."

"Too many fucking people and not enough resources. Handout

city, I call it. But it's still the center of the universe with all the shit." She paused and continued her inspection.

"What do you do?"

"Me?"

Jenny had, of course, been prepared for the inevitable question, but not the way in which Connie delivered it, as if she were throwing down a gauntlet. Jenny was not happy with her initial response. Of course me, she thought. Who else?

"Where do you work?" Connie pressed.

"Right here," Jenny said, trying to put a spin of humor on her answer. "For the moment, I'm just a little old housewife." She resented having to add the phrase *for the moment* as if it implied something temporary.

"Doesn't it bore the shit out of you?" Connie asked.

"Not at all," Jenny replied.

"Wait'll you have kids. We've got two. You'll kill to get out of the house."

"Well, we're not there yet," Jenny said.

"You're young yet. Why rush it?"

Jenny shrugged, knowing that Connie's interrogation would continue.

"What did you do in Indiana?" Connie asked.

"I was . . ." She hesitated. She wanted to say "a nurse" but could not bring herself to lie outright. "I worked in a doctor's office." Might as well put this behind us, she thought.

"Did you?"

Jenny could sense the woman's retreat, like a lawyer saying "No more questions, Your Honor." There, you have the full picture, Jenny told the woman silently, feeling the full weight of her intimidation.

"Anyway," Connie said, as if it were an expression of dismissal, "this is one helluva move for all of us."

"Yes, I suppose it is," Jenny said, almost relieved that they had reached the heart of the matter between them.

"Tough racket, advertising. Dog eat dog. Frankly, I've encouraged Vincent to make this break. No percentage in being a flunky to another man's ego. Seize the day, I always say. Hell, Vince developed the accounts, and from what he tells me, your Larry is one helluva shrewd executive. Really organized. Someone to look after the details. Vince stinks with details. He's more the creative type. Perfect team, don't you think?"

"Mr. Inside and Mr. Outside," Jenny said, hoping to fake her knowledge of the situation.

"Vincent agonized over it for months," Connie went on. "Couldn't sleep. Couldn't eat." She lowered her voice. "A little withdrawn in other departments as well, if you get my drift. Finally I couldn't take it anymore. Fuck ethics, I told him. You're in advertising, for chrissake. There's no ethics in advertising. It's all kissy-ass at the top. And the product is simply bullshitting the public, making them buy things they don't need." She paused suddenly. Obviously this new business venture was the paramount question among the four of them. It was also apparent that Connie knew a lot more about what was happening than Jenny, which put Jenny at a distinct disadvantage. "Takes a lot of balls to do what our guys are doing, don't you think?"

The question took Jenny by surprise. "It does take courage."

"It'll leave Payne and Magruder with their pants down. I'd love to see their faces. They'll wake up one morning and see half their business gone south. And the good personnel will go with Vince and Larry. That's the way new agencies get started. Steal the business. Maybe 'steal' is too harsh a word. Let's say 'transfer.' All that noncompete legal shit won't stand up in court anyhow. And how do you like the new offices? Of course they haven't signed the lease yet. Why pay the extra month with D day August first? Clever the way they've kept it under wraps. Don't you think?"

Larry had mentioned office space. And that other? Noncompete? What did that mean? Her lack of information and knowledge made her tongue-tied. It crossed her mind that perhaps the woman was aware of her ignorance and might be flaunting her knowledge. In response, all she could do was to sip her drink, nod, and try to keep her expression from revealing the extent of her ignorance.

"Do you like the proposed logo?" Connie asked.

"Logo?"

"I'm not too keen on the way they looped the *z*'s. Also the colors don't seem right. What do you think?"

"Maybe so ... "

"I hate beige," Connie muttered. "Plain white stationery is always appropriate."

Jenny felt that she had been deliberately set adrift on some unknown sea. But she had recovered enough to feel the first faint bubbles of anger rise in her chest. Somehow all this information provided by Connie, once the initial shock had been absorbed, seemed to touch her innate sense of unfairness.

She felt genuinely abused, deliberately left out. Not just kept in the dark, but left out, isolated. All right, she told herself. Business is his turf. House is mine. But this woman knew everything that was happening with the new business, and she, Jenny, knew nothing. Less than nothing. To make matters worse, she did not approve of the idea that they were going to start a business by stealing accounts from their employer. It was against her principles, her values.

Anger seemed to speed her recovery and lessen Connie's aura of intimidation. To deflect the conversation, Jenny took Connie's near-empty glass and her own and interrupted the men's conversation in the den.

"If you're going to play bartender," she told Larry with a forced smile, "then you've got to watch the ladies' glasses."

"Sorry, Jenny," Larry said. He got up and went to the shelf that served as the bar, and Vince followed her into the living room.

"Larry's talked to Barbara Hawkins," Vince said. "She's ready to jump ship."

"Is that wise?" Connie asked. "She could be a fourteen-karat bitch."

"She knows where the bodies are buried," Vince countered.

"Especially her own," Connie said. "Most of the bodies have been buried in her." She looked toward Jenny and winked.

"I'm inclined to go along, Connie," Vince said. He looked toward Jenny, who had never even heard of Barbara Hawkins. Then he turned away and shrugged as if he were still uncertain about the decision. Jenny wasn't sure whether her expression gave away her ignorance. Controlling her anger, she refused to show them her lack of knowledge. Fortunately Larry arrived with their drinks.

"I think we can trust Barbara," Larry said, handing the women their drinks. "But I do have a queasy feeling about Sam Shuster." Another name Jenny had never heard. "He's an asshole," Larry continued. "He'd be the first one to run with an account."

"If we gave him the chance," Vince said.

"But he's a talented asshole," Connie interrupted, her eyes shifting to Jenny as if she were looking for alliance. Jenny nodded stupidly, then turned to Larry, who seemed to look right through her.

"I wouldn't approach him until the very last minute," Larry said.

"He may be an asshole, but he's nobody's fool. He confronted me yesterday, said he heard rumors."

"Screw rumors," Connie said, again casting an eye toward Jenny. Was she expected to comment? She wasn't sure. But she sensed that there was only one course of action for her at that moment. Besides, there was no point in waiting for Larry's signal, which might never come, and totally ruining her dinner.

"I'd better see to dinner," she said.

In the kitchen she forced her concentration to the task at hand, but she did feel, if not ignored, then certainly, as she had heard Larry say on occasion, out of the loop.

She spooned the fettuccine Alfredo onto plates, then checked to be sure that the chicken Kiev, the sauce, asparagus, and potatoes au gratin would be ready with assembly-line precision. She had timed everything carefully so that one dish would follow another and she would be able to play the dual role of hostess-cook. Now she wasn't so sure that she was needed as hostess. She uncorked the wine, which had cooled in the refrigerator, poured herself a long draft into a tumbler and drank it down in one gulp, then went into the dining room and placed the plates of fettuccine Alfredo on the table.

"Soup's on," she called to the others, who were still locked in conversation. When no one stirred she called again in what she thought was her most ingratiating tone. "Dinner is ready." Again they didn't respond. "It'll get cold," she said, raising her voice to match the level of her frustration.

"In a minute," Larry snapped.

The three of them appeared to be intensely involved in some momentous decision. She could hear them mentioning names and subject matter that she had never heard before.

"Please," she said firmly. "You can talk over dinner."

"Jenny, this is important," Larry said. "The dinner can wait."

"No, it can't," Jenny said. Her throat had constricted and her voice had tightened to a whisper. She felt miserable. In desperation she sat down at her place at the table and gulped some wine.

"I still don't think so, Larry," she heard Vince say, the words bouncing without meaning in her mind.

"Why don't you guys cool it," Connie said. "Rome wasn't built in a day."

"Clay Barnes is a schmuck, and Milton Hines is a company loyalist. One of those 'my shit don't stink' guys. I don't trust him," Larry said. "I've seen his memos. He's a back stabber."

"There's nothing worse than cold fettuccine Alfredo," Jenny cried, finding her voice again. She was sitting alone at the table. She poured herself another glass of wine and took a deep gulp.

"In a minute," Larry said, raising his voice.

"Well then." Jenny shrugged. "Forewarned is forearmed." She poured herself more wine, then began to eat the fettuccine. "Not bad," she told herself, washing it down with another heavy draft of white wine. She was nearly finished with the fettuccine when they came to the table. Larry gave her a look of disapproval as they took their seats.

Jenny watched as Connie tasted the fettuccine. "Wonderful," she said, playing with it with her fork but eating little.

"A little on the cold side," Larry said.

"Not bad," Vince said, but he too was playing with it with his fork.

They began to talk among themselves, only now they didn't even give her the courtesy of an occasional glance. Their conversation was growing increasingly distant, as if they were talking a foreign language.

She dutifully poured the wine into their glasses, then collected the plates and went into the kitchen to put together the main dish. Although she was beginning to feel light-headed, she still had the presence of mind to keep the meal on schedule. Timing was crucial.

Larry came into the kitchen to fetch another bottle of wine from the refrigerator. As he uncorked it, he whispered his criticism through clenched teeth.

"The pasta was too cold and too damned rich. People don't eat rich food in New York these days, in case you hadn't noticed."

"I thought it would be festive," she said, hoping she was hiding the heaviness in her tongue.

He opened the oven, in which the chicken Kiev was baking.

"That also looks too damned rich," he snapped.

"If you think that's rich, wait until they have the dessert. It's strawberries Romanoff."

He studied her with disapproval and shook his head. "You've got a lot to learn, Jenny," he said with a sigh.

"Better get back to your crew," she said. "They could hire someone while your back is turned." Larry glared at her and flushed deep red. She was surprised at her own tone. Dutch courage, she decided, feeling a giggle rise in her chest.

"What's that supposed to mean?" he asked. But she had turned away, busying herself with the chicken Kiev. She felt him watching her as she arranged the portions on plates.

"We'll discuss this later," he told her ominously when she did not respond. She heard him move out of the kitchen.

"Yes, we will," she whispered to herself as she picked up two plates and brought them to the table, repeating the operation, then seating herself.

"Super," Connie said, picking at the chicken Kiev. Jenny again noted that she was playing with her food, moving it around without appetite. Connie ate a tiny bit of the chicken and one asparagus spear but didn't touch the potatoes au gratin.

"You're one helluva cook... uh, Jamie," Vince said.

"Jenny," Jenny said politely.

Larry also ate sparingly, occasionally glancing at her with a mad look. Jenny forced herself to finish everything on her plate. Just because they were on diets didn't mean that she couldn't enjoy what she prepared. The fact was that she didn't enjoy it at all. It was merely a way to seem busy while they talked about things she didn't understand, and it did mitigate to some extent the effects of the wine.

They paid little attention when she rose to clear the dishes, although Connie did make a disinterested offer to help.

"You're my guest, Connie," Jenny responded, and Connie, looking relieved, quickly returned her attention to the others.

When Jenny came out of the kitchen with the strawberries Romanoff, the others were completely absorbed in their discussion and totally ignored her presentation. But by then she had sufficiently reined in her frustration. She knew she was still slightly drunk but felt she was carrying out a good imitation of sobriety. Besides, what would it matter if her tongue was heavy? She wouldn't be saying anything that they cared to listen to.

"There's no way we can get the loan without personal signatures," Larry said as Jenny spooned the strawberries Romanoff onto their plates. It was quite obvious that they couldn't have cared less. "Mine and Jenny's signatures and yours and Connie's. I've explored every avenue, interviewed other bankers. It's our only option."

"Doesn't mean I have to like it," Connie said.

"It's a business risk," Vince said. "With that kind of line, they'd be crazy if they didn't ask for all our signatures."

"Mine, too?" Jenny piped. She was surprised to have heard her name mentioned in a business context.

"Of course yours, too," Larry said with irritation, glaring at her and shaking his head as if he were embarrassed by her sudden intrusion. His words sounded like a stage aside, which the others had barely noticed, and he quickly resumed his conversation.

"Must I?" she interrupted.

"Must you what?" Larry asked impatiently.

"Sign something," Jenny said.

Larry sighed. "Of course you must."

"What exactly will I be signing?"

"Jenny, will you please keep out of this?" Larry snapped. He turned to Vince and Connie. "Believe me, we'll find the bank. Trust me on this."

"Without the loan, we're kaput," Connie said.

"Listen," Larry continued. "Even in this climate, banks have to make some loans, and it won't be long before we have the cash flow to keep it rolling over."

"Would really throw a crimp into things if the banks turned it down," Vince said.

"Let me handle that," Larry said.

"I'd like to know—" Jenny had wanted this business of her signature explained, if only to make herself part of the discussion; but at that moment Larry rose and reached for the champagne bottle that was cooling in a bucket beside the table. They all watched in silence as he popped the cork and carefully poured the champagne into the fluted glasses.

"I just love Dom Pérignon," Connie said, watching the bubbles settle in her glass.

"The perfect stuff to launch our ship," Vince said. "And if we're lucky, there will be plenty more where that came from."

When Larry had filled all the glasses, he picked his from the table and remained standing.

"This calls for a special toast." He raised his glass in the direction of Vince and Connie. "To the success of our venture."

"Here here," Vince said, touching his glass first with Larry's. Jenny had lifted hers, but when she saw that no one intended to touch hers she brought it up to her lips and drank. But Vince wasn't through. He turned toward his wife. "And to Connie for pushing me into this craziness. For better or for worse, kiddo." Connie touched glasses with Vince and then with Larry. If there was any intention to include her, it was aborted by the sound of the buzzer.

"I'll get it," Larry said. He went into the foyer, where the intercom was located. She heard a voice come over the intercom, then Larry's response. A few moments later the buzzer to the apartment sounded and she heard the door opening and closing.

"A package for you, Jenny," Larry said, bringing with him a fairly substantial-looking package. "The messenger was all contrition. Some foul-up with the address. Anyway, it's addressed to you." Jenny had forgotten. It was Myrna's package. She hadn't expected to be confronted with this situation, and her panicky reaction cleared her head instantly.

"Just some clothes I ordered," Jenny said.

"Henri Bendel," Larry said, reading the letters on the box.

"Bendel's?" Connie exclaimed, her head cocked as if in disbelief.

"A little on the pricey side," Vince volunteered.

"What is it?" Larry asked, inspecting the box. He looked genuinely puzzled as his eyes met Jenny's.

"Just a little something," Jenny said with mock cheerfulness, hoping she was appearing calm. Beneath the calm she was seething. It was none of their business.

"Like what?" Larry pressed. He looked at her suspiciously, knowing that it was totally out of character for her to buy anything at Bendel's. Besides, her allowance wouldn't cover it.

"Come on, Jenny. I'm dying to see it," Connie trilled as if it were a challenge.

"I'd rather not. I'm not sure that it fits."

"Well, try it on and we'll see," Connie pressed.

"No," Jenny said firmly.

"No harm in opening it," Larry said.

"I said no. Absolutely no."

She got up, walked around the table, and took hold of the box. Larry continued to hold one end of it, and for a moment a tug-of-war ensued.

"Oh, don't be a shit, Larry," Connie said. "It could be a surprise. You know, something that she bought for your eyes only." She winked. "Something sexy."

"Is it that, Jenny?" Larry asked. His lips were pressed together, and she knew he was holding back his anger.

"I don't want to show it," she said, forcing herself to remain calm. "Anyway, it's coffee time in the living room."

"Really, Larry," Vince said. "You should respect her wishes. If she doesn't want us to see it, that's her right."

"Damn straight," Connie said. "Stick to your guns." Jenny could detect their patronizing tones.

At that point Larry released his grip on the box and Jenny quickly took it to the bedroom and slid it under the bed, out of sight. She felt awful, as if she had betrayed Myrna, even though she hadn't. Nor would she, except under duress. The only glimmer of hope was that Larry might forget about it until tomorrow and by that time she would have brought it upstairs. Then she'd tell Larry that she had sent it back to Bendel's. It occurred to her that this was a real lie, but she dismissed it as necessary to keep her word to Myrna.

They moved into the living room, and she served them coffee in demitasse cups.

"Is it espresso?" Connie asked.

"Afraid it's good old American decaf."

Larry glared at her. His look said: I'll attend to you later.

She noted that after one sip they all put the cups aside. But even as the coffee grew cold, they continued to discuss the matter between them. Since they didn't include her in the conversation, she made no effort to decipher what they were saying. Her mind was more engaged with the matter of the package lying under the bed in their bedroom, hardly a hiding place. It was, she decided, too late for that.

After a while Vince and Connie stood up.

"We've got to go," Connie said. She turned toward Jenny. "It was a perfectly wonderful dinner, wasn't it, Vince?"

"You've got quite a little lady there," Vince said. "Connie can't boil water."

"But there are some things I do exceedingly well," Connie said, winking toward Jenny. It occurred to Jenny that most everything that Connie said to her was accompanied by a wink.

Larry shook hands with Vince and kissed Connie on the cheek as they edged toward the door.

"Don't forget," Vince said. "Early tomorrow morning at my place. There's lots of decisions to be made."

"I'll buy the bagels and make the coffee," Connie said.

"No. I'll make the coffee," Vince said. They all laughed.

Since she didn't seem to be invited to this last-minute tête-à-tête, not to mention not being invited to tomorrow's early-morning meeting, Jenny headed for the kitchen, where she began to scrape the dishes and load the dishwasher. The rush of water from the sink faucet drowned out any other sounds in the apartment.

She forced herself to concentrate on the process of scraping the dishes, loading them, and, after a while, washing the stemware, which she would not trust to the dishwasher. Such attention to detail crowded out any postmortems about the dinner. What did it matter? She knew that she would soon undergo a plethora of postmortems.

Looking at her watch, she noted that it was much too late to call her mother. She needed to do that, to touch those people who kept her, as they say, in the loop. There was another reason as well. She'd have to break the news that she couldn't be with the family on the Fourth of July. Larry had nixed it. Too crucial a time in their life, he had told her.

After picking up the phone, she hung it up again. It would be eleven in Indiana. Her parents were always asleep by ten. No need to upset them.

"Who are you calling at this hour?" Larry bellowed. He stood at the entrance to the kitchen, holding out a spectacular fur coat.

"I was thinking of calling my mother," Jenny said.

"And how would you explain"—he lifted the coat by the collar and shook it—"this?"

"You had no right to open that," Jenny cried.

"No right? It was addressed to my wife."

"That's right. To me."

"We are husband and wife. There are no secrets between husbands and wives." He was speaking slowly, articulating each syllable for emphasis.

"Oh, yes, husbands and wives. Only your rule is that only wives should inform their husbands, not vice versa."

"What the hell are you talking about, Jenny?" Larry asked.

"The new business. You've told me nothing and Connie knows all about it."

"I knew it. One meeting and you're already suspicious of her.

The fact is that she's a lawyer, and because of that Vince clued her in."

"And me?"

"You're evading the issue, Jenny. Who gave you this goddamned coat? It probably cost a bundle."

She considered a number of answers, none of which would be satisfactory to him. Besides, they would be more lies.

"I can't say."

"Of course you can't," Larry fumed.

"It's not what you think," Jenny said. "You've got to trust me on this."

"Trust you?"

"You say that all the time. Isn't that the basis of all contracts, especially marriage contracts?"

"I used to think so," he snarled.

"Would you believe me if I told you it was delivered to me but isn't really mine?"

"Now I've heard everything."

"It's the truth."

"Some truth. What do you take me for? The message is coming through loud and clear. All the time my thinking I had married this sweet little thing from Indiana, my true mate, my goody-goody homemaker. Who sends a coat this expensive to a housewife, for chrissakes? Then to stand there and say it wasn't meant for you. Maybe you think I'm one of your Indiana deadheads, stupid enough to swallow that story. And here I was out there working my tail off for our future, and what were you doing? Come on, Jenny, who was the lucky fucker?"

She inspected his face, appalled by his suspicions, hoping he might be joking. He wasn't. Then, looking at the beautiful coat, she softened and forced herself to give him the benefit of the doubt. It could, indeed, seem like a tall story. But the point was that it was the true story, even by virtue of who was telling it. Just who she was in relation to him should be all he needed to believe her.

"Your imagination is running away with you, Larry," she said, determined to remain calm. It seemed to enrage him still more.

"I want to know who he is, Jenny," he fumed. "How could you,

living under the roof I pay for, eating the food I pay for? I can't
believe it. I guess you got bored with all that time on your hands."
When he had first confronted her, she had been carefully wiping
the stemware. Turning her back on him, she returned to her task.

"I told you the truth," she said as if addressing the glass she was
wiping. "It was only delivered to me, not meant for me. And you
should know better than to accuse me of... of that."

She felt a sudden yank at her right shoulder, which caused her
to drop the glass she was working on. It fell to the floor and
shattered.

"Waterford, Larry," she said, sighing.

"So what? What did you know about Waterford before I married
you? Besides, I paid for it. Now I want you to tell me about this
coat."

"I can't." Jenny turned to face him again. She felt her lips trembling. "And I don't want you to ask me. Can't you just trust me?"

"I've heard that before," Larry snickered. Without another word
he took a box of safety matches from a shelf above the stove, took
one out, and scraped it against the wall. The match burst into
flame.

With his left hand he held up the coat. With his right he held
the match. His objective was unmistakable as he brought the flame
toward the coat.

"You wouldn't," Jenny cried.

"Doesn't matter to me. I didn't pay for it."

"It has nothing to do with you," Jenny pleaded.

He brought the match closer. She watched it, peering into the
yellow flame, mesmerized for a moment. When it burned too close
to his fingers, he shook it out, then scraped another one into flame.

"Who is it from?" Larry asked.

"I can't say. I promised. It wasn't for me." She felt a tightness in
her chest that seemed to drown her words.

He brought the match closer. It was merely inches away from
the fur.

"I think it's even better than mink. Sable. I think it's sable."

"Larry, please. I gave my word."

"Of course you did."

He brought the flame closer. Her nostrils quivered at the first faint aroma of singed fur. Reaching out, she slapped the hand that held the match.

"All right," she said.

"Well. Well. So who is the lucky fellow?"

"It's not a fellow," she whispered, watching his face. His lips were curled into a snarl, his eyes blazing and unforgiving. Obviously he expected the worst. "No, nothing like that." She wished she had it in her to be more aggressive in her own defense. But how could she have allowed him to burn the coat? "It belongs to Myrna Davis from upstairs. And I feel awful telling you about it because I promised I wouldn't."

"You can't be serious," Larry said, his eyes narrowing as if he were unable to shake his nagging suspicion. His brows knitted in confusion. "Hard to swallow, Jenny. Why send it here?"

"Think about it."

"Didn't you ask?"

"I didn't have to. She admitted that it was a present from someone who does not want it traced back to himself." She wanted him to know only the bare minimum.

"That makes you a part of it," he said, shaking his head, apparently taking another, more benign tack.

"I did a favor for a neighbor," she began.

"I don't believe this, after all the warnings. Can't you understand that this is where involvement leads to?"

She raised both palms. "Please, Larry. I've heard all that before. Frankly, I didn't see the harm in it."

"You should have consulted me."

"You would have said no."

"Damned straight."

Having dishonored her word, she felt humiliated, angry. Nor was she willing to face any further lectures from him on the subject.

"I know you don't approve, Mr. High and Mighty," she began. She had always eschewed confrontations, but this was one time, she told herself, that she could not turn the other cheek. "It's too neighborly, too decent a thing to do for a neighbor, a stranger. Don't look at me that way. I didn't exactly commit a murder."

"No, you didn't," he said, appearing to soften. "You just got involved as a kind of shill, a go-between for a man and his mistress. You've been used. Can't you see that? Do you know who the man is?"

"That's none of my business." She paused. "Or yours."

"My business happens to be your business," Larry said.

Suddenly the events of the evening roared back into her mind.

"Sure, Larry. I saw that policy displayed tonight. Your business doesn't happen to be my business. It works okay for the goose but not for the gander. Frankly, I think it stinks."

"You wouldn't understand it," Larry said. He was showing signs of contrition, but it didn't faze her. "Connie is a lawyer," he muttered. "She understands what we're doing."

"And you all think I'm a dumb ninny?"

"Just not experienced in these matters."

"Can't you teach me?"

"I intend to," he said. "Someday, okay? Now let's get back to the coat."

"Nothing to get back to. I told you about it. Now let me put it back in the box. Tomorrow I will deliver it and the incident will, I hope, be forgotten." She paused and took a deep breath. "And I thank you for your trust and confidence. It's a wonderful feeling for a wife of four months."

She took a broom from the closet and began to push the broken shards of glass into a scoop.

"Considering the circumstances. My wife gets a coat from an anonymous someone. What is a husband to think? Look at it from my point of view." His tone had a hint of pleading about it. "I just hope you learned your lesson."

She threw the glass into a garbage bag, then turned to look at him. "What lesson is that?" she asked.

He sighed and shook his head, and his eyes danced everywhere but on her face.

"Never to get involved. Now you see where it leads."

She pondered the ad infinitum so-called lesson for a few moments, and as if something suddenly clicked in her mind, she no longer feared his disapproval.

Perhaps it was for that reason that she allowed him to apologize. It had happened at about 3:00 A.M. or, more precisely, 3:05 by the digital clock that stood on her dresser. He had turned to her, folded himself next to her like a spoon, and whispered in her ear.

"I'm so sorry, Jenny. I've been a shit. Can you forgive me?"

She let the digital clock register another three minutes before she responded, attributing his sincerity more to the urgency of his erection, which she felt against her buttocks, than to any feelings of contrition. It troubled her that such an idea should enter her head.

Nevertheless she demonstrated a kind of semiforgiveness by her acquiescence and her lovemaking fervor. In her heart she wanted to accept his apology. Her reaction to the events of the night continued to be troubling. She wondered if her own sense of inadequacy had set off an unworthy chain reaction of her emotions. Surely she wanted her husband to succeed in his career. Unfortunately both the method and the people he had chosen to achieve this success were, to be kind, suspect. The very suspicion about such things was equally bothersome.

Perhaps, she decided finally sometime around dawn, she had overstepped her role, invaded his turf, been childish and presumptuous, allowed jealousy to warp her opinions. After all, wasn't Larry working for their future and the future of their unborn children? She was out of line, she rebuked herself. Business had its own rules, its own morality. She was a neophyte in this area. How dare she intrude her negativity on his plan to better them financially? Wasn't he, as her father said, a go-getter?

In the morning, feigning sleep, she felt his cool lips kiss her forehead. Moments later she heard the door to the apartment close, and she got out of bed. She didn't want to rehash last night's events. Actually she felt a nagging sense of embarrassment. Hours of reflection had convinced her that she was a victim of her own unworldliness, a true Hoosier hick.

What she needed to do, she decided, was expand her horizons. She knew that Larry meant well with his protectiveness, but all this isolation had left her mentally pinched, hemmed in. Not that she wasn't respectful of his advice and counsel about living in New

York. But it was clouding her judgment about people and their motives. What she needed, she decided, was to be open to her own observations. Not that Larry was wrong in his assessment of the New York culture. Her problem, she decided, was that she had no personal frame of reference to understand his evaluations. It was time to embark on some observations of her own, see things through her own eyes.

Myrna Davis had said that she should deliver the package around noon. This gave her a few hours simply to roam the streets, walk around, with no goal in mind, no task other than to soak up the environment, observe, fill the data bank of her mind.

She giggled at the idea. The weather was sunny and pleasant, the streets less crowded than on an ordinary weekday. She slipped into jeans, a T-shirt, and sneakers, slung a leather pocketbook over her shoulder, and, pumping herself up with an air of determination, set out on what she now characterized as her private adventure.

The slight morning chill was bracing, and she walked fast, turning south onto Third, heading downtown. She sensed that her eyes were jumping at every sight, soaking them up, slotting them in her mind.

Images and sounds crowded into her consciousness. A young Korean man dressing, moistening, and literally shining the fruit on display on the sidewalk in front of his fruit stand; a dark-skinned, Indian-looking man setting out the papers on a newsstand; a middle-aged, paunchy man using a long winding tool to open the canopy over his jewelry store; a young woman in long tights and bouncing pigtail jogging on the sidewalk; a teenage black man, sporting a cocky lope, with a ghetto blaster on his shoulder; green plastic garbage bags, like boulders strewn haphazardly after a violent earthquake, lining the curbs. Through glass windows of cheek-to-jowl restaurants, with a United Nations choice of cuisine, she observed men and women cleaning up, preparing for the new day.

She tried smiling at the pedestrians she passed, a normal ritual back in Bedford. Unfortunately those people who did not have earphones stuck in their ears seemed equally intense and self-absorbed in their own concerns.

It struck her that even on Saturday mornings the street energy level was intense. Car horns honked, brakes squealed, and footsteps and voices melded into the din. Sparkles of sunlight cast odd shadows along the high buildings, and an occasional sunbeam caught on a spire, giving it the appearance of a huge match bursting into flame.

Store windows seemed to overflow with displays of abundance: food, jewelry, clothing, computers, cameras, eyeglasses, artwork, liquor bottles, glassware and plates, stationery—a cornucopia of riches. She felt the contagion of energy, of bigness.

Occasionally she caught glimpses of despair, men and women squatting on the sidewalk, their eyes glazed with fatigue and disorientation, or roaming aimlessly through the streets. Lost souls. Yet her compassion seemed blunted by overexposure, and for the first time she sensed how it was possible to become inured, to ignore, screen out, the idea of another's pain and suffering.

In her mind everything, sights, sounds, smells, seemed magnified, exaggerated, and, after walking twenty-odd blocks, overwhelming. The agenda of this city, she realized, was set by its energy level, emanating from what seemed, even on a comparatively quiet Saturday morning, an overpowering variety of people engaged in an equally overpowering series of events. Even the unseen millions who lived in buildings that lined the way were an undeniable presence, living participants in her observations, both conscious and subconscious.

There was, she realized also, a sense of laissez-faire lurking in the streets, a lack of formality and discipline. People did not wait for traffic lights to change before dashing between moving cars to cross streets. There were no discernible walking corridors even on the sidewalks, where people simply chose a path to follow without regard to others going in the same direction. Except for the neatly laid out street block patterns, the living tissue seemed to operate in a helter-skelter fashion, like cars bouncing against one another in an amusement-park ride concession.

Those people who were not self-absorbed seemed feral, their eyes on the alert for predators. She wondered if such thoughts were influenced by Larry's warnings about being defensive.

There was no taking it all in at once. The city was too alive, too fluid, too varied, to absorb completely, like powerful light refracted through crystal. On weekdays when she shopped in the neighborhood stores, she had been conscious of the crowds and activity but had not opened herself up to observation. It was more manageable, safer, less confusing, to hide behind mental blinkers and Larry's catalog of admonitions.

Feeling hungry, she went into a coffee shop and sat at the counter, ordered cream cheese on a toasted bagel and a cup of coffee. The man behind the counter filled the order swiftly and indifferently. He was a thin man with a knobbed, bony face and a splotchy complexion that her father would have characterized as a "drinker's" look.

Although there were other customers at the counter, there was no conversation. All seemed lost in their own thoughts and the task of eating.

She was nearly finished with her bagel when she noted that the man behind the counter had narrowed his eyes and was concentrating on something happening behind her.

"Out," the man behind the counter said, his face flushing. "Get the hell outa here."

"All I want is a cup of coffee," a voice said. She turned and faced an unshaven man in shabby clothes, obviously one of the army of homeless that roamed Manhattan's streets.

"One lousy cup of coffee," the homeless man said. "To take out. What's the big deal?"

"Do I have to come out there and throw you out?" the man behind the counter said. Jenny noted that none of the other customers, after a cursory look at the altercation, paid any attention.

"God bless you, pal," the homeless man said with sarcasm, turning to leave.

"I'll pay," Jenny blurted suddenly, startled at her sudden outburst. The man behind the counter shot her a look of disdain and shook his head.

"Bless you, my dear," the homeless man said, showing a gap-toothed smile. He was unshaven and looked about forty, and she could detect a sour, urinous smell that seemed to cling to him.

She started fishing in her purse.

"Make it a large," the homeless man said.

She slipped a five-dollar bill from her wallet and put it on the counter.

"One born every minute," the man behind the counter said as he pulled a large Styrofoam cup from a shelf and filled it with coffee from a silver urn.

"You couldn't by chance see your way clear for a sandwich, lady, could you?" the homeless man said. Not a single customer raised his head to watch them.

The man behind the counter shook his head with disgust. "Don't be a dammed fool, lady," he muttered. "Comes in here once, twice a week to stage this scam. Sometimes, like now, he hits a sucker."

"He should know what it is to be without means," the homeless man said to Jenny.

"It's all right about the sandwich," Jenny said, feeling oddly combative and resentful toward the man behind the counter.

"Can I see a menu?" barked the homeless man.

"Sure. Be my guest," the man behind the counter said, handing the homeless man a menu.

"Look at him. Able-bodied. Youngish. He's working a scam out on you, lady."

"Steak sandwich, okay?" the homeless man asked.

"Why not? Top of the line. Not his dough," the man behind the counter said, pointedly smirking at Jenny. "If I was you, lady, I'd cut my losses. Make him go for the egg salad."

"I hate egg salad," the homeless man said.

"Picky bum," said the man behind the counter.

"It's all right about the steak sandwich," Jenny said, feeling her throat constrict. She felt less combative now. Customers came and went. She noted that some of them exchanged glances with the man behind the counter and shook their heads. Jenny wondered if they were passing judgment on her. In Bedford this would be considered simple charity, an expected act of compassion.

"You're a real lifesaver, ma'am," the homeless man said, sidling

130

onto the stool next to her at the counter. His odor at that proximity was nauseating. "People don't understand what it means to have nothing, not even a roof over your head."

"Get a job," the man behind the counter said as he threw the thin slab of steak on the griddle. It quickly began to sizzle.

"No jobs out there," the homeless man said.

"Not in his line, right?" The man behind the counter threw an angry glance at the homeless man. "I mean, how many jobs are around for brain surgeons? Or are you a nuclear physicist?"

Jenny felt another stab of nausea. She had to get out of there. She cleared her throat.

"My check, please," she managed to say.

"Hey, you don't have to go," the homeless man said. "Stay here while I eat my sandwich."

"You ain't eating that sandwich in here, pal," the man behind the counter said without looking up. He turned the steak over and split open a slab of soft bread, which he buttered, and laid out tomatoes and lettuce.

"I'd like some sliced fresh onion," the homeless man said, turning his big gap-toothed smile on Jenny.

"Would you, now?" the man behind the counter said, stealing a glance at Jenny. "Give them a finger, they'll take your arm."

"When you're down and out, they treat you like scum," the homeless man said.

Jenny tried to ignore him, wanted to ignore him. The problem was to keep from smelling him. She waited for the man behind the counter to give her her check.

"In a minute, lady. First I gotta give Prince Albert here his sandwich."

"Then just take this," Jenny said, putting another five on the counter.

"You'll have nearly two coming," the man called from the griddle.

"It's all right."

"You leaving the change for me?" the homeless man said.

No, she thought. She didn't want to do that. She felt embarrassed. Worse—humiliated and slightly ashamed.

"She says for me to get the change," the homeless man said.

"It's all right," she mumbled.

She had to get away. Unable to utter another word, she left the coffee shop. For a moment she was disoriented, not knowing which way to go. It took her a moment more to get her bearings, then she headed northward, away from downtown, toward the town house. As she walked, she felt herself collapse inward. Her observation portals narrowed.

She walked swiftly, but before she had gotten a block or two away from the coffee shop, she was overwhelmed by the feeling that she was being followed. At first she dismissed the idea, although she refused to look back. Just to be sure, she speeded up her pace, then began a loping jog. She cut across the street diagonally, hearing screeching brakes and an angry horn, knowing for certain that she had caused the sounds. Still she didn't look behind her. Her fear was two-pronged. She dreaded seeing someone, perhaps the homeless man, following her. But what she dreaded most was that she would see no one following her, a sure sign of galloping paranoia.

Sweat was running down her back as she reached her street. There was her town house half a block away. With a burst of energy, as if she were running speed laps, she made it to the steps of the town house. At that moment she slowed down but did not make the sharp turn to run up the steps. Instead she ran past the building, deliberately, a clearly defensive gesture. Above all, she did not want whoever might be following her to know where she lived.

Only when she reached the corner of Second Avenue did she finally muster the courage to look behind her, although she continued to run.

"Christ," a woman's voice squealed as Jenny slammed into her.

Turning again, Jenny saw a portly, middle-aged woman carrying a bag of apples. Fortunately the woman did not go down, but the apples hit the sidewalk and began to roll into the gutter.

"Oh, my God," Jenny cried, holding on to the woman for support. "I am so sorry."

"Where's the fire, you crazy girl?" the woman said. "You coulda killed me."

"I am so, so sorry," Jenny cried again, disengaging. She bent and ran after the apples, noting that some of them were badly bruised.

"Please," Jenny said. "I must pay for them. I absolutely must."

The middle-aged woman was only mildly placated, but she shrugged her acceptance.

"This is very embarrassing," Jenny said. "I live down the street. I was just..." As she spoke she opened her purse and looked in her wallet. "Oh, my God. I haven't got any cash. Please. I'm just down the street. I..."

"Figures," the woman said. "Never mind."

"But I insist."

"I don't. Just let me pass. Forget about it."

"It's my fault, I—"

"Are you a nut or something?" the woman replied, turning quickly and walking north on Second Avenue. Jenny stood there, rooted to the sidewalk, embarrassed, feeling leaden and stupid. When the woman was a block away, she turned, looked toward Jenny, and shrugged, more in pity than in anger.

Only then did Jenny start walking toward her town house. What she had done was childish and illogical. She was thoroughly ashamed of herself, of her mindless fear. All she had done was help out a poor homeless man. Where was the harm in that?

No, she told herself firmly. I must not let that incident color my feelings about the city. What she had done, she decided finally, was to allow the incident with the homeless man to exaggerate her vulnerability. Larry was always telling her to act defensively. She had simply overreacted. Hadn't she?

It seemed obvious when she finally observed the full length of her street that no one was following her. She had capitulated to blind, foolish, and illogical fear. Larry had apparently succeeded in making the city itself an enemy. She vowed never to give in to that feeling again.

When she got into her apartment, she noted that three hours had slipped by. Myrna had said to deliver the package around

133

twelve. She got it from under the bed, marched upstairs to Myrna's apartment, put it against the door, rang the buzzer, then went downstairs to her apartment.

New York was confusing, she told herself, finding humor in the events of the morning. It was a self-deprecating kind of humor. She giggled. It made her feel better.

8

ON MONDAY morning, just after Larry had left on his jog to work, Myrna Davis rang her buzzer. It was at about the same time as when she'd visited last week. As then, she was dressed with immaculate taste and in the height of fashion. Dressing for success, Jenny thought, but without envy.

"It is divine," Myrna said. "And I simply must show it to you."

"Really, it's not necessary, Myrna," Jenny demurred. After all, she had already seen the coat.

"I insist."

She took Jenny's hand, and they proceeded up the stairs to Myrna's apartment, which was beautifully furnished with antiques.

"They're mostly English," Myrna explained, noting Jenny's interest. She left the room, leaving Jenny to observe and fondle the furniture. When she returned she was wearing the coat, posing like a model. It looked beautiful on her, elegant. Apparently, in her euphoria, she hadn't noticed the slightly singed area, which Jenny had inspected carefully when she'd repacked it. Fortunately, the damage was barely visible unless you knew exactly where to look.

"You're a knockout in it, Myrna," Jenny said as Myrna pranced around the room.

"I didn't take it off all weekend, not even when we...I must tell you, Jenny, it really does something for your libido. Maybe the wearing of the animal skin conveys some of the property of the animal."

"I wouldn't know anything about the habits of sables," Jenny said. Yet she liked Myrna's forthright attitude on the subject.

"Would you like to try it on?"

"I'm much smaller than you. I'd look terrible."

"Terrible? How can anyone look terrible in sable?"

After much persuasion she tried it on, and it did indeed feel good on her body, despite its being too long.

"You've been great about this, Jenny," Myrna said as they left the apartment. "I told you. No big deal. Was I right?"

"No big deal," Jenny repeated, hoping Myrna wouldn't probe too deeply about her promise.

As she started down the stairs, Myrna paused for a moment as if wrestling with an intruding thought. "Oh, and my friend really appreciated your help in this as well. Really. Someday you may even get to meet him—that is, someday in the future, not necessarily the near future. There I go. I've said enough."

Myrna continued down the stairs, then paused again, sniffing.

"What is it?" asked Jenny.

"Gas, I think. I've got one of these super noses."

Jenny sniffed but couldn't detect any odor.

"Maybe my imagination," Myrna chirped, heading down the stairs. "Anyway, you're home all day. If it gets worse, just call the gas company."

Although it was mostly true, Jenny did not appreciate the remark about her being home all day. She had begun to note that people treated her differently when they found out that she spent her day being a homemaker. Maybe it was because she and Larry lived in Manhattan and hadn't any children as yet. People had a better understanding of what a homemaker did when there were children around. And yet her mother had continued to be a homemaker long after the children had left the family nest. And was proud of it.

"Nothing, but nothing, is more fulfilling for a woman, Jenny," her mother had told her many times over. "It's a woman's role in life. That's the way it used to be. Was the world worse for it? No, it wasn't. It was better. More people should realize that. Why should a woman have to give up her role as nurturer just to satisfy blind ambition or make a few more bucks?"

It was, of course, a grandiose notion, but Jenny believed that there was a great deal of truth in it, despite the armies of female naysayers. No matter what, she told herself, she would continue being a homemaker, and to satisfy not just Larry but herself as well.

Someday she would bear children and be the bedrock of her family, fulfilling a woman's true destiny. She knew that to many women, especially those who lived in big cities like New York, such a fate was considered a form of imprisonment or worse. She had no illusions about how people assessed her, an underachieving clod, a dumb ninny who wouldn't or couldn't compete in the real world, wherever that was.

And like her mother, she had firm ideas on the raising of children. There was simply no excuse for any woman who could afford it not to stay home with her children, to rear and nurture them, to provide them with the love and affection they sorely needed. Lots would disagree, she knew. Mothers who weren't prepared to do this shouldn't have children. Was it better for a child to be dumped into a day care center while the mother worked all day? She doubted it.

All right, she supposed she was being intolerant toward woman who had to work, who couldn't afford to stay home with their children, who were the sole support of their family. Why were there so many single mothers in the first place? How had this tragedy come about? Why did it take two salaries in an intact family to make ends meet? These were just a few of the pressing questions that ran through her mind.

It was humiliating to have to be defensive about her values and her goals. Most of the time she was afraid to voice them, afraid that people might think her, well, inferior. People like Connie Mazzo would, and who knew what Myrna Davis and Terry Richardson were really thinking? The proof of the pudding would be to see how their children turned out in the end.

At this thought Jenny felt a slight tug of uncertainty about her future with Larry, but she let it pass. Every marriage was subject to stresses and disagreements. How were couples to get to know each other if they did not establish parameters and boundaries? Wasn't it better to bring these differences into the open instead of letting them fester beneath the surface?

On Sunday, for example, she and Larry had had a serious conversation about the new business he and Vince were going to start.

"Believe me, Larry, I'd be proud to be the woman behind the man. A wife has to be a helpmate, and sometimes her point of view can be really helpful." Thinking of Connie, she deliberately avoided saying "woman's point of view." "But to give you the benefit of my opinion, I've got to know what's happening before it happens."

He appeared to agree. In fact, he seemed willing to agree to almost everything in his contrition, or so she imagined. By the end of the weekend she was even willing to admit to herself that a little conflict and the subsequent ritual emotional apology was an excellent sexual stimulant. He promised never to speak of the incident of the coat again, and taking advantage of his current pliability, she asked him also to promise her not to lecture her again on how she should behave toward the neighbors. She wasn't completely sold on his keeping either promise, but it did make for a pleasant weekend.

She wasn't in her own apartment ten minutes before she began to smell the gas. Checking her kitchen, she noted that all the gas jets were closed. Sniffing, her nose alert, she went into the hallway again. The odor was faint but unmistakable and seemed to get stronger as she moved upstairs. On the second floor, where Myrna Davis's and the Richardsons' apartments were located, the odor seemed to grow even stronger. She knocked on the Richardsons' door. As expected, there was no answer.

She started up the stairs toward the Stern apartment, and it quickly became obvious, because of the strength of the odor as she rose, that it was coming from the third floor. Clipping her nose with the thumb and forefinger of her left hand, she pressed her right hand over her mouth and held her breath. When she reached the Stern apartment, she banged on the door.

"Hello," she cried. "Anybody home?"

No answer came from within the apartment. She tried the door-knob, surprised to find that the door opened, but no more than an inch. It was fastened securely from the inside by a chain. Someone was obviously inside. Again she banged with her fists against the door.

"Please answer," she cried, trying to break the chain using her shoulder as a battering ram. The door wouldn't budge. Don't panic, she told herself, forcing a mental clarity that allowed her quickly to go over her options. There was no time to call the gas company. No time to call the police. She had to get that door open. And fast.

A crowbar! Her brain flipped over possibilities. An idea popped into her mind, and she ran down the two flights of stairs to her own apartment. She flung open the window, sucked in fresh air, then scrambled to her bedroom where Larry had his weights. She grabbed a bar that had been stripped of weights. Despite its heft, she managed to get it up the two flights.

Shoving the bar into the space between the door and the jamb, she put all her weight against it, and the chain lock separated from the wall.

Sweating profusely, her chest aching, trying to stop herself from inhaling the toxic fumes, she moved swiftly through the apartment. She began to feel faint and light-headed but through an effort of will made it to the kitchen.

Mr. Stern was seated on a chair, elevated with telephone books. His head was in the oven. First things first, she told herself, sustained by the charging adrenaline in her body. She shut off the open gas jets, then ran around the apartment like a madwoman, flinging all the windows open.

That done, she turned her attention to Mr. Stern. She grabbed
the back of the chair and lowered it to the ground. Mr. Stern was
breathing and showing signs of consciousness. His eyes opened
and closed.

"You're alive," she whispered.

He opened his eyes again, then nodded. His lips moved, but she
could not make out what he was saying.

"Just rest. You'll be fine."

Rushing to the nearest window, she put her head out and sucked
in deep gulps of air until her light-headedness disappeared, although her chest still ached. Sweat was running down her cheeks
and her back, and her clothes were soaked through with perspiration.

But as the adrenaline subsided, so did her clarity. She wasn't
sure what to do next. This indecisiveness went on for a few moments, her eyes roving the kitchen until they lighted on the telephone. Running to it, she grasped it and dialed 911. Standing there,
waiting for the buzz at the other end, she looked at the man. He
had raised his head and was watching her.

"Please, no," he said hoarsely.

"You need help," she said. Someone answered the phone.

"Not that. P-please," he stammered.

She hesitated a moment, watching him. The color was coming
back to his face. His eyes were open, and he seemed to be filling
his lungs with the good air that had replaced the gas. He sat leaning against the wall, watching her, his expression glum. She heard
voices at the other end of the phone, then she hung up.

"Don't say it," she said.

"What?"

"That I should have let you die."

He stared at her silently for a moment. There were deep, dark
circles under his eyes. Then he lifted his hands, covered his face,
and began to sob.

Watching him, she wasn't certain of any course of action. Her
first instinct was to give him a pep talk about standing up to life.
She decided against that, not knowing the man's story. Suicide was
something she knew little or nothing about. She had never been

exposed to that kind of total desperation. Instead of acting or saying anything, she just stood there waiting for his hysteria to run its course, which it finally did.

"I'm sorry," he said finally, removing his hands from his face, wiping away the tears with the cuffs of his shirt. Shakily he started to rise from the floor, using the wall for support. She ran to help him, but he waved her away. "It's okay." When he had gotten up, he shook his head a number of times. "Back from the dead," he mumbled. Then he looked toward her and, incongruously, actually smiled. "Looks like I bungled this like everything else."

"How do you feel?" Jenny asked.

"Nauseous and shaky," he said. Using the wall as support, he moved out of the kitchen. She followed him until he arrived at the bathroom and shut the door. Listening, she heard him retch.

"Can I get you something?" she called to him.

He didn't answer, and after a while he came out. His hair was damp and his skin blotchy, but he seemed to have regained some of his strength. Their eyes met, and he shrugged.

"You want to talk about it?" she asked. It seemed a logical question.

"You really want to hear it?" He chuckled wryly, then shrugged again.

"I make a good cup of coffee," Jenny said, offering a smile.

Mr. Stern looked about him with uncertainty.

"Why not?"

She went out the open door of the apartment, pausing in the doorway.

"You'll have to fix this," she said. "Sorry." But when she turned he was not behind her. Before she could call out, he was back, folding an envelope and putting it in his side pocket.

"My suicide note. I'm too embarrassed to read it again."

In her apartment, he sat at the kitchen island while she measured out the coffee and water and turned on the automatic coffee maker.

"Nice of you," he said. She could feel his eyes studying her.

"I don't often get a chance to have a coffee klatch with a neighbor," she said, hoping that the light touch might cheer him up.

"I don't mean that part. I mean what you did."

"Oh, that."

Facing him, she noted that he turned his eyes away and began to look at his hands as if they conveyed something of profound importance.

"It seemed like the only alternative," he said.

"That was apparent," she said.

"Something just came over me. Everything seemed so bleak and overwhelming. Sally's . . . my wife's illness. My business going under. The eviction notice. Oh, yes. I got this eviction notice yesterday. Pay up or get out. I haven't got a job. I can't pay up. Then this business with Teddy."

"Teddy?"

"My son. I'm sure you've seen him around."

"Yes, I have. Sweet kid."

"Too sweet, maybe," he said, looking off into space. He reflected in silence for a moment. When he lifted his eyes toward her, he seemed frightened, as if he had revealed too much. "Never mind. It's not important."

"You may be just imagining . . . " She found it difficult to continue. What she wanted to say but couldn't was: Teddy's not what you think.

The coffee was ready, and she poured a cup for him and one for her. Shakily he brought the cup to his lips and sipped.

"You're right. It's pretty good."

"I've got the coffee touch," she said, sitting down on the high chair beside him. She looked at him and smiled. "Mad at me?"

"At you?"

"For saving your life."

"God," he said. "It's embarrassing. I can hardly believe it. Why did I do it? I even wrote this stupid note." He took it out and tore it into little pieces, which he put on the surface in front of him. Then he sighed and shook his head. "This morning after they both left, I just blundered into it, I guess. Obviously, in my haste, I chose the wrong method."

"I wouldn't know," Jenny replied.

"I should have used pills."

"Would have saved me a lot of trouble," she said.

"Crazy talk," he said. "Can you believe this?"

"Maybe this is what people talk about when they come back from the dead," Jenny said. Oddly, she suddenly thought of Myrna and her sophisticated repartee. She felt imitative, yet strangely superior, morally superior.

"You must think I'm pretty weak," Mr. Stern said, as if he had been reading her mind.

"Who am I to make any judgments like that?" Jenny said. "I guess it happens. People get overwhelmed and lose their courage. I'm not exactly an expert on it. Except..." An idea was forming in her mind, the branch of an idea rooted in her life, her values, back in Indiana. She imagined she heard her father's twang, her mother's words.

"Except what?" he asked.

"I...I don't want to set you off...make you run off and do it all again." She watched his expression for any sign of that, not that she could have told if there were a sign.

"No. That's over. Definitely over. Temporary insanity, let's call it." He sucked in a deep breath. "Please. Please don't say anything. Not to..." His eyes looked up, his message clear. "Not to them, especially. I'll be eternally grateful."

"I was about to say," Jenny said, "that it was an act of extreme selfishness." There, it was out, and she felt better for it.

"Who can argue with that? You can't imagine how small I feel. It's not the end of the world. Hell, so we get evicted. I'll get a job. I can be quite an earner. Damned recession kicked me in the butt." He looked up suddenly. "Bet I sound like a kid whistling in the cemetery. Shit." The color drained from his face, and he seemed to Jenny to be sinking back into a suicidal depression. Can't have that, she told herself, feeling somehow responsible for the man, as if saving his life gave her some proprietary interest over him.

"Just put it out of your mind," she said. "Remember that song from *Annie*. The sun will come up tomorrow."

"It's up," he said, frowning. "And I've got to move, lock, stock, and barrel. Uproot." He shook his head. "If only..."

"If only what?" she asked.

"A little breather is all." He sighed. "The miracle is that I was able to stall them for four months. Sally has no idea about the eviction. The family finances are my bailiwick. Her salary goes for Teddy's tuition and putting food on the table. Oh, she knows things are rough, but not that rough." He looked up at Jenny. "I didn't want to upset her. That's a laugh. Just look what I was about to present her with."

"Your corpse," Jenny said with a touch of sarcasm.

"It was either the eviction notice or that," he said. "The latter somehow seemed less painful."

"The easy way out," Jenny said, looking at him archly.

"So here I am." Mr. Stern chuckled wryly. "And I've still got to explain the eviction notice. No way out on that one." He grew pensive, as if he were carrying on an imaginary internalized conversation. Even his lips moved soundlessly. "Now where the hell can I come up with the back rent?" he blurted as if responding to the hidden voice. "All I need is time." He blew air between his teeth. "Fat chance." He looked up, flushing. "Babbling away like an idiot."

"You'll come out of it," Jenny said, adopting her cheerleader mode again. "You look pretty smart to me and, judging from your quick recovery, reasonably healthy and strong. I'd say you were the kind of guy that will make it."

He upended his coffee mug and seemed to linger behind it for more time than it would take him to swallow. Sensing his embarrassment, she berated herself for her Pollyannaish attitude. Somehow her words seemed hollow and unrealistic, as if she were talking to a straw doll instead of a flesh-and-blood human being feeling terrible pain and about to lose the roof over his head. In a strange way, she felt responsible for the man. Hadn't she brought him back to life? Rescued him? What now? She couldn't imagine why she was addressing such questions. The man was a total stranger.

Often her parents had preached the doctrine of sharing with the less fortunate, of being helpful and kind to those in need. When their neighbors the Robinsons had gone through hard times, with Mr. Robinson out of work and Mrs. Robinson deathly ill with pneumonia, hadn't her parents come to their rescue, taking Jenny's best friend, Penny, to live with them and providing the family with food, nursing help, and, Jenny was certain, money to tide them over?

"Good deeds come back tenfold," her father had told her. Actually it was a family litany. Being a good Christian didn't mean going to church, they had preached. And the Golden Rule was invoked at every opportunity. She remembered suddenly the incident with the homeless man. So what if he'd wanted more? Desperation made people crazy. Hadn't she just witnessed such an act?

Watching this wretched, defeated man whose life she had saved, Jenny felt a great wave of compassion wash over her.

"And Teddy," she remembered the man had said, too ashamed to confront "that" issue in front of her, although it was obviously a heartache for him.

"I have something to ask you, Mr. Stern," she began tentatively. "And I hope it won't embarrass you." Above all, she thought, she mustn't take away his dignity.

"To ask me?"

"Would you be upset if I offered to lend you some money? You know, to tide you over until you can pay me back."

She watched as the man's eyes seemed to wobble in his head, then became moist. His lips trembled as they tried to form a kind of smile.

"You would do that?" he managed to say, his voice gravelly with emotion.

"Only if it didn't offend you," she said.

Coughing into his fist, he cleared his throat. He shook his head in disbelief. "But why?" he began, wiping away his tears.

"Let's say I feel..." Jenny searched for a word. "Responsible. And surely you'd pay me back when you got on your feet. I have no doubt about that."

Did she really? she wondered. Or was she superimposing her own moral sensibilities onto him?

"I can't believe this," the man said as if he were once again starting to converse with some being inside himself.

"Just a loan, remember."

"I don't know what to say."

"Say nothing. That would be a condition of the loan. Not to your wife. Or Teddy. And especially..."

In her mind the idea of Larry's disapproval loomed menacingly, and she tried to dismiss the thought. This was her money, saved by herself. Suddenly she regretted having told Larry that she had it. Hadn't he acknowledged to her that it was hers to do with as she wished? The memory gave her a stab of resentment. Why did she need his permission? Considering his general attitude about neighbors, she wouldn't expect consent anyway. None of his business, she decided militantly, remembering her anger at not being included in the discussions about his new business.

"As long as we keep it between ourselves," she continued, hoping he would catch her meaning without further explanation.

"Between us. Of course," Mr. Stern said, his eyes dry now. "I wouldn't have it any other way."

Without another word, she went into the bedroom and took her checkbook and a pen out of a drawer, then came back into the kitchen. With the checkbook open on the kitchen island, she started writing, then paused. It suddenly occurred to her that she didn't know the man's first name.

"To whom should I make it out?" she asked.

"Barry Stern," Mr. Stern said.

She wrote out a check for $19,000, which left approximately $1,000 in her account, then tore it out of the book and gave it to him, acknowledging to herself that in handing over the check, she felt good, as if she were fulfilling something fine and valuable in herself. The man looked at the check for a long time.

"I can't believe it," he mumbled.

"It won't bounce, either," she said lightly.

"I...I feel very funny about this. I mean, I barely know you. And here you are..."

"I told you. It's a loan."

"Of course it is." His eyes roamed the kitchen as if he were looking for something. "And I should sign some paper acknowledging that."

"That won't be necessary," she said. "I feel quite certain that you'll pay me back."

In her heart, which was bursting with magnanimity, she felt sure of it. Trust was trust. What difference would a piece of paper make? At the same time she wondered whether this was another test, a true test of her own judgment about people, a midwestern, not a New York, judgment. Or was it defiance, defiance of Larry and his opinions about the human condition?

"I...I don't know what to say," Mr. Stern said, tears brimming in his eyes once more. "I don't really feel I deserve this." Reaching out, he took one of her hands and moved it to his lips. "You're a saint, Mrs. Burns, a true saint. You've saved my life twice today. I feel..." He began to sob, and she gently removed her hand from his grasp and patted his head with it.

"It's all right," she said. "You'll be fine. I know you will."

"This is the greatest vote of confidence a man could have," he said.

"I hope so," she said, trying to head off any additional show of gratitude, fearing that the memory of it might embarrass him later.

He folded the check and put it in his shirt pocket, patting it to be sure it was still there. Then he stood up.

"It's like the first day of the rest of my life," he said. "I'm sure it's the beginning of a turnaround." He smiled, took her hand again, and kissed it.

"Now, now," she said, smiling. "And remember our bargain." She put a finger on her lips. In response he repeated the gesture, patting the check in his shirt pocket once again. He turned and moved toward the apartment door.

"And Mr. Stern," she called. Despite her gesture, this thing with Teddy still nagged at her.

He turned in response, his look expectant, as if he feared she had changed her mind.

"About Teddy," she said.

"Teddy?"

"He's..." She hesitated. It was impossible to get the words out. Need she do more for this man? she asked herself. "He's a fine boy,

Mr. Stern. I'm sure everything will work out." Sooner or later he would discover the truth. Quite enough salvation for one day, she decided.

"Who knows?" Mr. Stern said. "You could be my lucky charm."

She smiled inwardly, knowing it was probably true. She liked that. She had performed the greatest good deed of all, saving his life. It felt wonderful to be a good luck charm.

"I hope so," she said.

He nodded, their eyes locked for a moment, then he left the apartment.

9

THE RICHARDSONS?" Jenny exclaimed, flabbergasted by the request.

"Nothing overboard," Larry said. "Just a pot luck kind of thing. No pressure. Just a neighborly get-together."

"Neighborly?"

"You're supposed to be this big fan of neighborly, I thought it might be appropriate to give your instincts fair play."

He had wandered into the living room from his den, where he had been working while she was watching reruns of "Dallas" on television. Sitting beside her for a while, he had watched the program without comment, which was unusual for him since he detested television in general, especially "Dallas."

"How can these airheads possibly have so many complications in their lives?" he had once commented. And here he was sitting next to her on the couch, actually watching the show with her. It was during the commercial break that he'd made the startling suggestion.

"Do you object?" he asked when her response seemed less than enthusiastic.

"No. I think it's a fine idea," she said. "I'm just surprised."

She liked Terry Richardson, although she did not feel much admiration for her husband, Godfrey, who was obviously carrying on adulterous relationships with numerous women. Jenny could not forget his little midday tryst with that bimbo. And who knew how many times he cheated outside the apartment?

Lately, in her chance encounters with Terry in the hallways, she had noted that Terry looked tired and wan, as if she were either sick or carrying too great an emotional burden. Considering what Jenny knew, she could certainly empathize with her.

With Godfrey she was polite but never truly friendly. He didn't look so hot himself these days, she had observed. How could he, considering the double life he had been leading?

"When would you like to do this?" she had asked.

"Sooner the better." His response puzzled her, but then he had mused aloud: "Once you make your mind up, it's better to act on things."

Perhaps he was having a change of heart on the issue of neighbors, she decided, although he hadn't seemed to have had a change of heart on much else. Nearly two weeks had gone by since the dinner with Vince and Connie Mazzo, and he hadn't mentioned much about the new business, except to say that everything was going according to schedule. And he hadn't lectured her on the issue of the neighbors, which did indeed represent that he had kept at least part of his promise. This new wrinkle in his attitude might mean that he was beginning to discard some of his cynicism and paranoia about other people.

Jenny extended the invitation to Terry on the telephone, and after a few moments of hesitation Terry accepted, although not without some guilt.

"We should be reciprocating," Terry said. "After all, you had us first months ago."

"Don't be silly," Jenny said, although she knew that there was a lot of truth in the allegation.

"It's just that we're under such pressure. Besides, all we do these days is work and jump into bed in exhaustion."

"Well, then make an exception," Jenny said. "It will be good for both of you."

"Don't make a big deal," Terry said.

"I was thinking spaghetti and meatballs," Jenny mused, happy for the acceptance.

"Good. I'll make my super sauce."

The Richardsons showed up on time a few evenings later. Terry carried a pot of sauce, and Godfrey carried a bottle of red wine.

"Not bad," Larry said, eyeing the label and offering an uncommonly broad smile of greeting. In fact, Jenny had noticed, he had been oddly absorbed by the impending dinner, dropping strange hints of concern and worry.

"Remember, low-key," he had reminded her on a number of occasions.

"Does that mean paper plates?" she had joked. He hadn't laughed.

"Not that low-key," he had answered, looking at her archly and not smiling. Lately he had seemed more self-absorbed than usual, which she attributed to the pressures involved in starting the new business. Still, he had continued to be less than forthcoming on that subject, and she had deliberately not added to the pressure by probing too deeply.

Both Richardsons looked tired, and although Terry seemed cheery, her sad eyes belied her upbeat manner. Jenny dismissed any further analysis, although based on her observations of Godfrey's behavior, it did cross her mind that they might be having serious marital difficulties.

Jenny and Terry went into the kitchen, leaving Larry to play host to Godfrey in the living room.

"A few little odds and ends yet to get the sauce up to prize-winning par," Terry said. "Needs a couple of nice Bermuda onions."

Jenny brought out the onions and put them on the chopping block. She had already put up the big pasta pot to boil and had rolled the meatballs and put the salad makings into the wooden salad bowl.

As she sliced away at the onions, Terry kept up a steady patter of talk.

"This is one great idea, Jenny. I can't remember how long it's been since I had any fun. We really should do this more often, don't you think? Only next time I want you and Larry to come up to my place." Her talk went on and on while Jenny supplied the acknowledgments in the appropriate places.

After a while Godfrey came in with a bottle of opened white wine and two glasses. He poured each of the women a glass and put the bottle down on a corner of the cutting board. Jenny noted that he stopped for a moment to observe his wife, whose eyes were tearing from the onions.

"You okay?" he whispered.

"Of course I'm okay," she snapped. "It's these damned onions."

"You promised," he whispered.

"I told you, it's the onions."

Jenny felt embarrassed at overhearing the exchange and tried to appear as if she hadn't heard by mixing the salad with more enthusiasm than was warranted. But after he had gone, Terry seemed less bouncy.

"Wine's good," she said after a deep sip.

Jenny noted that Larry had opened his very best white, which by his own word had been bought to be used only for special occasions.

"Damned onions," Terry said, rubbing her moist eyes with her sleeve.

"Let me," Jenny said.

"No. It's fine." She had turned away from the cutting board and upended her wineglass. Jenny took the bottle and came around to refill Terry's glass. Facing her at that distance, Jenny noted that there seemed to be more to her tears than the onions. Also her hands shook as she proffered the glass for the wine.

"Jesus, look at me," Terry said. With her other hand she steadied the glass and brought it up to her lips, taking another deep sip.

"Are you all right?" Jenny asked, deliberately trying to appear unprovocative.

"Do I look not all right?" Terry said, a slight tremor noticeable on her lips as she spoke. Then she shook her head vigorously. "No. That is an unfair question."

"I can finish the onions," Jenny said, hoping to avoid the confession that she sensed was about to emerge. She hated the idea of having to listen as Terry recounted her husband's infidelities, as if somehow her silence made her culpable. She resumed chopping the onions, aware that Terry was studying her, perhaps trying to determine whether or not to confide her misery.

"Jesus, Jenny. It's been awful." The woman began to sob, her shoulders shaking as she braced her palms against the sink. Jenny's heart went out to her, and she felt it impossible not to respond.

"Really, Terry. It couldn't be that bad."

Jenny imagined herself in that position, imagined her reaction. Betrayal, she supposed, hurt a great deal, as if something valuable were lost. She wanted to embrace Terry, comfort her. As she was about to do so, she realized that her hands were moist with onion juice.

Terry bent over the sink, turned on the tap, scooped up water, and patted her face. Then she stood up and, facing Jenny, sucked in a deep breath.

"I promised him. He sees me like this it will only make things worse."

Jenny was confused by the statement and must have shown it.

"It's not his fault, you see," Terry said, her reddened eyes beginning to clear.

"Not his fault?"

"Actually I blame myself mostly for waiting too long. Pursuing my career. My fucking career."

Jenny thought that Terry would begin crying again, but she somehow recovered, finished her wine, then poured herself another glass. Even though Terry seemed to be speaking in shorthand, Jenny realized that her unhappiness didn't appear to have anything to do with infidelity, but with infertility. Apparently they hadn't had much luck on that score.

"It's...it's psychological. Common, the doctors say. Oh, I feel terrible about even telling you, but who the hell can you talk to about this, except doctors, and all they can say is that there is nothing organically wrong."

"That's good, then," Jenny said. "Isn't it?"

"Good? Horrible. Worse than horrible."

"Well, if there's nothing organically wrong..."

"Jenny," Terry said, her tone on the cusp of intimidating, "don't you understand? He can't get it up. He can't fuck. He can't even masturbate. In case you haven't heard, the sperm is in the ejaculate. And nothing seems to help. Nothing." The outburst disintegrated into hysteria. "We're going crazy over this. It's frustrating, maddening, and the damned clock keeps ticking away."

Now Jenny was totally confused. The man was philandering and he couldn't have intercourse? God, she thought, did I have that wrong.

"Jenny, I swear. I'd do anything. It sounds bizarre, doesn't it? I adore Godfrey. I love him. I want his baby. Our baby. All he needs to do is come and take the ejaculate to the fertility clinic for processing. Sounds simple, right? It's not. Dammit, I'd let him do it with anyone just to get the right stuff. I'd welcome it. But I'm scared to death to even suggest it."

Watching Terry agonize over the situation, Jenny could barely correlate the information. She berated herself for being smug and judgmental, even sanctimonious. And yet, observing Terry's genuine pain, she still harbored doubts. It was possible that the woman who came up to meet Godfrey was nothing more than a sex object, hired to induce his orgasm. Such a situation was simply out of her realm of experience, although it did have a logical twist that made her feel ashamed of her original assumptions. The perception of evil in terms of Godfrey disintegrated, and her sense of compassion accelerated. She apologized in her heart to Godfrey. Nothing in Manhattan is ever as it seems, she thought, wondering why she had never encountered these matters in Bedford. Not that they weren't happening, but it was the kind of thing that Bedfordians kept hidden and suffered silently.

"So here I am laying it on you," Terry said. "Godfrey would be enormously embarrassed if he knew I had told you. It's worse for him, since it strikes, well, right at the heart of his manhood. Believe me, I've learned a lot about men from this experience. Men really define themselves by their hard-ons. It sounds awful to the ear, almost obscene, but it's a fact that we women don't fully comprehend. Erection, insertion, ejaculation. It's programmed into their maleness, and if the first fails, the others go down like dominoes. I can cry for every time I turned him down. Not that we girls are

supposed to be blindly compliant, but a little insight and understanding could have gone a long way. A man really needs the
comfort of this triad. Probably more so than a woman. Damn, I
sound like a shrink. I feel so terrible for him. The next step is an
impotency clinic, although he's not quite worked himself up to
go. Listen, how many times"—Terry lowered her voice—"how
many times when you were single did you confront...you know
...a temporary failure? Remember how reassuring you were, probably saying it's okay, even when you were hot as a firecracker.
Well, I've reached the limit of reassurance with poor Godfrey."

Terry's words, Jenny admitted to herself, were indeed harsh on
the ears. She had never heard such direct intimate talk from another woman, nor had she ever confided such things to anyone.
By no means was she a sexual prude, not in her actions, but putting
it into words made her uncomfortable, although it in no way
diminished her sympathy for the plight of her neighbors.

"Sex used to seem so forbidden, exotic, a secret thing, even
deliciously dirty," Terry continued, her voice now a whisper. She
had moved her face closer to Jenny's, who felt the breeze of her
words and smelled the scent she used, less subtle at this distance.
"A lot of my girlfriends hate sex. I love to fuck. I love to come. I
love to make him come. Tell you the truth, I've tried everything.
Everything. When he's sleeping I peek under the covers and look
at those lovely involuntary hard-ons, which happen when normal
men sleep, but as soon as I make my move, down it goes again."
She looked squarely into Jenny's eyes. "I'm at my wits' end. Now,
for example, right now, it's right in the middle of my cycle, the
perfect time. I feel so damned..." She paused for a moment, and
her voice rose. "So inadequate. So helpless. My heart goes out to
him. I don't know what to do, and I'm scared to death that his
libido may be permanently deceased."

Jenny hoped she had hidden her sense of shock, which was
compounded by this latest revelation. She could remember only
two times in her single life when a male had failed to function,
and yes, she had said those things that Terry had mentioned. But
they were exceptions. Her general experience with the four men
she'd been intimate with before her marriage was that men reacted,

got hard. Sometimes they needed a little help, but invariably they rose to the occasion. The episodes of impotence had been temporary, very temporary. In her experience they'd all had the opposite malady.

Jenny could not possibly be as blunt as Terry in assessing her sexual needs, but the truth was that she had learned to like sex. She liked it a lot, and she had been an apt pupil, especially with Darryl, the older married man with whom she'd had an affair. The most important thing he had taught her was that nothing was forbidden during the sex act between consenting adults, although she admittedly liked both the fore- and afterplay and a sense of mystery and romance to go along with it.

She and Larry had sex often. It wasn't satisfying every time, especially lately, which Larry attributed to having weighty things on his mind. At the beginning of their relationship, they would think nothing about having sex two or even three times a day. During the past few weeks, they hadn't made love more than three or four times. Not that she would complain. That would be unwomanly.

He liked her to be wanton and sometimes aggressive and had often told her he wanted her to act like a whore when they were in bed. She wasn't sure how a whore was supposed to act. To satisfy him, she used her imagination, and she could tell by his reactions that he enjoyed great pleasure through her special ministrations. Not once did he ever have a problem getting an erection. How terrible it would be for Larry, Jenny thought, picturing him showing off his lovely erect cock. Man's best friend, he called it. A girl's, too, she told him often, and she was never shy with her compliments about his equipment.

"I have no doubt we'll find the key to it someday," Terry said, winding down the confession. To Jenny she seemed the better for it, and the subject receded, at least verbally, as they proceeded with the preparation of the meal.

Jenny set up the food buffet style, and they helped themselves and brought the plates back to the table, which Jenny had set nicely with lighted candles. She noted, too, that Larry had opened three bottles of their best red, for which he had paid nearly fifty dollars a bottle. When everyone had filled their plates and sat down at the table, Larry hopped up and lavishly poured the expensive red.

"This is one great idea," Godfrey said, rolling the spaghetti on his fork.

"You can thank Jenny," Larry said, which wasn't the truth at all.

"You know better than that, Larry," she told him playfully. His response was a look of extreme displeasure, which conveyed the puzzling message that she was not to pursue the matter further. To divert herself from observing his strange conduct, she drank deeply, deliberately not looking in Larry's direction. For the Richardsons he played the perfect host, refilling their glasses almost, it seemed, after every sip. She had never seen him so alert and attentive to strangers.

"Anyway," Larry was saying, smiling broadly, addressing himself to Terry, "Godfrey has been filling me in on the ins and outs of the art business. I think I've persuaded him to be my agent when I get enough cash flow to seriously collect, which is one of my major goals." Such an objective was news to Jenny and only added to her confusion about the dinner.

"Always ready, willing, and able," Godfrey responded. It was clear that he had bought Larry's assurances.

"I really envision a great collection," Larry said after he had opened yet another bottle of the expensive red and had poured for the third or fourth time. "Our new agency, if all goes well, will generate lots of cash flow. We expect to open our doors in about a month."

"Brave man," Terry said, her speech just slightly thicker than it had been in the kitchen. "Start-ups being so hazardous, especially now." She had successfully masked her anguish, although it was obvious that she was drinking more than might be usual for her.

"It's not exactly a start-up," Larry said, explaining, with full concentration on Terry, what he called his business plan. "So you see," he continued, "we don't qualify for the usual definition of start-up. We have the accounts, the creative talent to carry out our programs. And, of course, the facilities and the management."

"What about capital?" Terry asked, still, despite the wine, in full charge of her faculties.

"We're interviewing banks," Larry said almost offhandedly, as if he were indifferent to the process. "Actually the technical management side is my turf, the creative and sales, my partner's."

"Mr. Inside and Mr. Outside," Jenny blurted, feeling the first signs of alcoholic euphoria. The slight buzz had not interfered with her logic, since it had suddenly occurred to her what this dinner was all about, a revelation that was remarkably sobering. The name of the game was, as she had learned by her very cursory exposure to the advertising business, to set up Terry for a pitch, which, with Jenny's help, Larry had done quite efficiently.

Jenny watched as Larry bore in on Terry, whose level of alertness seemed, oddly, to have increased with her imbibing. To Jenny, Terry's attitude, despite her anguish and drinking, spoke aeons about her career commitment.

"Anyone for seconds?" Jenny asked, eliciting a menacing look from Larry.

"They'll take it if they want it," Larry grumbled.

"I've got to save something for dessert," Terry said. Larry shook his head and shot Jenny a look of exasperation. She knew why, of course. She had interrupted his pitch.

"Basically," she heard Larry say, "we're looking for a revolving line, say three hundred thou to begin with. Signatures, naturally. Interest only for the first year. One point above prime, max. Of course later, if we're both happy, we'd expect prime."

Terry nodded and was silent for a while.

"Compensating balances?" she asked.

Jenny had the urge to find out what that meant and began to speak.

"What are..." she began, swiveling her gaze toward Larry. He shot her a vicious look, and she beat a hasty retreat, although she exchanged glances with Godfrey, who appeared to be frowning, as if he didn't approve of Larry's attitude.

"Not off the bat," Larry replied with a shrug.

"Tough deal," Terry said, shaking her head. She held out her glass for Larry to pour.

"I'll see about the dessert," Jenny said.

"Dammit, Jenny!" Larry erupted. "We're trying to talk important stuff here."

"Dessert *is* important," Jenny snapped, getting up.

"Need any help, Jenny?" Terry said, starting to stand.

"She'll be fine," Larry said, patting Terry's hand. "No need," he told her, smiling. She sat down again.

"Let me," Godfrey said, getting up.

"Really, Godfrey," Jenny protested, but mildly.

"We'll let these two do their tap dance," Godfrey said.

"Homemade apple pie à la mode coming up," Jenny cried, forcing herself to be cheerful. "Vanilla or strawberry, folks?"

"Strawberry," Terry piped.

"Anything," Larry muttered, scowling at her. "You pick it."

She went into the kitchen. Godfrey followed her.

"You scoop, I'll slice," Jenny said.

She busied herself with cutting pieces of pie while Godfrey scooped the requested flavors out of the boxes. She noted that he had scooped up a ball of vanilla for himself. As he did so, he seemed to be studying her intensely.

"Is he always that uptight?" Godfrey asked.

"I guess the pressure's getting to him," she replied.

"Pressure. Yeah. I know what you mean. He should be thankful. He's a lucky man to have such a pretty young wife."

Bells went off in her head. Was he coming on to her, being flirtatious or just friendly? Then she remembered what Terry had mentioned about his problem, which made her more curious than uncomfortable.

"And you're a lucky guy to have a girl like Terry," she said.

"Yes, I am," he said in agreement, "but that doesn't prevent me from admiring beautiful, sexy women."

"I thank you for the compliment, kind sir," she said, moving back into the dining room. Larry and Terry were still absorbed in their conversation. They barely looked up when she and Godfrey sat down.

"There's room for talk," Larry said, obviously having recovered his momentum and now launching yet another assault of salesmanship and charm. "We admit to being aggressive and highly creative and wanting to do business with banks and other entities, with people who are winners. People like yourself, Terry. People with brains and savvy. Watch our dust. We've already expanded our client base, and we won't be in business for a month yet."

"I assume you've got personal statements," Terry interjected.

"Of course. Mine and my partner's," Larry said. "We've got a detailed package of papers that will pass any loan committee. Believe me, the risk will be minimal, and we'll grow into terrific customers for any bank. The day of the super ad agency is numbered. We're specialists and perfectly positioned in the right place at the right time, just after an industry shakeout."

Jenny and Godfrey ate their desserts silently, exchanging glances occasionally while Larry and Terry pursued their business discussion. Noting that she and Godfrey had finished theirs, Jenny collected the empty plates and went back into the kitchen.

At that moment the inside door buzzer rang.

"Would you get that, Larry?" Jenny called from the kitchen, pretending that she was too busy to answer it. She wanted to break up their conversation.

"Can't even have a quiet dinner at home," Larry grouched, shaking his head. He got up from the table and flung open the door. "Oh, Christ. Not again," he muttered.

It was Jerry O'Hara from downstairs, looking harassed and apologetic as he always did when looking for his cat.

"I'm so sorry to interrupt—"

"No cat here. Just us folks," Larry muttered, beginning to close the door in Jerry's face.

"Thank you, but you see—"

"Why don't you chain him to a pipe or something?" Larry snapped. "This is getting ridiculous."

"Chain Peter?" The man looked aghast.

"Or worse," Larry said. He turned to the Richardsons. "You see his damned cat?"

"Afraid not," Terry said without rancor.

"Have you tried the Sterns?" Godfrey volunteered.

"Actually, Teddy Stern is out combing the neighborhood. Peter is such a bad boy."

"Yes. Such a bad, bad boy," Larry mocked, moving his arm, the wrist deliberately limp.

"I know it's a nuisance and I apologize for that, but he does mean a lot to us."

"Considering all the trouble he causes," Larry sneered, "you might consider sending him off to the glue factory." He looked to the others, obviously hoping for laughter. None came.

"I can see you're not a cat person, Mr. Burns."

"Well then, there's nothing wrong with your eyes."

"Not at all," O'Hara snapped, sucking in a deep breath and turning away. Larry pushed the door shut with a slam.

"Damned fairies and their fucking cat," Larry said sourly, going back to the table.

"Here we are," Jenny said, hiding her own disgust at his conduct. She marched in with a tray filled with little cakes, cookies, a coffeepot, and cups and saucers. Larry was having difficulty hiding his exasperation.

Shaking his head and shooting Jenny still another disgruntled look, Larry got up from the table and took a sheaf of papers from the breakfront drawer and laid them in front of Terry. He moved her pie à la mode dish to give the paper more room. Then he pushed aside his own plate with what Jenny thought was a note of dismissal, rejecting the dessert as a kind of punishment aimed at her.

"It's a pro forma," Larry said, trying with some success to regain his poise. "And I know how bankers view pro formas." Terry studied the papers as she ate.

"Coffee, anyone?" Jenny trilled.

"I'll have a cup," Terry said, her attention diverted.

Jenny poured out a cup for Terry.

"And I'll have one," Godfrey said. He seemed to have entered Jenny's little game of interruption.

"If you have any questions—" Larry began.

"Cream or sugar, Terry?" Jenny asked.

Peripherally she could see Larry's features tighten with exasperation, but she deliberately kept her eyes averted from his.

"Just black, thank you," Terry replied.

"But I'll have cream," Godfrey said.

She poured the cream into his coffee. Terry concentrated on reading the pro forma while Larry peered over her shoulder.

"Coffee, Larry?"

"Just pour it, Jenny."

"Cookies, anyone?" Jenny asked.

"Jenny, dammit," Larry said, making an obvious effort to hold his temper. "Can't you just leave us alone for a moment?"

"Good idea," Godfrey said. "Let's take our coffee into the living room while these tycoons mull over their millions."

"They won't miss us," Jenny said. It was her turn now to shoot Larry a nasty look. He was too absorbed to notice.

"So how's the art business?" Jenny asked when they were seated side by side on the living room couch.

"Lousy." Godfrey shrugged, sipping his coffee.

"Boom and bust," she said, smiling. "What goes down comes up and vice versa."

"So I'm told," he responded gloomily. He looked toward the dining room, where Larry and Terry were intent in their discussion. Then he turned toward Jenny and studied her.

"What is it?" she asked.

"When I first saw you, I thought you were still in your teens." He laughed. "Curly mop. Small. Like—"

"Little Orphan Annie."

"You said it, not me."

"It's part of my charm. One of my old boyfriends used to call me his Lolita." She had thought suddenly of Darryl. "Lots of guys think there's something vulnerable about small women. When I was a kid, I hated to be smaller. Actually I'm not that short. Five two."

"And well made," he said, averting his eyes in embarrassment as he finished off the coffee. His obvious interest in her aroused her curiosity still further. Was this a man with a dead libido?

"So is Terry. From what I can see."

"Very. I can assure you. The most wonderful woman in the world."

Jenny studied him for some sign of his condition, an underlying sadness, perhaps, or some similar clue. She searched his eyes, imagining she was detecting his hidden pain. At the same time she was embarrassed by the knowledge that Terry had imparted about his deeply personal crippling condition.

As she observed him, she realized that something drastic had altered in her perception of him. Jenny could not imagine him being less than sexually functional. He certainly was attractive, with light gray searching eyes surrounded by dark lashes. His hair was blond, with natural waves, his figure slender and graceful. He filled out his jeans well, crotch included, and his open sport shirt revealed a patch of curly blond chest hairs.

Something else seemed altered in her perception. He appeared very masculine and sexy, not merely generically, but personally, which surprised her. Considering that she had just heard that he was impotent, she felt it incongruous that she was actually thinking such thoughts. Rarely did other men inspire such fantasies in her. Certainly not since she was married. But the telltale signs were unmistakable. Was it the wine? she wondered. Or had Terry's seductive words inspired such a reaction, along with an embarrassingly clear sense of challenge?

She wondered if her suggestive conversation with Godfrey was deliberately flirtatious. If she didn't know better, she might conclude that there was also an underlying motive in Godfrey's attentiveness. Was it possible? Had she turned him on? She looked toward Larry and Terry, both oblivious of this other drama in the next room. Which reminded her how resentful she was at Larry's using her to lure Terry into this trap. Hustling, they called it in Manhattan. Larry had instructed her well on the nomenclature of such aggressions, the meaning of which was becoming clearer by his own example.

Of course, there was no law that said Terry had to listen. She was responding according to her own agenda. Strictly business, Larry would explain to her later, noting that business ran on such relationships, people hustling people. Beware of such predators, he had urged. Watch out for users. And here he was violating his own admonitions. Use anybody who can help. Waste no time with people who can't. At that moment she had no trouble identifying a perfect example of the true predator. She studied Larry for a moment, a deliberately clinical observation.

Perhaps she might have felt differently if he had involved her, made her part of it, shown some respect for her judgment. Instead he had simply manipulated her sense of neighborliness, her idea of sharing, and her concept of friendliness. The fact was that his influence over her was eroding before her very eyes.

He would be appalled if he knew that she had lent money to Mr. Stern. Even her own second thoughts about that action were at last put to rest by this display of indifference to her participation in what was clearly of interest to both of them. If he knew what she had done, his lecture would run on for months, maybe years. As for what had happened between her and Teddy, she immediately put that out of her mind. Lectures would hardly be enough to extract his pound of flesh.

"Hey," Terry called to them from the dining room, "you two are awfully quiet."

"Would you rather we yelled?" Jenny replied.

"It won't be much longer," Larry called.

"Take all the time you want," Godfrey bantered, winking at Jenny.

"You're an extremely attractive person," he said, his voice lower, for her ears alone.

"Am I?" Jenny mouthed in a kind of soundless mime.

At that moment she sensed movement across the couch. He had reached out and caught her hand, which somehow had found itself a ready target. His touch was, no question about it, arousing, and she was totally flustered, although she did not remove her hand from his grasp, casting a quick look toward the dining room.

A harmless gesture, she decided. He was just holding her hand, for crying out loud. She felt an odd belligerence, as if she were answering Larry's accusation.

At that moment another thought crowded into her conscious-ness. Suppose all this was Terry's doing, her manipulation, throw-ing Jenny in Godfrey's path for the purpose of arousal? Clearly that was exactly what was happening, the arousal part. She wasn't quite certain of the manipulative part.

Then she realized that Godfrey was smiling, his eyes shiny with ... was it gratitude?

"Would you like some more coffee?" Jenny asked him, more as a subterfuge than a real offer.

"Yes, that would be nice," Godfrey said.

With her free hand, she reached for the coffeepot, then poured more coffee in his cup, which he held with his free hand. Then she felt the hand he was holding move closer to his body. There was no way to stop him. The coffeepot she was holding was poised in midair.

Suddenly the back of her hand was in his crotch. She let it lie there, wondering why she wasn't resisting. This was absurd, she thought, but she could not find her indignation. Her inaction was inexplicable, out of character, but she did not argue the point with herself. Curiosity was motivating her now, more than anything else. Concentrating her mind into the nerves of her hand, she convinced herself that the hard part on which her hand lay was nothing other than a full-blown erection.

A kind of miracle, she decided, offering a moment's caress while she watched his eyes, shining with such obvious joy that she wanted to shout out the news to Terry. She noted, too, that he had flushed deep red, and she observed that the hand that held the cup and saucer was trembling slightly, making a clattering noise.

"Your husband is quite a salesman," Terry said. Luckily her voice preceded her, and Jenny managed to disengage her hand.

"He told me he was in research," Jenny said with a touch of malevolence, turning to face Larry, who had just entered the room. His expression seemed much more relaxed. He was obviously satisfied that the objective of the dinner had been achieved. She chuckled wryly at that. She had, after all, achieved another, possibly far more important objective.

* * *

When Jenny finally finished the dishes and cleaned up the dining area, it was nearly one. She had deliberately taken her time, rubbing to a high polish the pot in which Terry had brought the sauce. The Richardsons had forgotten to take it with them. She hoped that Larry would be fast asleep when she arrived in the bedroom. She was in no mood for confrontation.

He was lying in bed on top of the covers, wearing only his Jockey shorts and writing on a yellow legal pad when she came into the bedroom. It both surprised and disappointed her. Fortunately he was so absorbed in his work that he did not look up, and she was able to undress quickly, put on her nightgown, and crawl under the comforter.

With her back turned to him, Jenny closed her eyes and longed for sleep. She needed very badly to get over the evening, not the part with Godfrey Richardson, which in her mind became a kind of pleasant highlight. She thought of herself somehow as a catalytic agent and hoped that the Richardsons had made love before going to sleep, maybe even had made a baby.

She wasn't sure how to describe her feelings about Larry. Was it disillusion? Had he always been this calculating and manipulative? The fact was that she was mostly disappointed in his character. As if to emphasize her thoughts, he spoke:

"The way I figure, the whole deal cost us three, three twenty-five at the most."

She had closed her eyes and was feigning sleep.

"Five bottles of wine, four reds at fifty per and one white at thirty per. With food, say another fifty. If she gives us the loan, I'll put in a chit. Say three hundred. I could probably get away with five. Vince wouldn't dare raise a stink. All in all, I'd give the night, say, an eight.... What do you think?"

Although she heard every word, she didn't answer. He shook her shoulder. Still she didn't answer.

"All those damned interruptions. I wish hereafter you would just keep your mouth shut when I'm conducting business. It was so obvious. And she was listening. Thing with these bankers, you got to get them on your side so they can sell your deal to the committee. That's the key to it."

He shook her shoulder roughly. If she was asleep, the gesture could not fail to rouse her.

"You hear, Jenny? I mean, you've got to be a little more sensitive to circumstances. Hell, this means as much to you as it does to me. Sometimes I actually think you're deliberately trying to put a monkey wrench into the deal. Hard enough putting it together without your being Madame Buttinsky. Are you listening to me?"

She could feel his movement as he got under the covers and moved closer to her, settling his body against her back. He had put his mouth against her ear.

"Anybody home?" he cried, the loudness jolting. She could smell his wine breath. His hand began to roam over her body.

"Please, Larry," she whispered. "Not now. I'm bushed."

Not once since the beginning of their relationship had she refused him. But at this moment she felt cold, without the slightest feeling of arousal. He did not desist immediately, but she could tell that her refusal had dampened his desire.

"I don't know what the hell has come over you, Jenny."

She didn't answer, but it was a relief to her that he moved away, although she sensed that he was still awake, brooding. She felt tense, rigid, unable to sleep. Nor did she have any desire to make it up with him. Was this the man she'd married? To love and honor?

As she lay there, knowing he was awake and brooding, angry with her, probably insulted, she felt her attitude soften. Perhaps she was being too harsh, too critical. Was she fulfilling her part of the bargain, knowing where his ambition lay? Of course, it would benefit both of them and their future children.

After all, he was the businessman in the family. He was the one fulfilling his obligation. Was it guilt corroding her resolve to punish him? Punish him for what? She had her secrets now as well. How could she blame him for not sharing when she had performed an act of betrayal? Or was she being too harsh on herself? Within her she sensed a battlefield emerging, with warring factions of raw anger and honorable duty confronting each other. Finally the battle sputtered, anger retreated, honorable duty advanced. She was just about to turn toward him when he said:

"And that fucking fag with his fucking cat."

The battle was joined again, only this time the results were very different.

10

HE must have been in a dead sleep when Larry left for work. Inexplicably her first thought was about Peter, the cat. Odd, she thought, how the cat's fate had become a pervasive aspect of life in this building. She had the urge to go downstairs and ask either Jerry or Bob if Peter had been found. Putting on her robe, she left the bedroom, walked into the living room, opened one of the casement windows, and looked outside, searching the branches of the sycamore tree for any sign of Peter.

At that moment Jerry O'Hara emerged from his apartment and, obviously with the same thought in mind, inspected the tree's branches. He glanced at Jenny, who could tell from his expression that Peter was still among the missing.

"Not yet?" Jenny asked.

"Afraid not."

"What do you think?"

"Bob and I are afraid to speculate," he said, shaking his head in despair.

"He'll turn up. You'll see," Jenny said, suddenly irritated by her own blind optimism.

"Makes you feel so helpless," Jerry said. "We've been searching all night." He opened his arms palms up in a gesture of resignation.

"I'm sorry about my husband," Jenny said.

"Let's just say he's not exactly a cat person." Jerry grimaced.

She wanted to explain further but could not think of anything worth saying that would mitigate the circumstances.

"Let's just hope for the best," Jerry said as Bob came out the apartment door. He looked up and shook his head.

"We're ravaged," Bob said.

"We'll give it another day," Jerry said.

"Then what?" Bob cried. He glanced toward Jerry in irritation. Jenny sensed that things between them were tense. Probably each blaming the other for Peter's disappearance.

"It's an absolute nightmare," Jerry cried.

"The worst," Bob agreed, shooting Jerry an angry glance. They turned away and headed toward Second Avenue, talking animatedly, probably arguing.

She went into the kitchen to make herself some coffee. As the coffee brewed, she poured a saucer of milk and, after overcoming some consternation, placed it on the living room window ledge as a lure, leaving the window open.

She was quite aware that this was a gesture of defiance against Larry. But this time the eternal debate about it was not long and concluded decidedly in her favor. She simply characterized the gesture as her right. This was her home, and the word *obey* had long been eliminated from the marriage ritual. Suddenly she felt giggly, wondering what Larry would say if he were to walk through the door at that moment.

By the time she returned to the kitchen, the coffee was ready. Normally the routine of the morning's comings and goings of the house did not enter her consciousness unless she concentrated on listening or if, for some reason, the routine had been violated, as in the case of Godfrey Richardson and his so-called girlfriend.

Today, for some reason, as she sipped her coffee she found herself on alert, listening, feeling on the edge of some vague expectancy. She deliberately did not dwell on the events of the previous evening, knowing in her heart that such a recounting would lead inevitably to a reassessment of her life, her marriage, her state of mind, her values. For the time being, one blatant defiance was enough.

Better to drift today, she decided, postpone. She had this urge to call her mother, to confide her dilemma, but that reality, too, inhibited her action. In the context of this new life in Manhattan, her mother was as much of an alien as if she resided on another planet.

The elevator revved up. The Sterns were on the move. Not Teddy, who would have left long before she had awakened. She never heard the Sterns' voices, only the movement of the elevator and the sound of their footfalls on the stone steps in front of the house. She hadn't talked to Mr. Stern since the day he had attempted suicide, but she had seen him through the window, rushing off to whatever appointed round her loan had made possible.

In his carriage and demeanor, she sensed more optimism and determination, which once again buttressed her opinion that she had done the right thing. Even Mrs. Stern looked less doomed. For a brief instant Jenny had even seen her smile.

Then she heard Terry's distinctive high-heeled hip-hop on the staircase as she descended. Jenny smiled to herself. Terry's walk, in heels, was something less than graceful, and although they had never discussed it, Jenny was certain that the obligatory essentials of dressing for success were not among Terry's happiest chores.

The telephone's ring interrupted the rhythm of her alertness, although she had begun to sense that something was different in the morning pattern of the apartment house. She picked up the phone. It was Larry.

"I just got in the office," he said, his voice thick with contrition. "I . . . I . . . feel rotten. It's the tension of this new venture. I'm not myself."

She wanted to tell him that maybe he should leave well enough alone, not try to set up this new business on such a morally reprehensible foundation. No, she decided, this was not something to be discussed on the telephone. Perhaps his conscience was giving him second thoughts, and he was trying to find his way back to higher moral ground. Maybe.

"I understand," she said, hoping that he would tell her that he had called off the new venture.

"You know I love you," he said, lowering his voice. "All I ask is that you bear with me through this period. I'm hyper and I can't stop myself. You know what I mean."

"Yes, I do," she said. Yet she could not bring herself to tell him that she loved him. Up to that moment it would have been her knee-jerk response. If he noted a change in the calibration of her emotions, he said nothing.

"Everything will be fine," he said. "I promise."

"I hope so," she whispered.

"Tell you what," Larry said. "I'll get home early. Say no later than six. You rustle up my favorite dish, your A number one Indiana meat loaf, and I'll open a bottle of one of those fancy clarets." He paused, lowering his voice, putting on his teasing manner. "We'll take it from there. Get my drift?"

"More or less," she said, offering no commitment. At that moment the prospect hadn't much allure.

"Good," he said, oddly satisfied. "See you later, alligator." She could detect the hollowness of his attempt at cheerfulness.

After she hung up, she made some effort to enter the normal routine of her day, the household chores, the dinner plans. The prospect of such tasks, which since moving into the apartment had always anchored her day, filled her with dismay. For what purpose? she wondered, feeling a sense of disorientation and despair. Was this what was meant by the housewife blues?

She felt herself sliding into, as her mother would put it, the black hole of self-pity. Never, never give in to that, she would caution, one more homily that fitted nicely into the family's value system. She knew that she must not give in to this momentary wave of disillusion, that certainly Larry, her husband and the potential father of her children, must be given the benefit of the doubt.

There was, after all, nothing wrong in being ambitious. Wasn't that also high up on the list of priorities? A man with ambition was someone to be valued. Didn't dreaming big dreams mean taking big risks? How could one have small dreams in Manhattan, the Big Apple? Why was she so upset? And what, after all, could she contribute even if she were consulted about his business plans?

Despite these reflections, she could not find the energy to begin her day. Instead she poured herself another cup of coffee and wondered if she might shake off the blues by getting dressed and going to the movies. The idea triggered a tug of guilt and left her confused and uncertain, and it was with a sense of relief that she heard the inside buzzer ring.

Before she opened the door, she knew exactly who it was. The vague expectation, which had been bothering her all morning, had finally reached the edge of her consciousness.

"May I come in?" Godfrey said.

She looked at him for a long moment, not responding.

"Of course," she said nervously. "The pot."

She turned and went into the kitchen, listening as his footsteps padded behind her. The memory of Terry's anguished revelation and last night's episode with Godfrey filtered back into her mind. She had known he would return. It seemed more like a natural consequence rather than betrayal or perversion.

Jenny reached for the pot on the stove, all clean and gleaming and ready for retrieval. Turning, the pot cradled in two hands against her belly, she confronted him. His eyes studied her, washing over her face and body like scanning beams of light. He made no move to retrieve the pot.

"Last night—" he began.

"I was a little high," she interrupted.

"I know...." He could not continue. He was clearly embarrassed, and a red flush had settled around his neck.

"Would you like a cup of coffee?" It seemed to Jenny a logical question to break the tension. As if to facilitate the offer, she put the pot on the kitchen island behind her. He looked at his watch.

"I...I don't think so."

He took a step toward her, closer, but still more than arm's length distance. Her urge was to respond by stepping backward, but her movement was constrained by the fact that she was leaning against the kitchen island.

"It's not what you think," he said, his voice halting as if he had decided on what he was to say but couldn't bring himself to speak the words. She knew exactly what he meant. I am an instrument of his desire, she told herself, feeling foolish, the voice in her mind a kind of student declamation. Yet she did not feel the same level of desire for him that she had felt last night.

"May I kiss you?" he mumbled.

"I'm sorry, I don't think..." she began. It had crossed her mind that his being turned on might have had its effect, moving him and Terry to make love. This was the moment in her cycle, Terry had explained. From the gloomy look in Godfrey's eyes, she could tell that nothing had happened between them last night. It saddened her, and she sensed something growing deep inside of her, an attitude of militancy against life's injustice and unfairness.

"Just hold you, then," Godfrey said, coming still closer until his face was barely in focus. She could smell his after-shave, different from Larry's.

"Please," she said. It was neither an entreaty to desist nor a sign of consent. Nevertheless, she did not make any attempt to resist after he put his arms around her and settled his body against hers. His breath was warm against her ears as he spoke.

"I don't understand it, and I'm not going to question it, either," he whispered, holding her, his pelvis grinding into hers. "It's something about you. Natural involuntary selection. If only you knew. I'm sorry, but..."

She let herself be kissed; then, as he moved his head away, he was about to say something, and she put a finger on his lips.

"No need," she whispered, fearful that if she revealed Terry's confession, it would have an adverse effect on... She did not allow herself to extend the thought. Men, she decided, were far more fragile than women. Things like this, she supposed, could be talked away.

"Believe me," he said, "just this once. I'll...I'll never bother you again." She did not ask: Why her? Things like this were nature's mysteries. She had fallen in his path at exactly the right moment of his greatest need, an accident of nature.

She wondered if he and Terry had talked it over, debated this action, deciding finally to pursue it on the basis of desperation. Where was the harm? Call it an act of charity. Certainly not betrayal or revenge.

Such thoughts roared through her mind as Godfrey held her, rubbing himself against her. His arousal was unmistakable.

"Please," he pleaded. "Just this once."

She reached down with one hand, surprised to discover that his pants were open and his penis erect. She touched it, caressed it. She felt no arousal herself, nor did he press himself on her, apparently content to be manipulated by her hand, a process that harked back to her early teenage days.

"Faster," he whispered, his breath coming in short gasps.

Applying more movement, she wondered with clinical interest how he was going to preserve the ejaculate.

"Yes," he said. "Oh, God, thank you."

His breath came in convulsive gusts, and his body tightened. Then suddenly he grasped her wrist and moved her hand away, turning his back, groping in his pocket, removing an object that appeared to be a small cup. It was obvious that he was finishing the process by himself. His body lurched in a long, twitching response. She noted that he had bent his head, watching what was happening below. When he turned again to face her, he held one hand behind his back. She tried to assemble her features in an expression of neutrality.

"Someday I'll explain," he said with obvious gratitude.

"No need," Jenny said.

"I've got to go," he said, bending toward her. He kissed her forehead. "You don't know how wonderful you are."

"Never mind," she said.

He turned and rushed out the door, leaving her to debate the question of her culpability. In a technical sense, she had not been unfaithful. For that she was thankful, although it did take a giant leap of faith to reach that conclusion.

She had, after all, deliberately masturbated a man other than her husband. Means, she had been taught, could never justify ends. On the other hand, she might have been the instrument for bringing happiness to a neighbor. There was some solace in such a possibility, although she wasn't completely convinced of her in-nocence. Nor of her guilt. She hadn't, after all, well...fucked a stranger. That, never, she told herself. A hot blush rose in her face.

In an effort to mollify her feelings, she began to perform the household chores that she had postponed. Her energy level soared, and for the next few hours she moved around the apartment in a fury. Not a square inch of the place was spared, whether it needed attending to or not. She polished the silver, oiled the furniture, buffed the exposed portions of the floors, washed the windows, and generally eliminated any morsel of dust that might have lin-gered even in the remotest corners.

It occurred to her during this housecleaning frenzy that maybe all this activity was designed to physically remove any witnesses to what she now referred to her as semitransgression. Now, that isn't fair, she rebuked herself. By mid-afternoon she seemed to have smoothed the outer edges of any guilt feelings and come to terms with the reality of her deed.

Later, when she soaked in the warm water of her bath, her sense of well-being accelerated. It was purely mechanical, she decided finally. Neither an act of personal indulgence nor one of spiteful-ness. Something about her, an aura, a suggestiveness, a mysterious attraction, made him react. She was purely a catalytic agent, and as a result she had simply helped him produce sperm for a fertility procedure. Nothing more. The bonus to Godfrey might be that he was also cured of his impotence. At least she hoped so.

Just as she stepped out of the bathtub, she heard a strange sound coming from the living room. Wrapping a towel around herself, she came out of the bathroom to check on the source of the sound. It was Peter hungrily lapping away at the milk in the saucer. Hear-ing her approach, the cat looked up for a moment to study Jenny's intentions. Obviously judging them benign, he returned to his meal.

Jenny, talking in soothing tones, moved toward the cat, then carefully closed the casement window, trapping Peter inside the apartment. Checking all potential points of escape, she went back to her room and dressed hurriedly. Her intention was to somehow get the cat downstairs into Bob and Jerry's apartment before Larry returned from work.

It annoyed her to worry over Larry's reaction, but she had no stomach for inciting his wrath. Especially not today. She wanted tension to subside between them, to reconcile their differences.

When she went back into the living room, the cat was nowhere to be seen.

"Peter," she called as she roamed the apartment. "Here, kitty-kitty." She looked under furniture, inside closets, in whatever nook and cranny seemed a logical hiding place.

After a half hour of searching, there was still no sign of the cat. It was getting late, nearly four, and she hadn't even begun to think about dinner. No dinner and Peter lost in their apartment considerably dimmed prospects of an evening of marital reconciliation.

It was then that she thought of Teddy. Surely Teddy's knowledge of Peter would save the day. She rushed out of her apartment, went downstairs, and pressed Bob and Jerry's buzzer. No one answered. Then she ran up the front stairs and pressed the outside buzzer of the Stern apartment. No answer there, either.

Frustrated, she turned the problem over in her mind again. Perhaps Peter had found some hidden opening through which he had escaped. Such a prospect offered little solace at that moment. Time was running out. Larry would be home shortly. The self-confidence of the evening before had wilted.

She stood at the entrance to the apartment house, her mind on the razor's edge of indecision, resenting the anxiety induced by Larry's litany of caveats. But before she could work up a good head of anger, she saw Teddy heading toward the building from Third Avenue.

He looked somber, crestfallen, self-absorbed, as if he were contemplating some weighty and gloomy problem. She waited for him to reach the building.

"Thank goodness," she said. "I've been looking for you."

"Me?" he asked, puzzled by the question. She quickly explained her dilemma, watching his face light up with optimism as she spoke.

"I've been looking everywhere," he said. "Cut school, too." He lowered his voice. "The boys chewed me out plenty. They blamed me at first. I never let him out. Never. When I come in, I always make sure he's okay."

"I put milk out," Jenny said as they moved quickly to her apartment. "Then I closed all possible escape routes. I think—"

"He's one smart guy, that tomcat."

It was nearing the time when Larry would be coming home, which increased her anxiety. Inside the apartment, Teddy began his search.

"Peter," he called in a kind of specially contrived falsetto.

Jenny followed him around the apartment. At one point he got down on his hands and knees but still couldn't lure Peter out of his hiding place.

"Could be he's found some exit to the outside," Jenny suggested.

"Oh, he's good at that." Teddy shrugged and continued his falsetto summons.

"Tell me," Jenny muttered, feeling the accelerating pressure of time. A salad, she decided. She'd make one of those California-style everything-in-it salads. And broiled chicken. She'd call up a nearby grilled chicken place that was always stuffing their mailbox with fliers. The Grillery, it was called. If she was clever, it might pass for her own. It struck her that this was yet another violation of Larry's rules.

"If you can't find him, just forget it," Jenny said, growing still more edgy. She picked up the phone and got the Grillery's number from information. "No longer than ten minutes," she told the man at the chicken place. "Otherwise forget it." Her own aggressive tone surprised her. Am I getting just like them? she asked herself.

"No sweat," the man at the other end said as he took her order. "One quartered chicken."

As she hung up she heard Teddy's shout from the bathroom, then an unhappy screeching cat sound. When she got to him he was on his hands and knees, groping under the bathtub. He pulled out a reluctant Peter by one leg. After a brief struggle, Peter rested comfortably in Teddy's arms. Teddy stroked the fur behind his ear, and Peter purred contentedly.

"Well then, the crisis is over," Jenny said.

"For now," Teddy said. He was obviously overjoyed. "I can't wait to tell them."

"They'll be happy, I'm sure," Jenny said.

Suddenly the image of Mr. Stern with his head in the oven rose in her mind. She studied the boy for a long moment, and he seemed to sense her evaluation.

"You and your dad . . . " she began.

"That's over," he said, blushing. "Thanks to—"

"Please don't," she interrupted.

"I didn't tell him, Mrs. Burns. I kept my promise."

"I never questioned that, Teddy."

"Dad and I have had some long talks." He lowered his eyes and continued to stroke the cat. "About . . . things."

"That's great," Jenny said.

"It's been a real turnaround for us," Teddy said. "Like it was a miracle."

Despite a feeling of satisfaction, she felt uncomfortable about her own curiosity, reminded suddenly of Larry and his prohibitions.

"Anyway, Peter is back." He turned to Jenny and smiled. "Because of you."

"I'm just a cornucopia of good deeds," Jenny said, laughing with a touch of self-mockery. At that point the outside buzzer rang, recalling her earlier anxiety.

"The chicken man," she muttered, relieved, guiding Teddy with Peter in his arms toward the door. As she let them out she pressed the buzzer to open the entrance to the building.

"I'm sure Bob and Jerry will be calling to thank you," Teddy said in the hallway.

"Please tell them not to."

"Mr. Burns?"

"More or less." She shrugged, not wanting Larry to know of her cat-finding activities. More secrets piling up, she thought, not without a tremor of fear. Teddy waved good-bye just as the delivery boy from the Grillery entered the building.

"Burns?" the boy asked in Hispanic-accented English.

"In a minute," she said, rushing into the apartment to find her pocketbook. As always, it was never where she thought she had put it. She combed through the bedroom, the kitchen, the bathroom. Then she entered the living room, where she found it lying behind one of the family pictures on the spinet. Just as she extracted a twenty-dollar bill from her wallet, her peripheral vision caught sight of Larry coming down the street toward the house.

Rushing to the open door, she gave the boy the twenty-dollar bill and he handed her the package of chicken and a bill for fifteen dollars.

"Keep the change," she said, briefly noting the startled look on the boy's face as she closed the door and moved quickly to the kitchen. She took the chicken out of the bag, put the pieces on a plate, and stuck it in the microwave, ready to be reheated for dinner.

Moments later she heard Larry let himself into the apartment. She felt tense, fearful, and a growing agitation as she heard his footsteps approach. It annoyed her to have to deal with such oppressive emotions. Why do I feel this way? she asked herself, deliberately repressing a note of protest.

"Anybody home?" he called cheerily, poking his face into the kitchen. She had busied herself with cutting cucumbers for the salad on the kitchen island. He approached her from behind, embraced her, and kissed the back of her neck.

"Got it," he said.

"Got what?" she asked.

"The loan, silly. Terry called late this afternoon. See? Business is based upon relationships. Just as I explained."

He dipped his fingers in the salad bowl and popped a cucumber round into his mouth.

"Sounds good," Jenny replied, making an effort to appear enthusiastic. Shouldn't she be? she wondered, feeling oddly distant and unaffected by his sense of victory.

"Good? It's great. Especially in this environment. Not to mention that we've had five turndowns by other banks. There's still some open questions and, of course, the paperwork, but Terry says it looks in the bag."

She resisted facing him, fearing that he would see the distance and lack of enthusiasm in her eyes.

"And don't let it be said that I didn't fill you in on the details," he said. "I couldn't wait to get home to tell you."

What details? she wondered, remembering the night with Vince and Connie. There had been talk of signatures, her signature, being required. A note of malevolence crept into her thoughts, which she quickly dismissed.

"So when do you actually open the doors?" she felt obliged to ask, as if she were really part of it.

"Soon as the loan is closed, Jenny. But why trouble your pretty little head about such things? The broad strokes are we're in business."

"I'm very happy for you, Larry."

The statement was flat, mechanical. Surely it was the wifely thing to say.

"For us, Jenny. For us."

She took that to be the proper husbandly response. The dialogue seemed performed, as in a stage play, with each actor playing a clichéd role.

"We should open the claret now," Larry said, moving away from her. "It will go great with the meat loaf." He started to fiddle with the bottles in the wine rack, looking for the claret.

"I wouldn't," she said, turning finally, irritated by a sudden on-slaught of panic. "I made chicken instead."

"No meat loaf?"

His smile dissipated for a moment, then quickly returned, as if it were a gesture of forgiveness. For what?

"Okay, then. Have we a white on ice?"

A tremor of nervousness washed over her, and she felt an internal trembling. "I forgot, Larry," she croaked, clearing her throat.

Again his smile faded, but for a longer time. Finally, obviously forgiving her again, he smiled. "No sweat. I'll ice one. It's celebration time."

She turned back to the process of making the salad, listening as he extracted a white from the wine rack, then filled a bucket with ice cubes and jammed the bottle into it. That chore done, he embraced her again from the rear, squeezing her breasts and rubbing his pelvis against her buttocks.

"I'm going to shower," he whispered in her ear, his implication clear. Another thing gone awry, she thought, sensing the absence of desire.

When he was gone, she busied herself with finishing the salad, setting the table, putting out candles, knowing that all this was merely the props for his version of a reconciliation ritual. Although she tried to work up some genuine enthusiasm for the process, she felt a hollowness and disinterest that worried her. It isn't right to feel this way, she told herself. Not wifely. Not dutiful.

He came to the table wearing a new yellow silk kimono and smelling of after-shave. The dampness made his curly black hair seem more curled, more jet black.

"You look nice," she said, knowing he was expecting the compliment.

"For you, Jenny."

On another occasion, wearing a kimono that revealed his hairs to midsternum would have been a turn-on. Not tonight. Inside of herself, she felt a mass of contradictions.

"To us," he said. "Up and away." They clinked glasses and drank. The wine was tasteless on her palate.

"Great chicken," he said, eating with his hands. "Good idea." He looked at her as he denuded a chicken bone. "You're something. What a great girl I have. Tell you the truth, I don't deserve you."

She shrugged, remaining silent.

Considering what she was feeling, she didn't want to hear this avalanche of compliments. Suddenly he pointed the now meatless bone in her direction. "This I promise." He raised his other hand. "Word of honor. I'm going to make sure you're clued in on everything. Business. Everything. And once we get things going, we're going to make a baby. Maybe two or three. Would you like that?"

She nodded but could not bring herself to speak. Feeling as she did, this was hardly the time to bring up that subject. She thought suddenly of Godfrey Richardson and smiled.

"I knew you'd be happy," he said, pouring them more wine, although she had hardly touched hers. "And when they come, we'll stay in Manhattan. Maybe we'll make enough to afford a town house. No bland 'burbs for us. No way."

She only half listened to his words as he spun out various scenarios about their future, her future, which only emphasized the extent of her powerlessness. It puzzled her how she had come to this state. Perhaps when and if they had children, it might free her from this vague sense of—what was it?—exile. From what?

It was the events of the day, she decided, a kind of overload. Her mother might call it one of her spells. That was it. She was having a spell and was, quite successfully, keeping it hidden from Larry, who continued to talk. She watched his lips move, heard his voice, but it all sounded unclear, like someone talking underwater.

But she knew from experience that all she had to do was nod and smile and appear to be listening. She would never, she realized now, ever be called upon to comment on her day, as if those events were too trivial, taken for granted. Today I did all the things you despise and worse, she spoke inside herself.

When the meal was finished, Jenny got up to clear the table, surprised suddenly by Larry's volunteering to assist her. He never helped with the dishes. That was her job, and although she continued to smile benignly, she felt an odd sense of resentment, as if he were usurping her prerogatives.

"No need, Larry," she told him as he scraped plates and piled them on top of each other.

"Why not? I want to."

Before she could find the energy to protest further, he was carrying dishes into the kitchen, rinsing them under the faucet, and putting them in the dishwasher. As he stood in front of the sink, she realized that beside it was the bag in which the chicken had been wrapped. Clearly printed in large letters was the name of the store: "The Grillery." It was impossible for him to miss.

If he saw it—and she was certain he had—he made no comment. She wondered if she had lied to him or simply allowed him to make the assumption that she had cooked the dinner herself. In his mind, even that would be considered a lie. She debated whether or not to bring the issue into the open.

Before she could make up her mind, he had finished the dishes and turned toward her.

"Well now," he said. "Let's put the topper on the celebration."

Reaching out, he gathered her in his arms and began the inevitable prelude, and soon they were in the bedroom and she was struggling to climb into the character of the whore, which was the role he had assigned to her from the beginning. It was difficult, but she knew she had to somehow get past showing any indifference. After all, it was his right, wasn't it? And she knew quite well the little ticks and sounds that conveyed ecstasy. When her body didn't react on cue, she helped things along by playacting. Apparently it convinced him of her interest. Now, she thought, she was lying on every level.

"You see?" he said when they lay back, after their lovemaking was over. "We're made for each other."

She did not nod until he turned to face her on the bed and repeated the question with an added kicker. "Aren't we?" She was dead certain that he was totally convinced of this.

11

FOR the next week, Larry left the apartment early and came home late. He explained to Jenny that he was busy planning the offices with Vince and, as he put it, putting the new agency "on the launching pad."

Actually she welcomed the respite, although she remained dutiful in performing her household chores. For her own dinners she ordered various carryout dishes from places in the neighborhood. One night she ordered pizza, another Chinese food, another sandwiches, another chicken from the Grillery.

Although she was always careful to eliminate any signs of the carryout packages, she did revel in the delicious defiance of his wishes. He would come home late, tumble into bed exhausted, and usually be gone before she woke up.

Whatever communication passed between them during the following week usually revolved around the new business, and most of her inquiries were answered with what she could tell were deliberate deflections. Despite his often-voiced promise, he offered little concrete information about his new venture. Somehow she sensed that it was not going as well as expected. Apparently they had not yet opened the new offices, nor had they, as yet, left the agency.

"What about Terry's loan?" she asked.

"Still in the works. It's not her loan, but Citibank's."

"It seems to be taking a great deal of time."

"It'll come through by next week. Terry has promised."

"Sounds good."

She did feel duty-bound to try to lighten his burden. He was, indeed, working very hard, for which she was sympathetic, despite her feelings about the ethics of the way he was intending to set up shop. Also, he seemed to be making a great effort to hide his concerns.

Above all, he is my husband, she told herself. And I am his helpmate in sickness and in health, till death do us part. She had begun to wonder why these vows needed constant reiteration. Admittedly, doubts about her future were troubling her. Worse, she could not find a single soul to whom she could voice her misgivings.

Telephone talks with her mother were becoming more and more platitudinous, although Jenny could not completely hide her concerns.

"You should be very happy that Larry has the gumption and ambition to want to be a success," her mother had told her during a phone call during that week.

"I am," Jenny agreed.

"So what's the problem?"

"It's ... well ... the method. Actually, he and another colleague at the agency are taking accounts from their present agency to set up their own business."

"You've lost me, Jenny. I have no head for that sort of thing."

"It's just not right," Jenny said.

"It's not like he was a gangster or anything, is it?"

"Nothing like that, Mother."

"Larry isn't breaking the law?"

"No."

"Look, darling. You're living in a big city, where there are sharp practices. I'm sure that Larry knows what he's doing. It seems to me that you've got a great opportunity there. Dad and I are so happy for you."

"Sure, Mom, everything is wonderful," Jenny said without conviction.

There was a brief pause as her mother mulled over Jenny's downbeat tone.

"As long as Larry loves you, Jenny. You should not bother your head about things you know nothing about. You're a newlywed in a strange city. Perfectly natural to feel...well, considering you're a small-town girl...different. Big-city people just think differently, is all. You just concentrate on making a wonderful home for Larry and everything will be fine, just fine."

Jenny listened patiently. It was the same drumbeat of hopefulness and good tidings that she had heard all of her life. Suddenly she smiled.

"I love you, Mom."

"And I love you, Jenny. Above all, Dad and I want to see you happy."

"I know, Mom."

"You know what it is...."

"I know." She had wanted to waylay it but wasn't fast enough.

"The housewife blues. Remember Gramma's poem."

"I know, Mom." There was no way to intercept it now. She listened as her mother's voice recited the family litany.

"The heart of a home is a loving wife
Who protects it always from trouble and strife
Her sacred role is to love and to care
Always to nurture and forever to share
As helpmate or more, she can never lose
Unless she surrenders to the housewife blues."

Jenny sighed. "Thank you, Mom."

"It's something we all need to hear every once in a while," her mother said.

Repetitive it was, but the conversation, her mother's loving voice, even the corny little poem, did provide a kind of subliminal reassurance that might have triggered some reassessment of her attitude. Did she really have the right to be holier than thou about business practices in the advertising industry? Of course, that wasn't the only source of her dissatisfaction. Was it? Finally, with a great effort of will, she did manage to put aside all troubling thoughts and focus on the necessity to be Larry's support system in this time of trial. For better or for worse, she told herself, once again invoking her sense of wifely responsibilities as outlined in her mother's poem.

Surely his love for her was true, as her mother had assured her. And her love for him? Were emotions, like life itself, always constant? Judging from her own experience, they weren't. Like everything else, even emotions and desires had their ups and downs.

Late Thursday evening she was awakened by the sound of voices coming from the street, familiar voices. Knowing Larry would be late, she had slipped into bed early and had fallen into a deep sleep.

Jumping out of bed, she moved in the direction of the sounds, which took her to the living room. Through the window, in the light of the street lamp, she saw Larry having a heated discussion with Jerry. After opening the casement window, she stuck her head out and listened.

"I don't give a flying fuck about your goddamned cat," Larry was saying. Obviously Jerry had caught Larry at the wrong time and place and had become a target for his pent-up frustrations.

"You don't have to be so rude," Jerry said in a high-pitched whine.

"I'll be as rude as I want, you fucking—"

"Homophobic, felinaphobic. What a hateful person you are, Mr. Burns."

At that point Larry grabbed a handful of Jerry's shirt and might have punched him if she hadn't intervened.

"Larry. Stop it!" she shouted.

Both men looked up at her, obviously startled by her sudden appearance in the opening of the casement window. After a moment's hesitation, Larry let go of Jerry's shirt.

"It's not my fault, Mrs. Burns," Jerry said.

"Everything's fine, Jenny," Larry said calmly. "I blew up." He turned to Jerry. "I'm sorry. It's just—"

"Never mind," Jerry said, hurrying back to his apartment.

"No problem, Jenny," Larry said. "All I needed was that cat tonight."

"Just come on up, Larry. I'll make you a cup of hot chocolate."

He nodded, and she watched as he came up the stone steps to the entrance.

"Never mind the hot chocolate," he said as he came through the apartment door.

"Is there something—"

"In the morning, okay?"

She followed him into the bedroom and sat on the bed as he roamed around.

"What is it, Larry?" she asked as he undressed. For the past week he had not been working out or lifting weights. She suspected that he was also not jogging to work. Nor had he shown much interest in sex. In fact, he seemed depressed, a far cry from the euphoria of the week before.

"I said tomorrow, Jenny." He put on his pajamas and crawled in next to her, turning his back, his message clear.

When she awoke Friday morning, she had a sensation of disorientation. Larry was running a bath. She couldn't believe it. He hated baths. She thought about it for a few moments, then dismissed it from her mind. If he wanted to take a bath, that was okay with her.

She tried going back to sleep but could manage only a half-hearted drowse. Then she heard another, more familiar sound. Larry was taking a shower. She assumed that he had opted for a bath, tried it, rejected it, then resumed his normal routine. Again she tried to sleep. She heard the bathroom door open, then Larry padding in his bare feet to other parts of the apartment. Perhaps he is making himself some coffee, she thought, annoyed at her own sensitivity to details, like her preoccupation with those sounds the neighbors made.

Perhaps she should rise and make his coffee, she wondered. But he was back in the bedroom before she could get out of bed.

Watching him dress, she noted that his fatigue of the evening before seemed to have disappeared. He seemed a lot calmer.

"Hi," he said cheerily, smiling.

"Well, here we have Mr. Merry Sunshine."

"I was tired as hell last night. Pressure gets to you, I'm afraid. You expect things to go smoothly, only it never happens. I guess I was just getting too impatient."

"Impatience builds up frustrations," Jenny said, hoping she was offering him sound analysis.

"It's the loan. It's still not in place," he muttered.

"But I thought—"

"You know what a bureaucracy is like. Has to go up the line. Then Terry was out sick for a couple of days." The fertility clinic, Jenny thought, recalling the incident with Godfrey, noting in herself not the slightest vestige of guilt. Apparently she hadn't been paying much attention to the comings and goings in the building during the past week.

"Then that accounts for the delay," Jenny said.

"Everything's in place, we just haven't been able to expedite things."

"Have you been in touch with her?"

"Really, Jenny," he said, his mood changing. He was tightening his tie, watching her face in the mirror.

"I was just asking," she said, pouting.

"I know. I'm sorry," he said, turning to face her. "It's frustrating, especially since we did sign the lease on the office space. In a way you might say the clock is running." He forced a smile.

She was silent for a long while as he put the finishing touches to his grooming. She was happy to see that his preoccupation with business problems hadn't affected his fastidiousness.

"Would you like me to talk to her? Tonight, maybe? When she comes home?"

"No way," he shot back, startling her.

"But the other night—"

"I can't seem to make you understand. That was business. The connection was made. Any personal involvement now could only hurt."

"I was just trying to help." She sighed, not quite understanding. Helpmate, remember? she rebuked him silently. He moved toward her and sat beside her on the bed. She could tell he was going to be patronizing, offering her one of his lectures.

"Must I repeat the stuff about the dangers of personal involvement with the neighbors? Our dinner, while it seemed personal, was, in the end, a business thing. Terry sensed it quickly and got into the spirit of the thing. I'm not saying that it doesn't have an apparent undercurrent of neighborliness and friendship. But it's not the way it is in good old Bedford, Indiana. The fact is that she and I are now both using each other for our mutual benefit. A good loan gives her brownie points with her bosses, and, of course, we need the money, and as we grow, our account with the bank grows. Get it? One hand washes the other." He paused, bent over, and kissed her on the forehead. "A way of life, Jenny. Moreover, if you get too personal, you might say something that would have a negative impact."

"You think I would say something that might harm the business relationship?" she asked. She believed that was what he meant, and it was irritating.

"Of course not," he said. "Not deliberately."

"Like what?" she wondered aloud.

He looked down, shook his head, and smiled, obviously holding his temper, which only made him seem more patronizing.

"Like..." He shrugged. "I could come home and mention that we were having a temporary spat with a client's representative. Could be a perfectly innocuous comment and have no real effect on the account...."

"And I would say something dumb like 'Larry and Client X were having a to-do,' and she would think from that remark that the loan was in trouble. Right?"

"You got it," he said, standing up. "You see, it's not really that hard to understand."

She supposed she should argue the point, but it seemed futile. Confronted with her silence, Larry bent over and kissed her on the forehead.

"It will all come out in the wash," he said. "You'll see. Nothing for you to fret over. Actually, I think I might be hearing from her today. Maybe we'll have something to celebrate over the weekend."

"Be nice," she said without conviction.

"I'll call you if I hear. In any event, I'll be real late tonight. Going over stuff again with Vince. Lots more to setting this up than I thought."

She stayed in bed and listened as he moved through the apartment and let himself out. Confronting Larry's logic was getting increasingly frustrating, and it took enormous willpower to abort any further reflection.

Terry rang her buzzer just as Jenny sat down in the kitchen for a cup of coffee. It was late, nearly eleven. To avoid thinking about Larry and their problems, she had gone back to sleep. Turning these things over in her mind endlessly was debilitating. Sleep was a wonderful escape.

Finding Terry at her door was surprising. Jenny hadn't heard her usually clumpy high-heeled walk on the stairs. For good reason: Terry was wearing sneakers. She had on a pink jogging outfit. Remembering her talk with Larry that morning, Jenny felt uncomfortable and hoped that she would not bring up the subject of the loan.

Terry, she noted, seemed equally uncomfortable. She was not smiling, and her eyes appeared to reflect an inner sadness. Jenny's first thought was that the visit had something to do with the incident with Godfrey.

"Got a minute, Jenny?" Terry asked, offering a forced smile.

"Of course," Jenny replied. "Coffee?"

Terry declined, which seemed a bad sign. But she did sit down on one of the high chairs beside the kitchen island. She looked worried and hesitant, another bad sign.

"Godfrey okay?" Jenny asked, as if probing for some sign of where Terry might be heading. Suddenly Terry's face brightened, which seemed to relieve Jenny's fears.

"In that department, a miracle," Terry said. "We had our first procedure early this week."

"Really," Jenny said.

"Things are looking up," Terry said cryptically, offering a wink. "And we're off on a weekend jaunt. I'm meeting him at the car rental place." She looked at her wristwatch.

"I'm happy for you," Jenny said, patting Terry's hand.

"Doctor said we're entitled to a little relaxation. We're going up to a bed and breakfast in the Catskills. Make up for lost time, if you know what I'm saying." She sighed, and Jenny could see that a darker subject had entered her mind. "Jenny, I've got a problem."

"A problem?"

That could only mean one thing, Jenny thought.

"The loan," Terry said.

"Should we be discussing that?" Jenny asked. Even on this issue, defiance of Larry's caveats quickly lost some of its previous luster. "I mean, its being a business thing and all that. That's Larry's department."

"Doesn't work that way, Jenny," Terry said haltingly. "I must tell you. I did have it in the bag. But in this climate, well, the tiniest things matter."

"I don't understand."

"They demand absolute candor."

"You'll have to make yourself clearer, Terry."

Terry's features arranged themselves as if she were figuratively biting the bullet, telescoping the difficulty of what she was about to say.

"Your joint financial statement, Jenny. Unfortunately it reflected, well, an inaccuracy. They bucked it back to me. We're under a magnifying glass these days. The examiners. Fact is, the loan is declined. I feel awful about it, but that's the way it is."

"But why?"

"A double whammy, I'm afraid. In the first place, the inaccuracy."

"What inaccuracy?"

"The statement validated said there was about twenty thousand dollars in your account. It happens to be an account in our bank, easily checkable. There's only a thousand or so in it. I know it seems trivial. You see, it reflects an attitude. I might have fixed it say two, three years ago. Now we're under strict guidelines. The banking business today is in crisis. Actually, if it weren't for the other, I might have saved it."

"What other?"

Terry hesitated, grimaced as if she had swallowed something bitter, then plunged on.

"The signature," Terry said. "Your signature, Jenny."

"Mine?"

Jenny's heart sank. Her simple question, she realized, was revelation enough.

"Not yours, Jenny. That's the point. It only made matters worse. It was an obvious forgery. Can't do these things in today's banking environment, I'm afraid. A signature is a bond."

"But, Terry," Jenny said, wondering if the situation could be retrieved somehow. "He didn't mean any harm."

"Probably not, I'll grant you. But that on top of the other only made things worse. It was out of my hands. I have supervisors. Everybody's frightened."

"But you see, Terry, he didn't deliberately lie. I withdrew that money," Jenny said, knowing it was futile. "And it's all right that he signed my name. He is my husband."

"Husband or not, it's still illegal. Oh, I know it's violated every day. But he didn't even come close to copying your signature. It was so transparently obvious."

Jenny sighed. "I don't know what to say."

"The point is . . . you should have signed it yourself. I might have intervened then."

"But he's my husband. He's entitled to sign my name."

"Not really. Not if you haven't given him power of attorney."

"What's that?"

"Jenny," Terry said gently. "Where have you been?"

"Been?"

"It's like . . . like you're somewhere else, like things have passed you by."

Jenny could tell from Terry's look and tone of voice that she was being viewed as an object of pity, as if she were a poor dumb ninny. She felt the anger charge up in her, some of it self-directed, since she knew perfectly well that she should have signed the document, was entitled to sign the document. It was, after all, her account, her money.

On the other hand, she reasoned, wasn't marriage a special case? Not that she was defending Larry in her mind. But surely married couples, being joined legally as one, could act as one. Couldn't they? Although she did not respond immediately, Jenny was conscious of Terry studying her.

"Don't look at me as if I were a retard," Jenny snapped.

"In case you hadn't noticed," Terry said with the kind of visible patience reserved for recalcitrant children, "the day of the 'little woman' is over."

"I'm not the little woman, Terry," Jenny said firmly. "I'm a married woman, and I made the free choice to be a homemaker." Something seemed to give way inside of her. "Why do you women who work outside the home think you're so superior? You make us, who choose to be full-time housewives or mothers, seem like morons. You have strangers keep your house, strangers take care of your kids, and you think you're better than us because you're making wages outside the home. Chances are that those wages are being paid to you by men who order you around. And if you really analyzed it, you'd realize that Larry would be creating more jobs for women like you." She wanted to continue but suddenly was confronted with all kinds of complicated contradictions.

"Jenny," Terry said gently, "I didn't mean it the way you think."

"Yes, you did. And I'm not so sure your values are better than mine."

"Neither am I." Terry sighed.

"Believe me," Jenny said, anger continuing to simmer, "I know all about the hunter-gatherers and the nurturers." In her heart, Jenny suspected, she was, right or wrong, defending her home and family. Maybe—she gulped over this—she was defending a lousy little shit of a husband, but Larry was her lousy little shit. The thought softened her courage, and her anger began to cool.

"He'll go through the roof," Jenny said, the reality of Larry's reaction sinking in. Soon she'd have to deal with still another level of confrontation.

"I'm sorry," Terry said, getting up. "One of the down sides to being a banker is having to dash people's hopes and dreams."

"Larry depended on it coming through. He'll be crushed. All because of me."

"You?" Terry said.

She wondered if somehow she might turn this around, motivate Terry to go the extra mile.

"I didn't tell him about the money I withdrew. He just assumed it was there when he made up the statement. It's not his fault. Can't your bosses find it in their hearts . . . " She felt herself quickly approaching the outer edges of panic.

"It doesn't work that way, I'm afraid," Terry said. "Everybody knows that bankers don't have hearts." The attempt at humor fell flat, and Terry seemed to agree. "Jenny, it's out of my hands."

Jenny tamped down an urge to be vindictive, to tell Terry what she had done with Godfrey. But that, too, seemed a confusion of values. Perhaps Godfrey had confided to Terry what had transpired between himself and Jenny. Apparently it had cured his impotence. Perhaps she could appeal to Terry on that score. After all, she deserved some credit for changing her and Godfrey's life for the better.

"Anyway," Jenny said, breaking a brief silence, "I'm happy things are better with you and Godfrey."

It was an abrupt change in context. Terry seemed surprised.

"So am I," she said, providing what appeared to be the minimum reply. Jenny sensed her distancing herself and was afflicted with second thoughts about invoking the Godfrey thing. It seemed somehow wrong, underhanded, and, probably, counterproductive.

"I'm happy for you both," Jenny said. Terry did not reply. She stood up.

"I'll be going," she said. Her awkwardness was apparent as she made her way to the door. Jenny watched her. Then she turned.

"The fact is," Terry said, her mannerisms more professional than when she had first come into the apartment, all business now, "the loan was marginal, Jenny. I was pushing it."

Yes, Jenny thought, not without a touch of inner sarcasm, you were just being neighborly.

"I wish I had never become involved," Terry said. "I know we would have been great friends. But now..." She left the words hanging in the air.

"When will you tell him?" Jenny asked.

"I was hoping you might."

"Really, Terry. I couldn't."

Terry shook her head and sucked in a deep breath. "I didn't think so."

"He—he was expecting his answer today," Jenny stammered.

"I never give bad news on Friday." Terry sighed. "I don't like to get it on Friday myself."

"So I'm the one who has to live with it," Jenny said, wondering how she could possibly get through the weekend carrying this knowledge.

"I thought maybe you'd need the time," Terry replied. She closed the door behind her.

Time for what? Jenny wondered. Time to soften the blow? Time to be miserable? What?

12

"TODAY is the day you worried about yesterday and all is well."

Myrna could picture the little plaque on the kitchen wall of her parents' apartment before they had divorced, an innocuous little homily that nevertheless could be summoned up in a pinch when a shot of optimism was called for. Well, she needed it now, because today was the day she'd worried about yesterday and all was not well.

Jack had just told her that they would not be seeing each other again until after the election was over, and she was buying only one-half the equation, the part about not seeing her. Only in her mind it meant forever.

It was significant, she decided, that he broke the news after their first episode of lovemaking of the weekend. As always, after these episodes, he was first to go to the bathroom.

A moving image of him flashed through Myrna's mind, picturing him completing the last stage of his postcoital "toilette," dabbing droplets of manly Polo scent on those hairy places where they would linger like a morning forest mist.

In a moment he would appear in his blue terry-cloth robe, a

near match to his remarkable cerulean blue eyes. Over the left breast of the robe was the little Polo player, his reassuring phallic mallet in midstroke, obviously poised to make the goal that would carry the chukker to triumph. There she was again, she thought, plumbing psychological depths, searching for barbs to prod her present discontent with him.

Anger boiled inside of her, growing more intense in his absence. A kiss-off, she was certain. It was terrible holding it in, bloating her. He hadn't even waited for Sunday. It was still only Friday night. She knew it was the way he did things, getting them out fast, political damage control. They would have two days to work it out. Only she didn't want to work it out. She felt used, exploited. Worse, she had been a toady to a man, been mesmerized by his powerful position, and she resented it, remembering her father.

He came out of the bathroom as expected, skin glowing, hair glistening in moisty black, thin lips poised in a satisfying smile. Then he moved smoothly into the kitchen, she following, and opened the refrigerator, pulling out the Dutch vodka that they drank.

"I'm pouring," he said with a wink. "You?"

She shrugged. He made an assumption of consent, reached for the glasses, and went through the pouring process with his usual smooth and measured expertise. She watched him, irritated by his precision.

"More in mine," she said. He stopped the process for a moment and looked at her, eyebrows raised. He shook his head and added more.

"Only until after the election. Four months. I'm being practical. It's a game, I know. Someone is bound to find out."

"It's a kiss-off."

"No, it isn't."

"I can tell."

"You're being very unreasonable." He sighed. "Why take the risk? It changes nothing."

"It will."

"No, it won't," he protested.

Clinking the glass he had handed her with his own, he took a long, hard gulp. She turned away from him, mostly to hide her unreasonableness. Politically speaking, he was right, which didn't help her growing paranoia. With weekends to look forward to, their relationship was anchored. They had carved out a place for themselves. Without that, she feared an ending.

"Would you like me to throw in the towel, then?" he asked.

Perhaps she should test the waters on that one? The question crossed her mind fleetingly, then retreated and disappeared. His expertise was manipulation.

"You know better," she muttered. "Although..." She paused and watched his face. "Well, that's another agenda." She felt a rising malevolence. Both she and her father were experts at substituting issues, disguising meanings.

"What other agenda?" he asked, falling into the substitution trap.

"The political agenda. One more hypocrite presiding over the decline of a constituency."

"Jesus, Myrna."

"Just look around you, Jack. Look what it's come to."

"Somebody has got to try and turn it around," Jack said, his standard response. "And stop baiting me."

"It's hopeless and you know it. Too many people rolling in like a black tide. Actually yellow tide, brown tide, Hispanic tide, rainbow tide. What magic wand have you got to solve the problems?" She was wound up in her substitution, attacking.

"I'll give it up, if you ask me to. Really ask me, sincerely. But before you make your request, think of what you'll be asking."

"I know. I know. The most exclusive club in the world. A great title. Ego satisfaction. Most of all, power."

"All that," Jack said, smiling. He put his hand behind his ear, as if it were being cocked. "Do I hear any requests to step down?"

She lowered her eyes, the substitution ploy dwindling in intensity. Finally she shook her head and shrugged, surrendered.

"Well then, leave it alone. It's best."

"Not best." She sighed. "Expedient."

"Necessary," he told her. "We'd be spending our time looking over our shoulders for investigative reporters, private dicks hired by the opposition, hordes of photographers. There would be listening bugs everywhere. Media wants your ass, they'll get you. Who would know better than you?"

"I surrender the point. You're right, dammit."

"Why take the chance?" he replied. "Listen, think of my deprivation as well. It will hurt like hell, Myrna."

"You'll have the campaign to keep you busy," she said.

"And you'll have your job."

"It won't be enough, Jack."

"For me neither."

"I'm frightened."

"Of what?"

She hesitated. It had been six months of joy beyond her wildest dreams.

"Losing you."

"Dammit." His voice rose. "Don't be such a worrywart. No point in us being self-destructive. So far we've been lucky, damned lucky. Hell, this is grist for the supermarket tabloids. If there's anything that can tear us apart, it's that kind of publicity."

She pouted. He was being sensible, and she was being a silly romantic, knowing it. Leave it alone, she begged herself.

"Would it, really? Might give me some cachet." She sensed her innate bitchiness rising, manufacturing those little wisecracking sarcasms that were the scourge of writers, photographers, and artists at the magazine. She felt herself approaching meanness and couldn't find the will to stop.

"At least I got a sable out of it," she said.

He paused, studying her, as if he were looking for the source of her malevolence. Take you down a long road, buster, she told him silently, another knee-jerk reaction to her frustration. Years ago a psychiatrist had told her that with men she was always deliberately putting herself into no-win situations, setting herself up for castrating dramas. No, she protested to herself.

"Emotional pain makes me a harridan, Jack," she said, trying to eliminate the nastiness of her intonation. She waited for the meanness to subside. "I didn't mean it. I'm sorry."

"No matter what, it's still a great-looking coat." He chuckled. "And I love to do you in it."

"Shall I put it on?" She giggled, the burst of meanness going.
"We'll save that one for last."

"Last?"

"Of the weekend," he corrected.

He came closer, and she could feel his body embracing her from behind, head to toe. "Bear with it. I love you."

"For now," she said.

"For always."

But his nearness did not make her fear go away. When she was hurting, her imagination became hyper and she could fantasize tragedy, separation, and grief complete with vivid details. Projecting their parting, she felt herself assailed by self-pity and despair. Finally the man of her dreams arrives, the one love of her life, her match, and now he was disengaging, letting her down easy.

From behind, he kissed her hair, her ear, his breath warm, tantalizing. With his fingers he played with the nipple of her right breast.

"How can we give this up?" she whispered.

"Only for four months. My eyeballs will start to float."

"Back to my vibrator. My electric bill will soar."

Pleasure was taking possession of her, taking the edge off her anger. The hurt was softening, then it was gone completely, and she giggled happily. He opened her robe and began to caress her belly, then lower, opening her with his fingers.

"It's just not fair," she said, feeling the pleasure accelerate. The fear of losing him, she realized, heightened her response. His as well. She could tell.

"My satyr," she cried, losing control suddenly, a little opening orgasm breaking over her like a soft wave, making her shudder. "Oh, God." The glass slipped out of her hand and fell to the floor.

It was a detail to be ignored. Odd sounds bounced in the air, like birds arguing. Her focus was elsewhere, in some soft beyond, far from time and place, her mind and body one, concentrating only on the deepening of pleasure. She felt him behind her inserting his penis. Expectation gave way to still another dimension of ecstasy. Her upper torso was sprawled across the kitchen table, and she was contorting her body to bring him deeper, as if she were bent on swallowing him up, sucking him into her from this point of entry, devouring him. Something really big began inside of her, coming at her with all the weight and heft of an oncoming giant train engine, heading for some waiting impact. She beckoned it. "Coming," she shouted, the echo reverberating as her body gave way, accepted it, surrendered.

Then she was making her way back, but something was awry, different. She felt the weight of him on her back. At first she told herself it was the natural reaction of his spent energy, a post-ejaculation relaxation. "As good as it gets," she whispered, waiting for her own deceleration to restore control to her mind. She did not move from the table, inert, emptied, relaxing, her heartbeat slowing, waiting for his voice. After a while she wiggled her behind, a playful sign for him to react, speak, remove his weight.

When he didn't, she wiggled harder.

"Jack," she called.

Was he teasing her? Her position, which did not work as well in repose, was getting increasingly uncomfortable.

"Come on, Jack, stop playing."

When he didn't answer again, she jabbed him playfully with her elbow. Instead of the expected reaction, he slipped off her and with a heavy thud fell to the floor. She turned, prepared to rebuke him. He was sprawled on the floor, his naked body unnaturally askew, like a puppet that had been carelessly laid aside.

"This is no joke, Jack," she said, standing over him. Bending down, she grabbed him by the shoulders, lifted him slightly, then shook him. His head wobbled lifelessly. "Jack!" she screamed. The jolting reality of his condition sank in finally. "My God." She cradled his head in her arms. "Jack, speak to me."

When he didn't respond, she lowered her ear to his chest. He was breathing with difficulty, each gasp labored. Instinctively, although she had never done it before, she ran to the phone and dialed 911, but when she heard a responding voice she hung up quickly. No, she told herself, surprised at this display of cool logic.

A series of action options crowded into her mind. Yet despite what was clearly a life-and-death crisis, the familiar paranoia still overrode all considerations. What was between them had to be kept hidden. Above all, dead or alive, he must not be found in her apartment. Tabloid headlines surfaced in her imagination. SENATOR DIES IN THE SACK. MAGIC RUNS OUT ON SENATOR'S WAND. SENATOR IN SEX OVERDOSE. SPRINGER TAKES ONE SPRING TOO MANY.

She owed him the avoidance of that, didn't she? Despite the nobility of such an idea, she did feel the tug of hypocrisy. Her reputation was at stake as well. Worse, people would find the ridicule in it. She could be an object of snickers and satire, like the woman who had been with Nelson Rockefeller when he died under similar circumstances.

Then suddenly Jack was moaning, clutching his chest. When she looked at him again, his eyelids were fluttering. But he was still gasping for breath. A glimmer of consciousness was returning. She ran into the bedroom, got a pillow, and put it under his head and kissed his forehead.

"It's all right, darling," she whispered. "Stay still." Gurgling sounds were coming from his throat. "Don't try to speak. I'll get help." An idea had emerged in her mind. Of course, Jenny Burns. Hadn't she helped with the coat? Jenny was already part of it, wasn't she?

She threw a robe over her naked body, then dashed down the stairs and pressed Jenny Burns's buzzer, leaving her finger on the button.

"What is it?" Jenny cried impatiently, responding to the continuous buzzing, opening the door. Seeing Myrna in what was certainly a hysterical state, Jenny reacted automatically, eyes widening with fright and confusion.

"Please, Jenny. I need help. Badly."

"What—"

"Please, Jenny, come up quickly. It's . . . it's him."

"Him?"

"I'll explain everything. I promise."

Jenny followed Myrna up the stairs.

"My God," she said, looking at the naked man. "You've got to call for help."

"A minute, Jenny. We've got to dress him first."

Jack's eyes were open, and he seemed to have regained more alertness, although his pallor was ashen and he was obviously in pain.

"Try to relax," Myrna told him. She rushed to the bedroom and gathered up Jack's clothing, socks, shoes, underwear, shirt, tie, the suit he had worn when he'd arrived. "Help is on the way, darling. Just hold on."

Jenny knelt next to her, and both of them began to dress him. It wasn't easy, requiring some gentle manipulation. Myrna wanted him to look neatly dressed. Jenny seemed puzzled by the care she was taking. Both women worked quickly, developing an efficient enough system so that Jack was fully dressed quickly. When they had completed the process, except for the tie, Myrna began to thread it under Jack's collar.

"That, too?" Jenny asked.

"That, too," Myrna replied. When it was clear she could not tie a proper knot, Jenny intervened and managed to make one that was passable.

"You've got to call someone," Jenny pleaded.

"In a minute—911. But first this."

Jack was still gasping for breath, but his eyes seemed to comprehend the situation fully, and he nodded consent for Myrna's action.

"You see, darling? Everything is being done, and help will be coming soon." She lifted Jack by the shoulders and sat him against the wall.

"We're going to get you downstairs," Myrna said.

"Is this wise?" Jenny asked.

"Please. I promise I'll explain."

Myrna pushed Jack gently forward, got behind him, and put her arms under his armpits.

"I'm going to lift you." She shot a glance at Jenny. "Stand here," she said, pointing to a spot on the man's right side. "Grab his right arm when I lift them and brace it on your shoulder."

"I wish I were tall like you," Jenny said. "But I am sturdy."

"One, two, three," Myrna said, lifting. Jack rose unsteadily to his feet, while Jenny draped his arm over her shoulder and held tight with both hands. She felt his weight, crushing at first, but then, as Myrna got to his left side, manageable.

"Easy, Jack," Myrna said. "Help us if you can. Try to keep us balanced."

Jack nodded as they struggled forward. Because of Jenny's smaller stature, he listed to the right, but they managed to drag him through the apartment door. Fortunately no one was in the corridor.

"It's going to be fine, Jack," Myrna repeated over and over again as they maneuvered his slumping body to the elevator. It was slow going. Jenny, grimacing with pain, was having a rough time. They braced themselves against the wall as the elevator lumbered downward from the third floor.

"We can do it, Jenny, I know we can," Myrna said, offering encouragement with a cheerleader's enthusiasm. "See, Jack? We're doing it," she said as the elevator door opened. "Just hold on. Please, Jack. It will be fine. Right, Jenny? Won't it?"

Jenny grunted, unable to respond, obviously saving all her energy for coping with Jack's weight. Myrna led them into the elevator, resting against the wall of the cab. She was sweating, and her robe had opened, but she paid no attention, concentrating on holding Jack and keeping up the patter of encouragement.

After what seemed like an eternity, the elevator reached the first level. With great effort, taking one cautious step at a time, they managed to move him into the corridor. At one point Jenny faltered.

"You okay?" Myrna asked.

After a moment Jenny nodded, and they proceeded to move toward the outside doorway.

"My apartment?" Jenny whispered.

Myrna shook her head. "Outside."

"Outside?" Jenny asked.

As they struggled to drag him through the outside door, Myrna turned to Jack. He was still ashen, but his eyes were open.

"Understand, Jack?" Myrna asked. Jack blinked his eyes in assent.

They paused at the top of the steps.

"Born under a lucky star, Jack," Myrna said. "No people, and it's dark." She called out to Jenny, "Hold on to the banister."

Jenny reached out and braced her arm on the stone banister as they struggled down the stairs. Finally they reached the sidewalk. The street was deserted, although there was pedestrian traffic on Third Avenue.

"Now," Myrna said. "We move to that lamppost."

They dragged him to the lamppost, let him drop to the ground in a sitting position, and braced him against the metal post.

"Now, Jenny," Myrna said, her heart pounding. "Go into your apartment and call 911. Tell them that you saw a man collapsed in front of the building—no, not in front. Near, nearer to the corner on Third. Got it? Tell them to send an ambulance."

"Do I give them my name?"

Myrna thought a moment. "Yes."

Jenny, obviously still reeling from the extraordinary effort, nodded and moved quickly back to the brownstone.

"Am I doing good, Jack?" Myrna asked when she had gone.

Jack's eyes were open and he was still fighting for each breath. But he did manage to nod his approval.

In a couple of minutes Jenny was back. "I did it," she said.

"Now please," Myrna said. She had stood up and moved out of the puddle of light into the shadows, leaving Jack leaning against the lamppost. "You've got to help me on this. Please."

"Haven't I so far?"

In the distance they heard the faint sound of sirens.

"They're coming, Jack. Hear?" Myrna said. Then she lowered her voice and whispered to Jenny, "I hope to hell it's for him."

"I was insistent," Jenny said.

"You stuck to the story, I hope."

"Of course."

"Now when they question you . . . here's the way it happened," Myrna said, speaking hurriedly and wrapping her robe tightly around her. The sound of the sirens seemed to be getting closer. "You saw him from your apartment window. He fell on the sidewalk. You called 911. You came out to help him. Nothing more.

I was not here. Do you understand? I was not here. I do not exist. Can you do this?"

There was a moment of hesitation as Jenny seemed too confused to answer.

"I can't stay here, Jenny. Don't you see?" Myrna pleaded.

"I understand," Jenny said, nodding. Yet Myrna sensed something tentative about her answer. At the same time it struck her that Jenny owed her no allegiance and, certainly, no favors. How can I possibly rely on her? she thought, wondering if she, Myrna, could be drawn into such a situation if the tables were reversed. No way, she thought, and yet she had to trust this woman, did trust her.

"You'd better disappear," Jenny whispered.

Yes, Myrna decided, she is into the spirit of the thing. And the sound of the sirens was indeed getting louder. She was thankful. The beginning of a sob bubbled in her chest, but she swallowed hard and the sensation disappeared.

"You see, Jack? It'll be fine. You'll see," Myrna said, addressing the man sitting on the sidewalk. His eyes were open, and although he continued to fight for breath, he seemed to comprehend. "You'll know how to handle it, won't you, Jack?" He blinked his eyes in obvious assent.

The sirens grew closer. Myrna could see the bursts of flashing lights in the distance.

"Thank God, Jack. We'll talk later, okay?" Myrna said, moving toward the stairs of the brownstone. Then she turned to Jenny.

"From the bottom of my heart," she began. Then, overcome, she rushed toward the brownstone and dashed up the stone stairs.

13

T MIGHT have exploded with less impact if Larry hadn't seen it first on the front page of *The New York Times.* Of course, she hadn't told him about it, knowing it would trigger an outburst, which she was in no mood to endure.

But there it was on the front page of *The New York Times.* She had been awakened out of a deep, dreamless, comalike sleep after spending most of the night trying without success to tame her revved-up thoughts about the strange turns her life was taking.

He had shaken her roughly, and she had scrambled into a sitting position, frightened and barely conscious. Even Larry's voice had not pulled her out of her disorientation.

"Read that!" he had shouted as he'd thrown the paper at her torso.

"What?" she asked, her mind still foggy.

"That," he said, pointing.

She picked up the *Times,* then looked at Larry with some confusion.

"That. That. That," he said, jabbing his forefinger at the paper. "The part about Senator Springer."

"Senator Springer," she said, startled, returning to full alertness.

SENATOR SPRINGER COLLAPSES ON EAST SIDE STREET, the headline read.
A long story followed, complete with the senator's picture. Apparently the senator was still in intensive care, and his office had released a statement that indicated it was one of the senator's pet eccentricities to walk the streets at night to observe city life and to illustrate the right of citizens to have free access to the streets, especially at night, and not be intimidated by reports of crime. "We must take back our streets from the hoodlums," he was quoted as having said.

Jenny shook her head in disbelief at the contorted reasoning, although the *Times* writer hadn't completely bought the explanation, even implying that the circumstances and the late hour were somewhat mysterious. The writer also made it clear that the senator had not been molested, which gave the story its only shred of believability, at least to her.

She supposed that the explanation made good political sense, and it was pointed out that the senator would further amplify the incident when he recovered, which was, according to a hospital spokesman, imminent. The heart attack was described as moderate to severe but not fatal, downplaying its impact on the senator's career.

She was more amused than angry as she finished that part of the story, then proceeded to find its continuation on another page. As she read, Larry stood beside her, observing her with an angry look on his face. She had to hand it to Myrna. She might have actually pulled off a clever political cover-up. Not that she, Jenny, particularly enjoyed being a party to it.

She had simply followed Myrna's directions. When the police and rescue people had shown up, she had followed her instructions to the letter. From Jenny's perspective, she'd merely told the police who questioned her little white lies, designed to protect the man's reputation. Simple as that.

Jack was rushed off to the hospital, and she was interviewed by the police. Naturally she gave her name and address and told them, as agreed, that she had looked out of her window and seen the man lying on the street and had called 911. Then she had gone outside and propped him up against the lamppost.

After the police had left, she had gone back up to Myrna's apartment and reported that she had complied with Myrna's wishes and that Jack had been rushed off to Mount Sinai Hospital.

"A true and faithful friend," Myrna had told her, embracing her and vowing sisterly fealty forever. "I'll never, never forget this. We've saved a family from terrible embarrassment."

"I'd like you tell me who this man is," Jenny had said.

"Not yet," Myrna had responded.

"Why not?" Jenny had protested.

"To protect you," Myrna had replied.

"Protect me?" Jenny had asked. It reminded her of Larry's attitude toward her on the issue of whether to approach Terry or not, as if she were some ignoramus who might say the wrong thing.

"Don't you see, Jenny? If you don't know who it is, you have the luxury of deniability. You'll be less a party to it. If somebody asks, you don't have to get involved."

"Like who?"

"Well . . ." Myrna paused. She seemed to be searching her mind for a way to express herself. "Take the press, for example. You did give your name."

"To the police. Of course. There was no way to avoid it."

"Exactly. You did the absolutely correct thing."

Jenny sensed she was being patronized, treated like the little woman again. "Why, thank you," she replied with just a tinge of sarcasm, which Myrna ignored.

"So you see, the press will find out. They will call. If I told you who he really was . . . well . . . you'd be vulnerable and might spill the beans." Myrna smiled as if to sugar-coat the message.

"You mean you don't trust me to handle it," Jenny said, but without the force of confrontation. It occurred to her that despite all she had done for this woman, she was still that nice little dumb housewife on the first floor.

"I didn't say that," Myrna said softly, still patronizing, stretching out a shaking hand, pressing a thumb and forefinger against both temples, a gesture of both exhaustion and exasperation.

Jenny shrugged, repressing on compassionate grounds any demand to know more, yet not at all comfortable with her surrender.

211

After all, it was obvious that she was participating in a cover-up. Did the woman think she had fallen off the turnip truck? It didn't take a genius to figure that out.

"Trust me on this, Jenny. I'm in the media. I know how it works."

She had heard "trust me" enough times in the past few months to last a lifetime. "And you don't think I can handle it?" she said.

"These reporters are tricky and clever. They can trap you."

"You don't have to worry," Jenny interrupted. "I'll be a good little girl if the media calls."

"What's come over you, Jenny?"

"It's all right. I didn't mean to upset you. I'm sorry."

"Believe me, I understand. It's all my fault. Bringing you into it. I have no right—"

"Let's just forget it, Myrna. It's okay. You have nothing to worry about from me."

Jenny studied the woman. She looked awful. Dark circles had suddenly erupted under her eyes, and she appeared to have aged ten years. No, Jenny thought, this was definitely not the time for a confrontation.

"You just try to get a good night's sleep, Myrna," Jenny said.

"I don't think that's possible, Jenny." She sighed and shook her head. "I'm even afraid to call up and check his condition."

"Would you like me to do that?" Jenny asked.

"God, no," Myrna snapped, as if to say, "Haven't I made myself clear?" But the anger was quickly repressed, illustrating to Jenny the bare bones of the woman's manipulation. No sense in getting Jenny pissed off. Above all, we must keep the dumb little housewife from blowing everything. Nevertheless, Jenny allowed herself to be embraced yet again by Myrna, enduring her repetitive gratitude and vows of perpetual fealty.

"I owe you, Jenny. More than you know. For now and forever," Myrna said as Jenny started toward the apartment door. "Just stand by me on this."

"Of course I will," Jenny replied. Under the circumstances, it seemed like the only possible reply.

"There is one thing, though," Myrna said, biting her lower lip as if to prevent what she was about to say.

"What's that?"

"Your husband."

"I told you. He's working late these days, setting up a new business."

"Yes. I remember. It's... it's the sharing part... you know..."

"You're afraid I'll tell him," Jenny said.

"Third parties water down secrets, Jenny. I mean, what's between us should remain between us. A sister thing."

There it was again, Jenny thought. Like the incident with the coat. Yet she had betrayed Myrna on that, had surrendered to Larry's intimidations. Worse, she wondered if her betrayal was transparent, visible to Myrna's inner eye. She felt both embarrassed and angered by the possibility of being perceived by Myrna as a diminished person, subject to a higher power... the man, the husband.

She was suddenly confused by the dichotomy. Didn't marriage mean sharing? Sharing everything? Including secrets? Yet Jenny had consented, had conspired, to hide things from her husband, eagerly conspired. It seemed somehow to undermine the entire concept of how she'd once viewed the marriage bond. She thought suddenly of her own parents, wondering what secrets they withheld from each other, if any. Was her vaunted value system crumbling under the weight of the big-city experience?

"Why put him in the loop?" Myrna pressed. "What he won't know won't hurt him." Jenny searched Myrna's face, as if looking for answers. But the fear and anxiety she saw there was unmistakable. "Trust me," Myrna said after a long pause. Jenny nodded, knowing it was without much conviction, then started toward the apartment door.

"Jenny," Myrna called before she could step into the corridor. Jenny stopped and turned.

"Best thing would be to take your phone off the hook," Myrna said, her mind obviously still concentrating on preserving Jack Whoever-he-was's reputation. "Everyone will know in the morning anyhow."

Well, Jenny could now confirm, she was certainly right about that.

* * *

"There. There," Larry said, jabbing his finger into the part of the newspaper that had the continuation of the story. Jenny was identified by name—"Jenny Burns"—as the woman who had called 911, along with her address. Apparently someone from the paper had tried to contact her, because it was pointed out that she could not be reached for further comment.

When she had returned to her own apartment last night, Jenny had, despite a repugnant sense of surrender, taken her phone off the hook. But then, with equal repugnance, she had put it back just as Larry had come in the door.

"So?" Jenny said. "I saw him there... collapsed on the street, then I called 911. That's all there was to it."

"And you didn't think that I was worthy enough to share this information?"

As usual he hadn't asked her about her day. She hadn't planned to tell him anyway, and he had fallen asleep immediately upon hitting the pillow.

"Frankly, I didn't think it was that important," Jenny said, quite aware of her duplicity.

"Not important? Senator Springer collapses practically on our doorstep under mysterious circumstances and you're the one that spots him and calls the police and you don't think that is important enough to tell your husband?"

"All right, I suppose it was important, but only because he's a senator."

"If he was only a bum and you were the one who called the police, wouldn't that be worthy of telling me about this event in your day?"

"I suppose I should have," she admitted, not wishing to provoke him further.

"And this cock-and-bull story about walking the streets at night. Dollars to doughnuts he was shacking up with someone in this neighborhood." He chuckled sarcastically, while Jenny felt her stomach knot. "Maybe even that *Vanity Fair* idiot upstairs."

She wondered if her features gave her away. But when she shot

Larry a glance, he wasn't concentrating on observing her, but was caught up in his own ranting.

"I wouldn't know," Jenny muttered.

"What a gas that would be."

"The fact remains, I didn't know who he was," Jenny said, remembering Myrna's statement about preserving deniability.

"Naturally not," Larry said with what seemed to be a deliberate attempt to diminish her, meaning that she was too uninformed to recognized Senator Springer.

"The little woman doesn't trouble her head about such things. Is that it?" she said. Under the circumstances, it was a question she couldn't resist. She felt her anger begin to simmer, but still she wanted to avoid any more confrontation, fearful that she might, in a fit of anger, blurt out this business about the loan.

"It's not exactly your bag," Larry said. "Notice I haven't tested you on who the other senator might be."

She was glad of that. She really didn't know, although she was quite aware of the two senators and her congressman from Indiana. Okay, she told herself, one for your side.

"What's the point, Larry?" she said calmly. "So I didn't mention it. Where's the crime in that?"

"No crime," he muttered. "Just indifference." He seemed unable to drop the subject.

"I said I was sorry. I just didn't think it was that important," Jenny said, no longer assailed by any constraints of conscience. She could only imagine what would have happened if he knew the complete truth.

"I have to read it in *The New York Times,* for chrissake."

"Well then, call it an oversight. I was too tired to talk about it when you came in. And you were probably too tired to listen. I would have told you this morning." She hoped that would put an end to it.

"It's indicative, that's what it is," he persisted.

"Indicative?"

"Of your inability to understand that in New York one does not volunteer involvement." He was off on that again. She sighed with exasperation.

"Are you saying I should have done nothing, turned my back on the man?" She had suspected it would come down to the issue of involvement. She chuckled to herself, realizing with some glee how far she had bent actual events.

"At least you wouldn't have had your name in the papers."

"Larry, can you spare me the lecture?" she asked, watching his face darken.

"How can one ever lecture on common sense? You either have it or you don't. Involvement has to be selective, well defined, like our involvement with the Richardsons. It has to serve a purpose."

A purpose, she thought with bitter irony, remembering her discussion with Terry the day before.

"Then where is my error?" she asked. "In not telling you or in getting involved in the first place?"

"A little of both," he said.

"Should I have let him die there in the street?"

"Sometimes that's an option."

She looked up and studied his face, searching his eyes for some hint of what he was thinking. But what she found there was a sense of insult to his maleness, as if his inbred sense of domination were under attack. Worse, he didn't appear to have any insight whatsoever into her state or mind, nor did he care. What he had done, she decided, was to force her into a kind of shadowland of deception, a place where she had to rearrange her own values and perceptions to accommodate his own view of the world. In some ways she acknowledged he had tried to make her into another person. Perhaps he had succeeded, she mused. Nearly. The concept troubled her.

Suddenly he grabbed the paper out of her hands and, folding it, threw it across the room. So he wasn't finished with it. She sucked in a deep breath, bracing herself.

"He was a fucking United States senator, Jenny. You were saving the life of a United States senator."

"I told you—"

"Don't you see, dammit! Brownie points. You saved his life. Quid pro quo. It's worth something. If you'd called me, I would have told you how to play it. These things don't come around that often.

I'm going into a new business. You botched a media event, an opportunity for name identification. The least you could have done is told the police that you were Mrs. Larry Burns."

"Something wrong with Jenny? I did use Burns."

"You're missing the point."

"According to you, I'm always missing that."

"Yes, you are. This was an opportunity. You should have at least consulted me."

"I told you. I didn't know he was a senator," she said, shaking her head in resignation, spacing the words in an effort to generate a sense of the sarcastic.

"And I would have told you to find out who this person was whose life you saved. That's the point. I know how to handle these things. You don't."

"I've heard that before," Jenny muttered, wishing it were over.

"Frankly, Jenny, I don't think you understand any of this." He snapped his fingers. "Not a whit."

"I agree, then. I should have told you," she said, hoping the hollow, and untruthful, concession might cut off further argument. His reaction, she had decided, was beyond her own perception of logic.

"Well, well," he said, smiling sardonically. "Do I detect contrition?"

"No," she said firmly. "No contrition." She felt a new kind of sensation emerging inside of her. Courage, perhaps. "The fact was I didn't need to consult you. Besides, I don't exactly get a full report of your daily activities."

"What is that supposed to mean?" he asked smugly, folding his arms across his chest in an unmistakable gesture of belligerence.

"We've been through that," she replied, not wishing to let anger cloud her judgment. Above all, she did not want to be goaded into telling him about her meeting with Terry and the rejection of his loan request. That bit of intelligence was on hold for Monday at the earliest. There was still the weekend to get through.

"It's all a matter of judgment," he said, calming somewhat, sighing as if confronted with a perpetually disobedient adolescent.

"With mine leaving much to be desired, I suppose."

"Let's put it this way," he said. "You've got a lot to learn. And I hope you don't screw up my new business life."

"How could I? I'm not part of it."

"You're right about that."

It seemed a parting word as he left the room, giving her a chance to privately assess the morning's events. Senator Springer. Admittedly it had amazed her, but she did feel that she had been true to her promise to Myrna to keep the secret from Larry. His suspicions were indeed well founded, but it troubled her to speculate what he might have done with that information.

After a while he came back into the bedroom. She had remained in bed, contemplating her own agenda. She admitted to disorientation and uncertainty about the direction her life was taking. Also, there could be no doubt that her value system had been seriously challenged.

"I'll be out most of the day," he said, his features hard and unsmiling.

"It's Saturday," she replied.

"Tomorrow, too."

"Oh."

"If you must know, we're moving into our new offices. Next week we're going to make the break and the announcement."

"Isn't that a big risk?" she asked, her heart pounding.

"Well, well," he said, turning as if to address some invisible person. "Now she's become a business adviser."

"And the loan?" she muttered, barely able to get the words out.

"I wouldn't trouble my pretty little head about that one, Jenny. It's in the bag."

"You think so?"

"I know so."

Again she was tempted to confront him with the truth, but she couldn't bring herself to be the messenger of misfortune and a continuing target of his rebuke.

After he left the apartment, she got up and made herself some coffee. She was not displeased that he would be gone most of the weekend. She needed to be alone. The telephone rang, but she did not answer it. When the ringing stopped she took the receiver off the hook.

A few moments later the door buzzer sounded. It was Myrna. She was dressed in a suit, her makeup was in place, and she had the air of someone in a hurry. She rejected Jenny's offer of coffee.

"I saw him take off," she said.

"He saw the *Times.*"

Myrna nodded and shrugged. "I can't stay. I'm out of here." Beneath the makeup her face looked ravaged. "Just in case this damage control blows up in their faces."

"Seems to be working fine," Jenny said.

"So far so good. But you never know. They start to really dig, he can be in deep shit." Myrna ran her fingers through her hair. "Anyway, just in case, I think it's better that I split for a while." She looked at Jenny. "No media types snooping around?"

Jenny pointed to the phone. The receiver was off the hook.

"Nobody show up on your doorstep?"

"No."

"If they do, just stay cool. Never mind. You will. I'm sure of it. Me, if it came to that, I couldn't face it. I'd look guilty. Everything shows." She studied Jenny for a moment. "You, on the other hand, could get away with murder. Scrubbed midwestern look, wide-eyed, innocent. Little-girl's voice. Small. A natural."

"A naive little housewife, right?"

"I used to think so. I'm not so sure anymore. But I sure as hell am glad that you were there when needed. You are something, Jenny. All in all, a tough lady."

"Funny, I never see myself that way."

"Part of your charm. Part of your charm."

"You'll be happy to know that Larry...my husband...has no idea—"

Myrna put out a hand, palm upward. "Stop there. I have no doubt about that, either."

It seemed a new tack on Myrna's part, but Jenny didn't challenge it.

"Also I know you won't ask me where I'm going. But I'll tell you anyhow. I've got an aunt in London with wide shoulders who has nursed me through these withdrawal blues before. Whole procedure usually takes ten days. Got it down to a science. Fact is, after mucho tears and hand-wringing, I've concluded he ain't ever gonna deliver the goods. His pussy is politics. That's his lech. I'm an interlude, no matter what he says. I hope he pulls through. Watch them all rally round, even the bitchy wife. I'd rather face the facts now than later. Besides, I feel morally cleansed by the action we took last night. Saved his political ass, we did. Anyway, Jenny, you're the beneficiary."

"Me?"

Myrna had spoken at breakneck speed, obviously hyper, barely taking a breath, and then she had stopped abruptly. "You."

At that point she moved to the apartment door, opened it, then brought in a box that lay leaning against the corridor wall.

"Ta-da," Myrna trilled, offering the box balanced on outstretched arms.

"That again," Jenny exclaimed.

"The very same. I want all tangible memories erased. Do with it what you will. Alter it and wear it. Sell it. Burn it. Give it to the homeless. Any of the above will do."

"Don't be ridiculous."

"I couldn't do it without dumping this." Myrna sighed. "Call it taking a stand. Being true to oneself. Whatever corn you concoct, it's yours. My gift to you, to whom it carries no personal connotations. Me? I can't stand having it around."

People crack, Jenny noted to herself. And Myrna had the kind of wild look in her eye that seemed to confirm the diagnosis. No point in arguing, Jenny decided. She'd keep it for Myrna until she got back.

"It's a fine gesture, Myrna," Jenny said, leaving it at that.

"Already I feel like a new woman."

Outside, they could hear the sound of a horn.

"Three beeps. That's for me. My chariot awaits." She embraced Jenny and kissed her on both cheeks. "Worth a double-cheeker, at least. You've been a brick, Jenny dear. I'm gonna wash that man right outa my hair."

Jenny felt Myrna's body shake with tears, then Myrna moved out of the apartment, picked up her suitcase, and walked briskly down the stairs to the street. Not looking back, she got into the cab, which pulled away from the curb with tires squealing appropriately for effect.

No sooner had Myrna left than Jerry came in the outside entrance. He looked forlorn.

"Still missing?" Jenny asked.

"'Fraid so," Jerry replied. "I waited for your husband the cat lover to leave. I need your help."

"You do?"

"Teddy told me about your saucer-on-the-windowsill ploy. It worked once. It might again."

In the bustle of events, Jenny had forgotten. "How long this time?" she asked.

"The longest, Mrs. Burns. Two full days and nights. Bob and I are fit to be tied. It's awful, as any cat lover could understand. The house is desolate and we're devastated. I know you can commiserate."

"Why do you put yourself through so much agony?" Jenny asked. "Peter is obviously incorrigible."

"With no regard for our feelings," Jerry said. "But then even the human species stick together while giving each other pain."

There was something deeply personal in the remark, and Jenny, of course, let it pass. But Jerry was not finished, obviously having plumbed the depths of the thought.

"As the song says, we've grown accustomed to his smile. We've been together through thick and thin. It's the ingratitude that flails the soul. The usual response of noncat people is that 'he's only a cat.' But he's not, really. More like a kind of person, a bit on the flouncy side and certainly inconsiderate, but lovely when he wants to be. Oh, God, I hope he comes home."

There were tears in his eyes, and Jenny felt touched by his attachment. "I'll put the saucer out immediately," she said.

"You're such a dear, I don't know how you ... "

He stopped in midsentence, and she completed it in her mind: "live with such an unfeeling boor." She had begun to wonder about that herself, but so far she felt she was still journeying with halting tread over the Rubicon.

"I hope it works again," Jenny said.

"I thank you, Mrs. Burns. You are wonderful."

She went back into the apartment, closed the door, then went through the process of putting the saucer on the ledge of the open window. By then the coffee she had poured into her cup was cold, and she threw it out and poured another one.

At that moment the buzzer to her inside door rang again. The activity astonished her, and she smiled to herself, once again remembering Larry's warnings.

It was Mr. Stern, looking remarkably fit, a far cry from the state he'd been in just a few short weeks ago.

"May I come in?" he said, offering a beaming smile.

"Coffee?"

"Love it," he said, stepping into the apartment, eyes surveying the surroundings, looking pleased. "What a wonderful place."

"Why, thank you, Mr. Stern," she said with a glance over her shoulder as she came into the kitchen. She poured him a mug of coffee and sat down on the high chair near the kitchen island. He sat down beside her.

"I saw Mr. Burns from my window," he began, then blushed. "Sounds awful, I'm sorry."

So Larry had become the building pariah, she thought, smiling. And well deserved.

"Whatever is between us does not concern him," she said, unable to mask her militancy.

"I was hoping that," Mr. Stern said. "Spouses do have their little secrets from each other. Like that bit of business a few weeks ago."

"Long forgotten, Mr. Stern," Jenny said, sipping her coffee. He sipped his and watched her.

"I appreciate that, Mrs. Burns."

She paused for a moment and grinned. "I was just about to say, 'Call me Jenny,' then I thought, You know, this formality between neighbors is nice and wonderfully old-fashioned. I'd like your opinion on that, Mr. Stern."

"I like it, too," he said. "I feel very easy about it, even though

you share the most important secret of my life. Yes, I like that."
He put down his cup and cleared his throat. "Now about that
money you lent me."

She was tempted to tell him about the troubles generated by
that money, but she held off.

"I hadn't expected things to happen so fast, Mr. Stern."

"Well, they did," he said. "You know, Mrs. Burns, real estate
people are true gamblers. I had planned to use part of the money
for paying my back rent. I really did. But then I said, What do I
do then? Then this building came on the block. Well, not exactly.
I simply made the owner an offer he couldn't resist. Everybody
who owns property in New York wants to sell. I used it as a good
faith deposit on the purchase of this very building. A real flier, but
the opportunity was there and I took the chance."

"Are you our new landlord?"

"Not quite," he said. "You see, I flipped the contract."

She had no idea what he was talking about, and apparently her
expression showed it.

"That's when you find a buyer who is willing to pay more for
the building than your contract calls for," he explained.

"And you did?"

"Yes," he said proudly, studying her reaction. She could sense
his pride and felt happy for him. "We won't settle for another
month, but I expect to make a nice profit."

"How absolutely wonderful."

"And," he said, pausing, focusing on her face as if ready to take
a snapshot of her reaction, "I'm going to give you double your
investment. That's nearly forty thousand dollars. You'll get a check
when we settle."

"My God, Mr. Stern. Have you lost your mind?"

"Maybe so, Mrs. Burns, but you helped me find my life again.
Mrs. Stern has stopped working. Doctor has prescribed lots of bed
rest, and he's preparing her for a bypass in a few months. After
that we're going to move to a place in the suburbs, let Teddy go
to a public school."

"Sounds great, but really, you don't have to—"

"Yes, I do. That's the point. I do. It's very important to me. They say virtue is its own reward, but charity and kindness have a market value. That I now can understand."

"But—"

"No, I'm not finished. There's Teddy."

"Teddy!" Oh, my God, Jenny thought. He didn't tell his father about that!

"I now can resume my normal tolerance for gays and, of course, all other minorities. It may seem hypocritical and selfish, but I was looking forward to grandchildren. Also, I no longer mind one whit about Teddy's friendship with the folks downstairs."

She remained silent, waiting with some trepidation for the punch line.

"I think he's showing a healthy interest in females. It sounds bizarre, I know, but I've found a slew of girlie magazines under his bed, and he's told me he has a girlfriend, although I haven't seen her yet. Now I've got other worries, but I think I can deal with them."

"That's certainly a bonus for you, Mr. Stern." She was relieved that he hadn't thanked her for stimulating Teddy's knowledge of his own sexuality.

He finished his coffee, stood up, and put out his hand. "I've always been a kind of a hustler, Mrs. Burns," Mr. Stern said. "And I probably will continue to be. But, you know, it makes me feel good to see that you've sort of helped me stake out a piece of myself that can still be called relatively pure. You understand what I'm saying?"

"I think so," Jenny responded, suddenly remembering another of her mother's trite little homilies: Do good and it will come back tenfold.

Mr. Stern started toward the door, paused, and turned. "If that Senator Springer recovers and gets reelected, he'll owe you a debt of gratitude as well, Mrs. Burns."

She started to respond, but he waved her silent with the palm of his hand. His knowledge surprised her.

"I've known about it for quite a while. Nearly sold the information to the tabloids."

"You wouldn't."

"More like I couldn't, Mrs. Burns. Shows that somewhere deep inside there was some good stuff."

"That's it, Mr. Stern. There's good stuff in all of us."

"You're a regular Joan of Arc, Mrs. Burns."

"Not by choice, Mr. Stern. Not by choice."

"She didn't have one, either," he said cryptically.

When he left, Jenny tried to absorb all the events of the morning. Myrna had given her a sable coat that she had no use for, and Mr. Stern was promising to return double the value of her loan. It was all so confusing. And this business with Larry. Well, at least she hadn't become like him, paranoid, manipulative, distrusting, and defensive. Could such attitudes be reversed? Could Larry's faith in people be restored? Certainly she could not go through life with a man who thought of human beings as the enemy? She needed to find answers to these questions, to think about them long and hard.

Taking a leisurely hot bath seemed the only obvious course of action. She needed to reflect, to sort things out. She sprinkled her favorite bubble bath into the tub, then ran the water, adjusting the temperature to her satisfaction. When things got overly complicated, she could always look forward to a lovely warm soak.

While the water ran she decided she needed to hear her mother's voice. In a few short months her conversations with her mother had taken on a purely informational aspect, as if she were getting news from a foreign correspondent covering another planet. This conversation was no exception, but it was pleasant and reassuring to hear her mother's voice and listen to her comforting platitudes.

As usual, her mother ran down the happenings dealing with her immediate family, her father, brother, his wife, their children, the neighbors, and the usual hometown catalog of vital statistics. But the reportage was taking on more and more of an air of sentimental nostalgia, of a past life. She felt far removed from events and people being discussed.

"No housewife blues, Jenny?"

"None, Mom."

That phase, Jenny decided, was long over. Indeed, she found herself listening as she might listen to music. It was pleasant, familiar, comfortable, but, for her, uninvolving. In a few months she seemed to have made a very long journey to that place where the concept of home had become more of a comfortable and sentimental myth than reality.

"I love you, Mom," she said when the conversation had run its course. Of course, that. Always that. "And my love to Dad and everyone."

"And I love you, Jenny."

Comforted, Jenny removed her clothes and slipped slowly into the tub. It took her some time to get used to the water temperature. Steam clouds floated upward lazily. Immersed completely, she felt her buttocks and lower back slide over the warm porcelain.

Yet something in the feel of the surface didn't seem quite right. There was a kind of debris that interfered with the smoothness of it. In a number of places where her flesh touched the porcelain she felt an odd grating sensation, like pinpricks. Searching for the source of the discomfort, she felt with her hand along the surface. With her fingers, she grasped what seemed like a piece of wire and brought it up to the surface, where she inspected it.

At first she thought it was a curl of pubic hair, but on closer study it had a coarser feel, like a snip of thin wire. She reached down again, slid her hand along the surface until she found another, then another. These, too, had the same wiry feel as the others. It didn't surprise her that she hadn't noticed them when the tub was empty. They were thin strands, coarse but thinner than human hair.

The steam inhibited a more thorough inspection of the objects. She remembered that yesterday morning she had heard Larry run himself a bath. It had been out of character for him. He hated baths. Then, she remembered, she had heard him run the shower and had assumed that he had rejected the bath and opted for his usual mode of cleansing.

But that would not have accounted for the little wiry strands of hair. What could they be? She rose from the bathtub and held the pieces up to the light above the medicine chest, rolling them between her thumb and forefinger. They had a kind of rusty color, and they had the feel of hair, but not really. They could not possibly belong to Larry. Rust, slightly orange under the light. If not Larry's, then whose? And yet they seemed vaguely familiar.

"Oh, my God!" she screamed.

She felt her insides congeal and a terrible nausea begin deep inside of her. Then she bent over the sink and vomited.

14

WHEN she got out of bed Monday morning, Larry had already left. She had heard him come in late Sunday night and, feigning sleep, managed to avoid any verbal or, for that matter, physical contact with him. Although she hadn't slept much, she had spent the night reviewing her present situation and reaching conclusions that would govern the near future. If everything in life was a learning experience, which was what she truly believed, then she was certainly eligible for a degree in higher education.

As she lay in bed, she found herself listening to the normal life of the building. She knew every sound by heart, and it was reassuring to be part of this familiar world. Teddy bounding off to school. Mr. Stern, resurrected now, off on his daily rounds. The Richardsons back from their brief vacation. She heard Terry clumping down the stairs, then Godfrey's familiar tread. Mrs. Stern, she knew, was no longer working and was probably also in bed at this very moment. There was some irony in that. Until the Sterns moved to the suburbs, Jenny would not be the only tenant at home in the building on a weekday. Myrna was in London by now. And Bob and Jerry, both with heavy hearts and a gnawing sense of anxiety and loss, would be off to their respective jobs.

Everyone in his or her proper place. "And all's right with the world," she said aloud, knowing, perhaps for the first time, where that myth ended and reality began.

She spent the greater portion of the day with her usual Monday household chores. She polished the floors, vacuumed the carpeting, dusted the furniture, changed the bedding, puffed the pillows, and, coping with the dry heaves but with great care, scoured the bathtub. That completed, she concentrated on a special chore that she had saved for last. By midafternoon she had finished the job.

The disposition of Myrna's coat occupied her mind for a time. She wondered if Myrna's assessment of any future with Senator Springer was correct. Only time would tell. How that situation turned out would determine the fate of the coat, which she had hung in her bedroom closet.

She went out during the afternoon, but not to do any food shopping. What she did do was go to a pet store to make certain inquiries, then she bought a newspaper and learned that Senator Springer was making an excellent recovery and would soon be able to face the press.

There was still some talk about the mysterious circumstances of his collapse, but it seemed to take a backseat to the basic issue of whether or not his health would preclude his running. His doctors assured the public that his condition was not serious enough to abort his political career. She wondered if they were telling the truth.

She was not sure exactly what time Larry would storm into the apartment, but she was fully prepared for the confrontation. She sat in the living room and waited, her mind empty of all distracting thoughts.

He arrived late in the afternoon. Through the front window she could see the lengthening shadows of early sunset. It was mid-September, and the leaves of the sycamore tree were almost fully turned to orange. Some had even floated to the ground.

He came into the living room, his face ashen, his eyes beady with anger, his lips curled downward in what was, she supposed, the exact opposite of a smile.

"Well, you did it this time," he said. She had turned over in her mind his various opening lines. It was reassuring to know that this had been one of them.

"Did what?" she said calmly, offering what she hoped was an innocent expression, wide-eyed, smiling benignly. Her hands were clasped on her lap, like an obedient schoolgirl.

"You blew the loan," he croaked. "Screwed me to the wall. How come you didn't tell me about that withdrawal?"

"Oh, that."

"All you can say, is it? We've made commitments. We've moved into our offices. We've already sent out press releases, and you blew the loan. It's more than just an embarrassment. Vince and Connie are fit to be tied and threatening to bail out. It's a disaster."

"You'll get another loan, Larry. You're a very resourceful man."

"And you are an idiot of a woman. A stupid lamebrained dumbass without a brain in your head. If I were you, I'd buy a one-way ticket back to Bedford. You haven't got the brains for the big city. What I bought when I got you was a fantasy."

"So were you," she said, but not without a tug of sadness. The fantasy, after all, had been wonderful and comforting.

He stood over her, menacing, his face red with anger and frustration. Then he turned away, and she calmly watched him pace the room. Suddenly he stopped and waved a finger at her face.

"You were a mistake, Jenny. A fourteen-karat mistake."

"That much," Jenny said.

"A housewife was all you were good for. I knew that from the beginning. I thought that's what I wanted. The little woman waiting at home to greet me with an apron, a smile, and a willing pussy. Damn, what a mistake that was. Thinking it was possible. I can't understand why I brought you into the business aspect of things. I was embarrassed in front of Vince and Connie, showing them what a dumb little bitch I married."

She listened patiently, having heard his words in her mind earlier, waiting for the moment, the right moment, the perfect moment.

"You're all ball busters, you and all the fucking sisterhood. And us poor guys are caught in the middle, between a rock and a hard place. You all want more than you can get. Not that any sane man can figure out what the hell you all want."

It didn't take much effort to maintain her silence. What was the point? Perhaps there was some truth in his point of view. His truth. Not hers.

"Do you know what that bitch upstairs accused me of? Forgery. Can you imagine that? All I did was sign your name. My wife's name. Is that forgery, I ask you? And you..." He turned to her again. Foaming spittle hung in the edges of his mouth. "Since when do I need to have permission to sign my wife's name?" He raised his arm in the direction of the ceiling. "You bitches are in league against us." He was a man obsessed, tormented. But she felt no compassion. It seemed the time. Now, she told herself.

"You killed Peter. Drowned him in our bathtub."

He stopped dead in his tracks and stared at her. If there was any hint of denial, it disappeared quickly.

"So what?" he said when he had recovered from the first shock.

"It was disgusting," she said, feeling the cap on her own anger loosen.

"It was only a cat, for chrissake. Besides, the damned thing was a pain in the ass."

"To you. Not to Bob and Jerry. They loved Peter. He was part of their lives. You can't go around arbitrarily hurting people. Not to mention the taking of a life."

"Oh, fuck," Larry said. "He had eight more." He chuckled at his little joke.

When she didn't laugh, he shook his head. "I told you not to get involved in other people's lives. Who cares about those fags downstairs, their fucking feelings? No law says I can't drown that little bastard. And that Davis bitch upstairs. And those goddamned Richardsons. People are out for what they can get out of you. And you're too fucking stupid to see it."

"If you're the norm, God help us all," she said, more with resignation than anger.

He squared his shoulders and looked at her with contempt. "You don't like it, go on back to jerkwater Bedford. Who needs you around here?"

She paused, watching him, gathering her thoughts, hoping she could say what needed saying without a tremor in her voice.

"I think you've got things a bit confused, Larry," she said. "This is my home. I'm the homemaker, remember? I made this home, and I'm staying. It's you who are leaving."

He had been pacing again. Now he stopped abruptly, his face beet red. A nerve palpitated in his jaw.

"You dare..." he began.

She stood up and studied him. Whatever had motivated her to marry him was gone. She felt nothing, not even an emptiness where his love had been. He had become the enemy.

"Yes, I dare," she said.

"You won't last a week without me," he sneered. "You'll be an alien here. They don't teach street smarts in Bedford, and what marketable skills have you got? You weren't even a nurse, just a glorified receptionist. That's minimum wage stuff in this city. You're a goddamned dependent. You'll always be one. Couple of months you'll be screaming for me to get you out of here, ship you back home."

He stopped pacing, stood directly in front of her, searching her face, as if looking for agreement with his assessment of her and her chances.

"I've packed your things, Larry, like the good little housewife you wanted. Everything. Even your electric toothbrush. As soon as you're settled I'll send you your weights and any other possessions I deem personal."

"You've got to be joking," he sneered. "You..."

"Me, the little woman. Get out of my house."

"Your house?" He laughed, but it was hollow, more like a cackle. "You lousy little bitch," he cried. "I paid for everything in this place."

"We, Larry. We paid for it. And I earned the right to keep it."

"We'll see about that!" he shouted. He turned away from her, and when he faced her again he had adopted a completely different expression, as if he were trying to conjure up haughtiness and ridicule, complete with a patently false smile.

"You've got to be kidding yourself, Jenny. This is the Big Apple and you're just a stupid hick. You want a fight? I'll give you one. Except there's no contest. Face it, kiddo, you haven't got a pot or a window to throw it out of. You can't even afford the rent on this place. If I were you, I'd reconsider. Pack up and I'll take you to the bus stop. Would you like some time to think it over?"

"Speaking of packing, you'll find your packed suitcases in the hall closet. All you have to do is leave." She looked at her wristwatch. "I estimate you can do it in less than ten minutes."

"Ten?" he shouted. "I can do it in five."

She turned away to look out the window. Dusk now settled over the streets. Angry sounds floated through the apartment as Larry noisily hustled his suitcases out of the hall closet.

"We'll see who gets the last laugh!" he shouted.

She heard the door slam and looked at her watch. He was right. He had made it in five minutes. She breathed a sigh of relief. Yet it did trouble her, not that he had gone, but because she felt no remorse.

After a while she looked out the window. There was no sign of him. Apparently he had quickly gotten a cab and gone to God knew where. She didn't care. It didn't matter. Not anymore. She walked through the apartment. Yes, she thought, this is my home. Except for the weights in the bedroom, his presence in it was swiftly disappearing.

It was already dark when she arrived at the pet store and picked up her purchase, a cute little tabby kitten with approximately the same markings as Peter's. She walked the few blocks back to the apartment building, descending the little flight of stairs to the doorway of Bob and Jerry's apartment. Before she could press the buzzer, the door opened. Jerry and Bob stood before her, startled.

"We were just going out," Jerry said.

"Look what I've got for you," she said, holding out the little tabby.

"Oh, my God!" Jerry squealed with pleasure, taking the kitten and stroking its head. Then he held it up with two hands and looked at it. "A he."

"He's beautiful," Bob said. "But why?..."

"Why not?" she said awkwardly. "He needs a home."

"And we've got a vacancy," Jerry said, cuddling the kitten.

The three of them exchanged glances. She nodded, sensing the silent understanding among them. They knew, she decided. There was no point in belaboring the unspeakable.

"Speaking for both of us," Jerry said, shooting a look at Bob, who nodded. "Well, we're overwhelmed and very, very grateful. We might never have had the courage to find a replacement for Peter. But a gift. That's something special."

"I hope he has a little less of a wanderlust," Jenny said.

"We're not going to have him fixed, no matter what," Bob said.

"Absolutely not," Jerry agreed.

"He can visit me anytime," Jenny said, clearing her throat of a sudden hoarseness. "I'm single again and can use some company now and again."

Jerry and Bob exchanged shocked glances. Then they both smiled broadly.

"Not to be missed," Jerry said.

Bob nodded agreement.

"Anyway, have a great evening," Jenny said. She started up the steps, stopped, then looked down at them.

"My door is always open to friends and neighbors," she said with a smile, then turned and let herself in the front door.

In her apartment again, she felt calm and happy, but, mostly, free. Feeling a pang of hunger, she sensed an urge to perform some act in honor of her independence. She opened the Yellow Pages, looked for a nearby pizza carryout, and punched in the number.

"Plenty of onions and anchovies," she told the man who took her order. For the first time since she'd arrived in New York, she felt completely in control of her own destiny. Tomorrow, she decided, she would confront her future. Not today. Today was for savoring the present. She deserved a hot bubble bath, and after all, the bathtub itself was merely an innocent device and deserved to be used for what it was intended.

But before she could draw the water, the apartment door buzzed. It was Terry.

"Is he here?" she asked.

"Gone."

"For good?" Frown lines deepened Terry's forehead.

"I hope so."

"I was afraid of that." Terry sighed. "He said lots of unkind things about you. And me."

They came into the living room. Terry wore her usual casual home clothes, jeans, sweatshirt, and sneakers.

"I'm so sorry," Terry began. "I—"

"Don't be. I'm not," Jenny interrupted. "It's not your fault. In fact, I'll survive." She felt exhilarated by the thought and must have shown it in her expression. As if to underline her resolve, she got up and brought out a bottle of champagne and two fluted glasses. She uncorked the bottle, poured, and gave Terry a glass. Their eyes met.

"You're a tough little hombre." Terry winked. "I'll give you that."

"For a housewife."

"Lucky you."

"You're not serious."

"I'm not sure. I used to be. But now..." Terry lifted her glass. "You're looking at a woman with a bambino in the oven."

"For sure?" Jenny asked.

"I tested today. Turned out old Godfrey was loaded with little spermatozoa."

Jenny laughed, hoping that she had helped in their extraction.

"He's a regular jumping jack now," Terry said.

"That's two things to celebrate," Jenny said gleefully. They clinked glasses and drank deeply. Terry put down her glass and stood up.

"Godfrey and I are off to a Chinese restaurant to celebrate. Want to come?"

"I'll take a rain check. I ordered a pizza."

Terry started toward the door, then stopped and turned. "I want you to know, Jenny. Godfrey and I are just one flight up. You'll never be lonely with us around."

"I know," Jenny said. "Nice to have good neighbors."

They embraced at the apartment door, and Terry bounded up the stairs.

Jenny poured herself another glass of champagne, undressed, and began to run the water in the tub. A warm glow had begun to suffuse her. She finished the champagne in her glass and poured herself another. She giggled. "I feel delicious," she said aloud.

Suddenly the outside buzzer rang. She put on a robe, and sipping her champagne, she answered the intercom.

"Who is it?" she asked gaily.

"Pizza," the voice answered.

She giggled. "I nearly forgot."

She rang him in and, still sipping the champagne, opened the apartment door.

"Welcome," she said to the young man bringing the pizza. "I'm famished." She had difficulty pronouncing the word and giggled, upending the glass of champagne.

"Eight fifty," the young man said.

Leaving the door open, she went into the apartment. "Gotta find my pocketbook," she said, leaving the man to wait in the doorway.

The pocketbook was in none of the obvious places. She inspected the various surfaces in the living room and dining room. She was not conscious of hurrying, expecting the man to remain patiently at his post by the doorjamb. She moved into the bedroom. No pocketbook. Then she came back into the living room.

It was only then that she realized he had moved into the apartment. Up till then she was conscious of him only as a young man, a pizza delivery person without identity. But inside the apartment he seemed to become more of an individual. Despite her tipsiness, she managed to note that he was Hispanic looking, a bit taller than she, with broad shoulders, a dark complexion, tight curly hair, tight jeans and cowboy belt, and a black leather jacket, the zipper pulled nearly to his chin.

"You havin' a party, lady?" the young man asked. His speech was accented, and his smile, when his lips parted, showed gaping spaces where teeth had once been.

"You might say that," she said, laughing as she took the pizza from him with one hand, balancing it on her palm.

It was then that she realized she was still carrying the champagne glass. She felt no sense of danger, and her cursory view of the man was nonthreatening. The man's smile, despite the gaps, seemed warm and friendly.

She walked past him, back into the kitchen with the pizza, saw her shoulder-strap leather pocketbook on the floor below the windowsill, where it must have fallen. She picked it up, laid it on the kitchen island, and inspected the contents of her wallet.

"Damn," she called to him. All she had was two singles. She had spent what cash she'd had on the kitten. Must learn to carry more cash, she told herself. "The best I can do is a check," she said, taking the checkbook out of her wallet and fishing in her pocketbook for a pen.

"Never there when you want it," she said, crossing the hallway past him. She moved to the living room secretary, where she stored her collection of mismatched ballpoints. Bending slightly over the open desk flap, she began to write the check, then, hesitating, looked up. He had moved a few feet into the living room. It was then that she noticed his sneakers, pure white with high-tops, not the slightest smudge to mar the white.

"What was it again?" she asked.

"Eight fifty."

"Made out to?"

"Pizzaland."

"If I add the tip to the check, will they give you your tip in cash?"

He didn't answer, and as she glanced toward him, she noted that he had moved still closer, but his attention was concentrated elsewhere.

"Nice paira jugs, lady," the man said.

"What?" Surely she was hallucinating. He couldn't have said that. Then she noted that her robe had fallen open. She cinched it closed with her hands, feeling the full shock of quickening sobriety. She shot him a quick glance. Actually, he would barely qualify for adulthood. Close up, he looked young, still in his teens. His youth did not, however, dispel the sudden sense of imminent danger.

Stay cool, she told herself, noting that the apartment door had been closed. He was so close now, she could smell his breath, garlicky. Maybe onions and anchovies. A trill of panic tightened her insides, and she thought suddenly of Larry. Where are you when I need you? Then, remembering, thinking: No, I don't need you now. Or ever. I can take care of myself.

"You and me, Maria," the delivery man said. "Chico can make you happy." She deliberately kept her eyes averted. Mustn't look. No eye contact. As if ignoring him visually might make him disappear.

"Here's your money," she whispered hoarsely, using the moment to hold out the check, which he took and put in his jacket pocket. Then she stepped away from him sideways, slowly, not wishing to alarm him with any quick move. But her mind was plotting an escape route. The apartment door seemed the logical—indeed, the only exit. She considered the bathroom, which she could lock from the inside. But he could smash down the door. She could scream, but that could panic him, turn him nasty. Besides, the three closest apartments to her were presently empty.

Again she thought of Larry, his warnings, his caveats. He would gloat over this. Perhaps he had set it up. She wouldn't put it past him. He had, she supposed, spoken the truth. She was just a Hoosier hick without street smarts. A damned fool. She hadn't acted defensively, like a true New Yorker.

The young man picked up the champagne bottle, which she had put on the secretary, and gulped down the remains. Then he wiped his moist lips with the back of his hand and smiled. Time to make a run for it, she decided, gathering her resolve, focusing her energy. Now! But before she could move, he had sprung pantherlike toward her, blocking any escape. Still smiling, he pulled open the bow that held the belt of her robe. Both sides of the robe came loose, revealing her nakedness from neck to toes.

"You mustn't do this," she said, forcing herself to remain calm.

He held open the robe, inspecting her nakedness. Then he pressed his body against her between the folds. She felt the cold leather against her breasts. They hurt from the pressure. His metal belt buckle against her belly felt like ice against her bare skin.

"You're hurting me," she cried.

He put his hand on her windpipe but did not apply any pressure. It was too late to scream now. Not that anyone would have heard.

"You feel what Chico got for you," he said, his arousal unmistakable as he dug the bulge of his crotch into her. "I gotta lotta ways to make you happy, Maria."

"I don't want what Chico got for me," she muttered sternly. "Before you get yourself into real trouble, I suggest you leave."

"We start a new party. You got more wine?"

"You're buying yourself real trouble."

His response was to grab one breast and move his thumb roughly over her nipple.

"I told you. You're hurting me."

"Don't look like that way to me."

"Trust me," she said, her throat taut with fear. She remembered how cavalierly Larry had used that phrase. Should she have trusted him more? It was too late for such contemplation. "This will ruin your life," she told the young man.

"Why? You got AIDS, Maria?" He laughed and tightened his grip around her, moving her backward toward the couch.

"You know the penalty for rape?" She resisted a major struggle, although she continued to squirm. Use your head, girl, she told herself. She felt a wave of nausea begin deep inside of her.

"Leave now and I'll forget about it," she pleaded. "Why throw away your life on a rape charge?"

"You talkin' rape. This ain't no rape, Maria. This is jelly roll. Real love."

He took her wrist and moved it to his crotch. "Feel that. You want I should let you suck it?"

"This is so wrong...."

She had raised her voice for the first time. The sound of it seemed to embolden him, and he put pressure on her windpipe.

"You think Chico wants to hurt you?"

"Well, you're doing a good job," she whispered, unable to raise her voice louder.

"We do this like I tell you." He pressed his hand harder around her windpipe. "You open my belt. You pull my zipper. You get it out. Simple. You got two good hands and I hold you here." He continued to press her windpipe. "*¿Comprende?*" She nodded in consent and did as she was told.

Suddenly the wave of nausea crashed. She gagged, and a bubble of champagne rose in her throat. He let go for a moment, and she expelled the champagne, turning her head away, letting it fall on the carpet. Then she had a coughing fit.

"Jesus, Maria," the young man said as he darted back a step to avoid being soiled by her throw-up. He looked ludicrous, his pants down around his knees.

At that moment her instincts reacted to the separation. She darted across the living room toward the apartment door, grasped the knob, and turned it. Again. The door would not budge. Panicked, she pulled at it. He had slipped the dead bolt. Behind her, she heard his movement, sneakers padding over the floor in pursuit.

Avoiding him by a hairbreadth, she felt the wind of his missed grasp and headed for the kitchen, moving like a magnet to the knives in their wooden sheaths on the kitchen island, pulling one out at random, then turning, lifting her arm. She felt the heft of the knife, a big one, with a heavy blade. Her ominous gesture stopped him in his tracks.

Lifting his arms, palms forward in a cautionary way, his eyes alert and predatory, he shook his head and smiled broadly.

"All right," he said. "It's okay."

Sensing his treachery, she moved backward, then circled the island with its wooden cutting board and sink, until it stood between them. She noted that her pocketbook was still open on its surface.

"It's okay, Maria," he said. "I no hurt you. I make a little fun is all." His fancy buckle dangled at the end of his unfastened belt. The top button of his pants was open, and his fly was unzipped, showing a sliver of white underwear.

"Out," she cried, her throat constricted, barely able to force the word. She had it in her mind to scream, but Larry's ridicule came back at her. No way, she told herself, brandishing the knife.

"You think I was gonna hurt you, Maria?" he said, mustering every effort at ingratiation, his lips still curled in a twitching smile.

She assessed the distance between them, alert to any sudden lunge. Then she noted that he was within reaching distance of the wooden knife stand. Without letting her eyes signal, she started to circle the island again to where she had started. Waving the knife, she moved, watching his eyes. Still smiling, palms out, he backed off. She stopped near the knife stand, taking some comfort in his stupidity.

"Just get out and I'll keep my mouth shut," she said, finding the full timbre of her voice.

"I didn't do nothin'," he said, his eyes obviously searching her for any weakness. She could tell he hadn't given up and was calling on his street-smart con to get at her.

"Now be a good boy and get out of my home," she said.

She noted that the hand that held the knife was shaking. His eyes seemed to observe this. By then, too, his scanning glance had taken note of the knife stand. She also realized that the island was not much of a barrier if he chose to leapfrog it. The assessment only made the trembling spread to every moving part of her. Her knees felt weak, and her pulse raced.

"Please," she began, only to discover that her throat had constricted again and her voice had weakened.

"I'm goin', Maria. I promise," he said, turning his body as if he were about to be true to his word. Instinctively she knew better. She lifted the knife, sensing that he would spring. He reacted on schedule. She saw his fingers splayed on the cutting board, to be used as leverage to lift his body forward.

But before he could move, she waved the knife, slashed hard. She felt the blade's flicker of resistance, then the actual sound of slicing. He looked down at his arm. The knife thrust had sliced through his leather jacket, and blood was pouring out of the opening. It took a minisecond for it to register on both of them, simultaneously. Their eyes looked up, met, turned away, hers in disbelief, his in pain.

Above her, the knife remained poised for another blow, a thin red line along its blade. The boy's face was ashen.

He looked up, his eyes boring into her. She saw more than horror there now, a fulminating disorientation. He shook his head, eyes narrowing as they searched the room, clutching his arm. She noted that the blood had begun to spill over the leather, like droplets of red paint.

"I warned you," she began hoarsely.

"It hurts bad," the young man said, clutching his arm. He looked at her helplessly, the swagger gone. She watched his arm, bleeding profusely.

"I can fix that," she said. She still held the knife poised for another blow if he came at her.

"No cops, okay?" He grimaced in pain, defeated.

"No cops," she whispered, knowing it was a hollow promise. At the very first opportunity she would certainly call the police.

His face was the color of mud, and he was losing a great deal of blood. "Help me, lady," he said.

She was still frightened, but the boy's pain seemed genuine enough. She felt Larry watching her, berating her for her compassion, her foolishness. Don't believe him, he would say. He has no conscience, no morals, no feelings. He tried to rape you, maybe worse. You're stupid, naive, a dumb little hick. His words raced in her mind.

"Dammit," she said, putting the knife down on the island.

"Please," the young man said. "I be good. I promise."

His pleading seemed sincere. Besides, he looked terrible. She moved slowly around the kitchen island.

"It's okay, lady," the young man pleaded.

He was leaning against the refrigerator door. When she reached him, she pulled down the zipper of his leather jacket.

"Easy," she cautioned as she helped him out of it. He grimaced, his features convulsed with pain. Then she unbuttoned his shirt and helped him move his injured arm out of the ripped sleeve.

Handling his dark arm gently, she inspected the wound. The blood was flowing freely, but it wasn't, thankfully, an artery.

She washed the wound with water, took a clean dish towel from a drawer, then applied pressure. The trembling in her hands, she noted, had miraculously stopped. Then she told him to keep the pressure applied while she went to the bathroom to get her first-aid kit.

When she returned, he was still leaning against the wall, his hand holding the dish towel, which was soaked with his blood. She removed it gently. The blood flow had eased. Using a bottle of peroxide, she washed away the blood. He winced with pain.

"It needs stitches," she said. "You should have it looked at."

"Who gonna look? I got no doctor."

"Go immediately to the emergency room at Mount Sinai," Jenny advised.

"They treat you like shit there. Ask too many questions," he said. "I been."

"You've got to have it treated and stitched," Jenny pressed, hesitating, wondering if she should mention her past experience. Suddenly tears filled the boy's eyes, spilling over his cheeks.

"Look...I ..." Jenny began, then stopped. "Dammit, why did you have to..."

The boy looked down and shook his head.

"I can stitch it," Jenny blurted. "I know how."

The boy straightened, and with the sleeve of his good arm, he wiped his face, cleared his throat, and looked at her.

"Please, lady, you do this for me. I'm sorry I done what I did. I musta been crazy."

"I'll agree with that."

"Please, lady. I ain't really that bad. I got crazy is all."

"It will hurt," Jenny said.

"Just fix me up," the young man said. "Please."

Again she imagined hearing Larry's voice berating her.

Jenny shrugged and looked into her first-aid kit. She had the makings for flesh-wound stitches, medical thread and an appropriate needle. She threaded the needle and sterilized it in alcohol.

Then she turned toward the young man. But first she ran the tap and filled a glass with water and gave the boy two codeine painkillers. He swallowed them and washed them down with the water.

"I told you, this will hurt," she said. "Just don't look."

She worked swiftly as the boy groaned with pain. At one point she thought he might faint. Somehow she managed to keep his arm steady until she'd finished the job. Ten stitches. Then she dressed the wound, put a bandage over it, and helped him put his leather jacket over his shoulders.

"Now go home and lie down. I still say you should see a doctor as soon as you can."

The young man nodded. Holding his good arm, she walked him toward the door. But before she opened the door, he turned and their eyes met.

"Bet you think I'm the crazy one, right?" she asked gently.

He shrugged his shoulders. "You gonna call the cops?" he asked, his voice weak.

"You ever going to do this again?"

He sighed. "You gonna believe me?"

"Maybe." She wouldn't put her hand on a stack of Bibles over that one, she thought.

"Don't call the cops, lady. Please. My mama got enough troubles."

"How does it feel?" she asked, pointing to his arm.

"Like shit," he muttered. He managed a thin smile. "Lucky I got stuck by a nurse," he said.

"I'm not a nurse. Just a glorified receptionist."

She chuckled, watching the boy's look of puzzlement.

"No cops, right? You're not going to tell?"

"Macho man," she said.

"I didn't mean to . . . " The young man paused.

"I did," Jenny said, looking at his wounded arm. "You're lucky it was only your arm." She hoped the implication of her words would sink in.

"Yeah," he agreed.

"Did you learn anything from this?" Jenny asked sternly.

"Yeah," the boy drawled. "Maybe."

She opened the door for the young man, then helped him open the outside door. As she did so she noted that his pure white sneakers were soiled by bloodstains. She did not point them out to him.

"Your pizza's cold by now," he said. Then, holding on to the stone banister, he walked slowly down the stairs. When he reached the sidewalk, he turned and raised his good arm in a kind of wave, then walked off toward Second Avenue.

When she got into her apartment again, she put up the chain and rolled the dead bolt into place. For a moment she leaned against the closed door. Cops or not? she thought. What would Larry have done? she asked herself. "Cops," she whispered, shaking her head in the negative. Then she brought the first-aid kit back into the bathroom and put it in the cabinet under the sink.

When she rose again, she saw her face in the mirror.

"No matter what," she told her mirror image, "never become like them."